InterPlay

Jennifer Watts

Copyright © 2017 Jennifer Watts
All rights reserved.

Second edition.

No part of this book may be used or reproduced in any form or by any means electronic or mechanical, including photocopying, recording or by any information storage and retrieval systems without prior written permission of the author except where permitted by law.

Cover Design by **Rita Toews** yourebookcover.com

Editing by **Kelsey Straight** creativestraight.com

This book is a work of fiction. Names, characters, places, and incidents are either products of the author's imagination or used fictitiously. Any resemblance to actual events or persons, living or dead, is entirely coincidental.

For the ladies of The Summit: Maryvonne, Cathy, Christina and Erynn. From PowerPoints to Platypus rules, Whistler would not be the same without you.

Chapter One

"Don't Go Away Mad (Just Go Away)"

Stevie

There is no feeling quite as gross as standing in the humid confines of an indoor pool building covered from head to toe in polyester. In my mind, the only thing more offensive might be the reason that I'm here–Granger Ellis.

I tug at the collar of my hotel-issued dress shirt while balancing a tray of drinks with my other arm. I can actually feel the sweat stains forming in my armpits as I wait for our VIP guest to finish swimming laps in the outdoor pool. A pool, might I add, which is currently closed to paying customers because some celebrity felt like taking a dip. Serving drinks is one part of my job that I normally enjoy, but there's something so mind-numbingly cliché about waiting on a rock star— correction: *Rock God*—that makes each passing second more painful than the last. Not to mention, I'll be out a few hundred dollars in tips today, thanks to him effectively shutting down both the indoor and outdoor pool service.

I love serving on summer mornings like this one though, when the landscape is all blue skies, emerald mountain peaks, and sunshine so bright that even a waitress feels courted by the divine. After all, whenever the sun is out, the guests are usually more generous with their gratuities. I sigh and wiggle my toes, which swelter inside my hot black orthopedic shoes. They're beyond ugly but a lifesaver when it comes to working on my feet all day. I try not to stare at the pool and the infamous musician gliding across its surface. He butterflies his way past the plastic divider in my direction. *Show off*, I think.

The hotel pool includes both an indoor and outdoor area, cordoned off by the slatted divider. Granger's sandy-brown hair, all wet and plastered to his head, appears almost black. I huff out a breath as he touches the wall and heads back in the opposite direction. The damn drink tray balanced on my arm is getting heavy, so I shift it onto my right arm, always careful not to jostle the half-dozen pints of beer and lone girlie cocktail resting on top. The glasses clink together but I bob and weave to avoid spilling them. The girlie cocktail almost tips over, but it's probably for some groupie so I have a good laugh, wondering how bummed she'd be if she never got one sip.

By all accounts, beverages should be considered gender neutral, but this one in particular—a *Lava Flow*—defies all rules, from the neon-red liquid to the equally ridiculous pineapple wedge. A retro-green umbrella spears three maraschino cherries near the surface and the whole concoction is like sipping on Type-2 Diabetes. Maybe I'm just biased, since I'm strictly a scotch-girl; and even then it must but be triple-distilled, aged in an oak cask, and peaty as can be. I glance back at the rock legend, watching him swim beneath the plastic divider and head back outside. When he reaches the pool's far edge, he pauses to catch his breath and braces both hands on the ledge. Through the steamy glass windows, I watch him gather his composure and free himself from the water, meanwhile trying very hard not to admire the pop in his tattooed triceps.

Inky-black sleeves decorate the entire expanse of skin running from shoulder to wrist along both of his arms. Tattoos aren't normally my thing, but on him...well...let's just say I could make an exception—that is, if I had one iota of respect for him or his music. As the lead singer of the alternative metal band *Actuator*, Granger is both well-known and well-photographed, particularly for his hard-partying lifestyle. He snatches a towel from the plush poolside lounger and wraps it around his waist before heading back inside. I straighten up, seeing him pad across the tile floor in my direction. He doesn't stop walking until he's uncomfortably close to my body, leaning forward to pluck his drink from my tray without speaking a word. To my amusement, he selects the red monstrosity.

"That's your drink?" I probably sound judgmental, but like, seriously?

"Of course it's mine. Who else?" He glances around like a human searchlight, his voice laced with a thick accent. I figured he wasn't an American, but I wasn't expecting him to sound so...*Scottish.*

"Just figured the beers were for you, I guess."

"Nah, they're for my bodyguards." He gestures to the supremely large, stoic men hanging around in a semi-circle by the pool. "I'd hazard that they're mighty thirsty by now."

I cringe upon realizing that I should've offered them the now sweating pints of beer right away, instead of gawking at their boss for five minutes. Well crap, there goes whatever little tip I had left. Not that I expected Granger to guzzle six drinks all at once, just that it was some celebrity excess-type-thing, like Madonna wanting the walls painted pink or J-Lo asking for all blue M&Ms in her dressing room.

He nods his head at the men, who converge on me together, lifting their room-temperature pints off the tray. Granger rocks back on his heels and studies me with drowsy green eyes. They're sort of a muddy green, like the colour of American money. He's tall, like definitely over six feet, and muscular, but not in an Incredible Hulk kind of way. His frame is lean from jumping around on stage all the time, which I hear is his "M.O." Per the hotel staff, he's been on tour for two-hundred consecutive days and just finished his final concert in Vancouver last night.

Apparently his presence in Whistler is with the express intention of resting for a few weeks, but whatever brought him here is less important than the way he's looking at me right now, with a half-irritated, half-amused glint in his eyes. My gaze travels over his face and down his body, taking in his wicked scruff, pouty lips, and trademark hairstyle—shaved close on the sides but full on top. He even has both nipples pierced. Sure, he's gorgeous in his own right, but I'm not at all intimidated. My second job is bartending in the village and I've come across all kinds in my time.

"See something you like?" he quips.

It takes all of my self control not to roll my eyes. "Yeah, your drink looks delicious."

He furrows his brow, as if making ski moguls in his forehead. "What's wrong with my drink?"

"I don't know. I suppose it's kind of feminine? I didn't expect it to be yours."

There's a long pause (during which I wonder if I've lost my job) before he throws back his head and chuckles like thunder in a very good mood.

"I promise you, love, I'm all man." This particular rock star looks just like a frat-boy when he smirks. "If you don't believe me, I can show you some other way."

"I believe you," I mumble, supremely embarrassed for saying anything at all.

His eyes drop to my chest, inspecting my work-issued lavender dress shirt. It fits one size too small and gapes open between my breasts, even with tons of safety pins and double-sided tape. Whoever invented dress shirts like this must have been a man.

"Care to get wet with me?" he asks, wiggling his eyebrows.

Up until this moment, a small part of me was actually intrigued by him, but a line like that makes my vagina crawl up into itself. "Can't. I'm working."

"Pity." He clicks his tongue, and it's such a cheesy move that I literally roll my eyes. I don't know why I expected more from Granger Ellis, since I hate his music and everything he stands for artistically, but somehow I did.

"Anyway, is there anything else I can get you, or will that be all for now?"

"You in a rush to get out of here, doll?" I can't help but snort, hoping that he doesn't hear me over all the music in his head. "Did I say something funny?"

"*Doll*? Really? Do I look like a glassy-eyed plastic toy to you?"

"I didn't mean anything by it." The cocky smile on his face reveals that his words aren't genuine, which makes me want to shove him backwards into the pool.

"I'm sure you didn't. But I have work to do so…"

"You don't, actually."

"I don't what?"

"Have work to do. I reserved the pool, health club, and spa, along with the staff's services for the next three hours, so I have the pleasure of your full attention." This time he grins widely. I hug the tray against my chest with all ten fingers clamped around the plastic edges.

"The pleasure is all mine. If that's all you need for now, I'll be waiting over by the reception area—if it's all the same to you."

"No worries, as long as you answer one question for me first."

I nod. "Of course."

"Why?"

"Why, what?"

"Why would you prefer to stand over by the door than with a triple-platinum artist like myself?"

"Because it's hot over here." I do my best to avoid his eyes. "I'm sweating like a pig."

"Interesting analogy," he says, studying me like the mountain snow report.

"It is interesting, especially given that even-toed ungulate swine don't technically sweat." I don't know why I'm telling him this, except that he's started to make me nervous. The scientist in me can't help myself. I haven't been in a lab in years, but I'll always be a scientist.

"Hmm. Take it off then." He talks as if he's solved the problem.

"Excuse me?"

"The uniform. Take it off. It's ugly anyway."

I know he's right, but the admission still stings.

"I'm not getting undressed for you."

"Not now, but later maybe."

"Trust me when I say not ever."

I can't believe he's being such an ass.

"We'll see." He looks so smug and satisfied to have the last word, thrusting his now empty glass towards me before letting his towel fall around his ankles and diving back into the pool.

I don't get home until after five, because the drive from the hotel to my place in Pemberton takes about forty-five minutes. The rock star bought out the pool for another two hours following the end of my shift, probably just to spite me. I'm upset because my shift was supposed to end at two o'clock, and now Toto has been alone for too long.

I pull into my garage and jog up the stairs to my townhouse, which I figure should count for some cardio after standing all day. As a rule, I don't do much cardio, but they say that every little bit counts. As soon as the door is unlocked, I rush over to Toto's tank and snuggle him in my arms.

"How's my baby?" I croon at my favourite iguana and pet his scaly back.

Once I've given him a sufficient amount of cuddle time, I set him down and pad over to the window, taking a long look at the mountain vistas. I start checking messages on my phone, finding one from my mom, two from my brothers, and one from Kit.

It's late August and the night comes on much sooner, signalling the first hint of fall. The sun has already begun its descent, bathing the snow caps of Mount Currie in a magical orangey glow. Despite growing up with this view, I'll never tire of it. It doesn't hurt that I absolutely love my townhome, with its two bedrooms, two bathrooms, gas fireplace, and an extra-large deck. It's the first major purchase I've made on my own, and I've never looked back for a second. It became mine—well, the bank's anyway—when I purchased it two years ago on my twenty-fourth birthday.

Having grown up in a three-bedroom house with four older brothers, not to mention having the full Whistler "apartment share" experience as a teenager, partying all night and sleeping on bunk beds in shifts, it was nice to finally call somewhere my own. In celebration of my big purchase, I also adopted Toto from the SPCA, who I renamed because "Princess" just didn't do it for me. Actually,

I'm not sure if Toto is a boy or a girl, but at least he/she bears the name of one of my favourite bands.

I decide to call Kit back first, even though my feet are killing me and my uniform stinks. He's my best friend and I could definitely use one of those right now. While humming the melody to 'Africa', I scroll through my phone to dial his number, and he answers on the first ring.

"Hey beautiful."

"Hey Kit. I got your message and your texts. Sorry I didn't get back to you sooner."

"It's all good, thanks for calling. I missed hearing your voice."

"Charmer," I laugh.

"You know it, babe."

Originally from Australia, Kit has lived in Whistler for the past ten years. We met while he was dating a friend of mine; that relationship—much like the friend—disappeared like lightning, but Kit and I kept going strong. He DJs at the pub where I work, having spun tables for the town since arriving on the scene. Being a DJ is more than enough to draw in the ladies. Add to that Kit's shaggy blond hair, light blue eyes, big dimples, and near perfect white teeth, and he's quite a hit with the female persuasion. I'd always thought Aussies were fair-skinned, but Kit has this perma-tan going on across his whole skier's body. He swears it's all from natural sunlight, but come on? *Natural* in the mountains, in Canada, from January through December?

"I texted you like five times. Where's the love for the Kit?"

"First of all, please don't refer to yourself in the third person." I sigh and rub my forehead. "I've had all the ego I can handle for one day."

"So I take it things didn't go well with the chart-topper?"

Of course, I already told Kit about covering the rock star's private pool day, along with my mom and eldest brother, Spencer, hence all the messages waiting for me at home.

"It was the absolute worst. I had to stay another two hours while he sat drinking cucumber water in the eucalyptus steam room before *fannying* about in the hot tub."

"You do know that fanny has an entirely different meaning to my people, right?"

"Please try and keep focused, Kit."

"Sorry, babe. Was he at least as good-looking in person, as all the chicks seem to think?"

"Don't ask me," I snort. "I barely looked at him." I sound so convincing that I almost believe myself. "Besides, he has too much ink and attitude for my taste. The guy is clearly in love with himself."

"Well, he has reason to be. His last album debuted at number five and his first single went triple platinum on digital download."

"Sixth."

"What?"

"He told me it debuted at number six."

"Hey, who's the DJ here?" he scoffs.

"Whatever, I've barely even heard his music before, so…" I trail off, and Kit just laughs.

"Sure you have, everybody has. Ever tune into a rock station on the radio, Stevie? *Actuator* is impossible to miss."

"I guess I've achieved the impossible then."

"So you're telling me that you've never heard songs like 'Insidious Inside,' 'Burned Alive,' 'Bat Shit,' or 'Seizure'…?"

"No, but those are some really charming song titles." I cannot keep the sarcasm from my voice. "Why don't bands make songs like they used to, songs that take their time with the slow build and hit you right at the core, songs like 'Every Rose' or 'Wind of Change'"?

I hear Kit's muffled chuckle crackling over the line. "I don't think the world loves Power Ballads like you do anymore, babe. You're probably the last fan on earth."

Like a baby storm, I huff out a breath. He's right that I'm a complete "hair band" junkie, but no way am I the only one left on the planet. I can't put my finger on what I love about that music exactly, but something about the era speaks to me.

"Look, Stevie, I'm sure your day wasn't *that* bad. Why don't I take you out for dinner, then you can fill me in on the rest?"

I sigh and glance at the clock. "I wish I could, but I'm due back at the hotel by nine o'clock."

"They booked you a split? I thought that cunt Richard promised he wouldn't pull that shit anymore?" Richard is my very mean and nasty manager, whom Kit has had the misfortune of meeting a few times.

"Language, Kit. Someone up and quit today; they're moving back to Toronto, so now we're short. Who knows if the hotel knows about the splits, but I really don't mind the extra money."

Kit falls silent for a beat. "Breakfast, then—Elements Cafe at ten o'clock tomorrow?"

"That place is too expensive," I protest.

"You're worth it. But babe?"

"Yeah, Kit?"

"Steer clear of Richard. That guy gives me the creeps."

"Duly noted. See you tomorrow."

I hang up the phone, managing to shower and snuggle into my sweats before hearing it ring again like an orchestra.

"Hello?" The way I yawn into the phone, you'd think I'd already worked a split shift.

"How is my favourite little sister?" Instead the voice of my second eldest brother, Smith, travels over the line.

"I'm your only sister," I remind him. I should also remind him that at a curvy, five-foot ten, I'm not so little anymore—but that wouldn't make any difference. To my brothers, I'll always be the baby.

"Uh huh. So what's this I hear about you and some Hollywood rock star?"

"You spoke to Spencer, I take it?" Being the eldest, Spencer is the most overprotective, but Smith takes a close second. My brothers: Spencer, Smith, Sam and Sean (apparently my mom liked *S's*) range from twenty-eight to thirty-five and all four weigh in at over two hundred pounds. All of them are weightlifters; one is even an amateur MMA fighter.

"I think he's Scottish, actually," I try to divert his attention, but he doesn't take the bait.

"I don't care where he's from, all I want to know is what he's doing with my little sis."

"God, the four of you are like a bunch of old biddies, the way you talk. The 'rock star,' as you call him, is Granger Ellis, and there's no him and me. He just happens to be staying at the hotel for a few weeks, and I just happened to have the pleasure of serving him today. Hardly the drama you were hoping for, I know."

"Well, I don't care how many gold records the guy has—he'd better stay away from my sis' or I'll bash his face in. I don't like these celebrity types."

"What celebrities do you know, Smith? Also, I don't think they give out gold records anymore."

"Just tell him to back off. If he tries anything with you, I want to know about it right away," he growls.

"Why? Are you going to drive to the hotel and punch him in the face?"

"I can bench three hundred pounds without breaking a sweat. That rock star's got nothing on me."

"I'm sure there's no danger of some celebrity being interested in me, so my virtue is safely locked up for now."

"Damn right, baby sis, exactly where it should be," he grunts again. Smith knows that I'm no saint—hell, he even bailed Spencer out of jail once, right after Spence beat up my former lying sack-of-shit boyfriend, but it makes him happier to pretend that I'm wearing a chastity belt under my clothes.

"Okay, well, I'll text you later tonight, after I get home from work." As a rule, I'm supposed to send a one-word group text to all four brotherly psychos whenever I work late. Just one word at the end of the night: HOME. If they didn't love me so much, I would disown them. I guess growing up without my Dad around threw them into fatherly overdrive.

"See you Sunday then, at Mom's for dinner. Love you, little one."

"I wouldn't miss it. Love you too, bro." I make kissy noises into the phone and hear him gag on the other end.

"Cut that shit out, Stevie."

I laugh and hang up without saying goodbye. Serves him right for being so overprotective. This little sis' only has one plan: to be free and alive by the mountains—and mountains have nothing in common with rock stars.

Chapter Two

"We're Not Gonna' Take It"

Stevie

The sun makes its descent down the slopes, disappearing into the earth as I park my motorbike in the employee lot. It's a beautiful August evening—not too hot, not too bustling—with the view of Blackcomb Mountain in the distance looking spectacular from every angle.

Whistler Village is a tiny resort town just a few hours from Vancouver, British Columbia, well-known for its world-class skiing and cozy mountain vibes. Most of the world knows it as the main nexus of the 2010 Winter Olympics, as hosted by the region surrounding Vancouver. Whistler has long been a draw to tourists, but since receiving international attention, room prices have skyrocketed and tourists are arriving in droves. The town is mostly known for its wintertime scene, but it keeps up appearances in the summer as well, with endless opportunities for hiking, biking, and just *being* amidst the crisp mountain air.

I throw my jacket and purse into my locker, still in the process of straightening my tacky bowtie when Richard breezes past me.

"You're late." He gives me a smarmy look, half-grimace, half-grin, which makes my skin crawl.

"It's two minutes after nine."

He grunts. "You're in the Mallard Lounge tonight."

"I'll be right out," I sing.

"Well, hurry up. Kim left five minutes ago and the drink orders are stacked to the ceiling."

I make a beeline for the lobby lounge and snatch my tray from Jesse, the bartender. He gives me a quick wave and points dramatically towards Kim's section, rolling his eyes. Kim is the new girl. She's always caught up in some drama, so it's not surprising that she bailed and left her tables high and dry.

The lounge is extremely busy for a weeknight, but there's an entertaining acoustic guitar player in corner. Still, the bar never draws a crowd quite like this. I don't think much about it, getting to work and trying to smooth the feathers of our thirsty patrons. Once all my tables have been sufficiently hydrated, I spot another guest sitting by the fireplace. I make my way over and groan when I see who's waiting for me.

"What are you doing here?" The words stream out before I can stop myself, but he seems totally unfazed.

"Well, I'm about to order a drink," Granger says.

"You have a private Gold Lounge upstairs, with free cocktails, appetizers, and a concierge." I should know, given all the bored businessmen and bratty kids I've served in our alpine-inspired VIP lounge.

"I like the view better here."

He winks at me until I roll my eyes.

"Um, people are staring at you?"

Granger shrugs off my comment. "People always stare at me."

"Fine, have it your way then. What can I get you, Mr. Ellis?"

"What's good here?" His eyes travel up and down my uniform, stopping short at my chest. "Did you forget your name tag?"

I glance down and find the plastic rectangle safely strapped to my chest. "No, it's right here. Why?"

"Your name is Steven?" He gives me the same confused look from his latest Rolling Stone cover (which I *might* have Googled last night).

"Yes, but I usually go by Stevie."

"So your parents wanted a boy?"

The high note of sympathy in his voice throws me for a loop.

"No, they wanted a girl—named Steven."

"Like *A Boy Named Sue*?"

"Huh?"

"You really don't have any taste in music, do you? The Johnny Cash song?" I stare at him like a tabula rasa. "You must have been raised by wolves."

"Actually, wolves were tamed in the Middle East about twelve thousand years ago. Humans realized that wolves could lead them to food, so they chose to hand-raise wolf pups, who then accepted humans as their leaders. Therefore, *technically* humans raised the wolves."

"You're an odd one."

His wide smile softens his words.

"That's what they tell me. Now, what can I get you to drink?"

"Tell you what, Stevie. I'll get on with it and order if you tell me the story behind your name."

I drop my tray and let out another stormy breath. "I have four brothers, so my family was expecting a fifth. Also, my mother is a huge Steven Tyler fan...so cue the *Aerosmith* jokes."

"Why would I joke? Your *Mama Kin* name you anything she wants." He winks and I groan. "So you're a music fan after all?"

I nod at him like a bobble-head doll. "I definitely am."

"What's your favourite band?"

"*Foreigner, Whitesnake, Toto, Twisted Sister, Guns & Roses...*" I trail off after a while, and for once he actually looks speechless.

"Are you fucking with me?"

"Why would I do that?"

"What about my music?"

"Honestly, I've never heard it."

"You must have heard something," he counters. "We get a lot of airtime. Maybe 'Hammer Down'?"

I give him another blank stare and he spouts off a few more song titles. But nothing sticks.

"Huh, that's strange," he muses.

"So, do you want a drink, or is there some other reason that you're here?" My eyes hunt through the crowd, noticing the flash of camera phones in my periphery.

"I just missed you," he whispers.

"Is that so?" I don't know if I should feel flattered or frightened— but the customer is always right, so I keep a good poker face.

"It's true. I changed tables twice before finding your section."

When he mentions tables, I remember that mine are getting restless. I need to wrap this up soon. "You don't even know me, Mr. Ellis."

"But I want to."

"Why?"

"Why not?"

"I can think of a thousand reasons. Look, my other tables probably need me so…"

"I'll take an Aberlour 15—neat please." He rattles off the order like his birthdate. I pretend not to be impressed that he likes good scotch.

"Coming right up."

I place his order with Jesse, the bartender, before having him run it back to my favourite customer. Sometimes it's easier to be a coward. Jesse is quick to oblige though. I just hope he doesn't get himself into trouble by breaking the hotel's *no autograph* policy.

The crowd encircling Granger Ellis disperses as the onlookers grow tired of ogling his highness, returning to their respective tables like children abandoning the bunny hill. Still we're busier than normal and I'm on my feet for the next hour. When I return to Granger's table, his glass is empty and he's radiating amusement.

"I figured you couldn't avoid me forever." His chuckle reminds me of my brother—not just one but *all* of them.

"I'm not avoiding you—I'm working. Can I get you another?" I grab his empty glass while trying not to check him out. His light brown hair is combed back from his face and he's rocking a black vest over a white undershirt with leather wrist cuffs.

"Sure—" He stops short with a glance over my shoulder. "My bandmates are here," he mutters, his mouth thinning into a straight line.

I turn around to find an equally rock-hard guy and girl heading in our direction. The guy sits down first, greeted by my gaping expression. Between his dark skin and stallion black mane of hair, he seems attractive, but I can't process much beyond his stretched earlobes and the impulsive tattoos across his face.

"This is Ravi." Granger introduces his bandmate, who shakes my hand. "Pleasure to meet you." His soft voice and demeanour are totally at odds with the stone-cold look in his eyes. I notice some extreme body art in the skin-carving designs along his flesh, the word *ouch* popping into my head like a ghost.

"And this is Jayne." The girl stares right through me. I match her evil eye with one of my own, but I can't deny that she's beautiful. Her petite frame, short spiky brown hair, and big soulful brown eyes speak wonders about her personality, but they're hard to reconcile with her permanent resting bitch face.

"Why are you sitting here?" Jayne asks Granger; like him, she has a Scottish accent, only thicker.

"Because I like it in here." He gives me his full attention, like I'm the best channel on TV. "I apologize for Jayne's manners. I think she's spent too much time in the Gold Lounge. Jayne is our bassist," he explains. "Ravi is the drummer."

"Are you missing someone then?"

I'd always figured that rock bands were made up of more people.

"We're just a three-piece band. I do vocals and lead guitar."

"You've never heard of *Actuator*?" Jayne asks. From her tone, it's as if I've just announced that I've never heard of Jesus.

"I've heard of you; I just haven't heard you." I wipe the table down right where Ravi has taken up residence.

"Well, that's something," Ravi says, shaking his head in wonder.

"She likes eighties' hair metal," Granger chimes, suddenly putting me on the spot.

"Retro stuff." Ravi nods in approval. "There are some great riffs and melodies in hair metal."

"Can we go now?" Jayne interrupts, and I can't help but notice that she hasn't sat down. "Chad is arranging a private party in your suite as we speak." She gestures to this one guy lingering by the bar. I crane my neck round to check him out, but all I can see is the balding patch on the back of his head.

"Why would Chad throw a party in my room without asking me?"

"It was supposed to be a surprise for the end of our tour," Jayne spits out.

"Of all people, Chad should know that I hate surprises."

"Well, it's too late now," Jayne protests. "Chad is talking to the bar manager about getting some help."

Dread takes root in my stomach, because I know we're short-staffed and Richard already hates me. I'll be the first one playing servant to these celebrities. I don't know why I'm even still standing here instead of doing my job, but my feet are glued to the floor. Right as I'm about to flee, Chad from the bar comes over and grasps Granger's shoulders from behind his chair.

"Ack, Granger, you should see the sweet cheeks I've assembled for you upstairs. It's like a pussy buffet—truly brilliant." Chad is short and stocky with a burgeoning beer belly, probably the result of partying too hard without working off the pounds with a little rock n' roll. Chad has a thick Scottish accent, too, so I figure there must be history there.

Granger studies at me like I'm sheet music. "Stevie, this is Chad, our manager. Chad, this is my friend, Stevie."

Chad looks me up and down but dismisses me right away. "Right, can you run and get me a vodka martini?"

I step away from the table, but Granger holds up one hand to stop me. "Don't be rude, Chad. We were talking."

"Then ya' can talk upstairs. The bar manager is sending a few of them—maybe even this one—upstairs for the evening."

"This one has a name," I pipe up, unable to stop myself.

"Of course ya' do, sweets, but right now I'm more concerned with whether or not you can make a martini."

I bite my tongue, stifling my anger before stomping back to the bar. Richard is rearranging the bottles and talking to Jesse. I brace my hands on the countertop before leaning forward to whisper-shout at my boss.

"Richard! I'm already working a split shift and I'm exhausted. You can't send me upstairs!"

Richard gives me a look and shrugs. "Granger Ellis is a VIP guest and his manager requested female servers only." He pauses and gives me the onceover. "He actually requested hot servers, but I guess you'll have to do."

It takes all of my willpower not to scream at him. What a revolting over-the-hill little maggot he is.

"If they keep me past midnight, I'm requesting double time." I spit the words out like bullets, but Richard simply returns the gesture with a patronizing smile.

"We will see about that."

Fifteen minutes later, I am up on the twelfth floor staring at the glittering lights of Blackcomb Mountain through the twenty-five foot, floor-to-ceiling windows. I stand off to the side with a tray of champagne flutes filled with a 1995 Krug that I happen to know cost more than a month's mortgage for me.

Tonight is my first time in the penthouse suite. I've seen pictures, but they hardly do it justice. The living room on the main floor takes center stage with its impressive fireplace, rusted deer-antler chandelier, and peaked cedar-log ceilings. Double doors open onto the Juliette balcony where the circular staircase winds up to the second-level master bedroom. I'm dying to take a look at the enormous bathroom, but being *the help* and all, I'm not allowed.

The party unravels in full swing. Chad was not lying about the veritable vagina buffet. From the looks of it, he must have invited every model-slash-actress in Vancouver to party tonight. The evening is a smorgasbord of long legs and barely-there dresses covering collar-bones. A group of women have already descended on Granger, crammed like sardines beside him on the couch. It would seem a true feat of nature if only their asses weren't the size of my outstretched palm. I'm exaggerating, of course (*I mean, sort of*).

I glance behind Granger and notice Jayne hovering around him, kind of like an electron. She doesn't seem impressed with the crowd occupying their force field, either. Across the room, Ravi stuffs his face with appetizers as some others snort blow off the glass coffee table. I didn't think coke was so popular anymore, but judging by the ski hill of white powder on the table, it's making a comeback. One of the servers from the lounge, Mandy, saunters by me with a tray of smoked-salmon crostini. Her gaze is part fascination and part horror, which is not surprising as Mandy is all of nineteen years old. I'm not missing the lecherous looks that these dirt bags are shooting her way.

"Hey Mandeep," I whisper, but she just mumbles something incoherent. Her hair is pulled into a tight bun and her face is makeup free. Not to mention, her figure is well hidden by the shapeless polyester uniform—but none of it masks her beauty.

Someone turns down the stereo and the conversation halts. Chad, his nose rimmed in white powder, stands on an antique chair to command the crowd's attention. "Now, what you've all been waiting for, I give you the unheard, acoustic version of *Actuator's* soon-to-be-released single!"

Granger jolts upright. "Let's not do this now."

"I promised them, man," Chad mutters back. Granger doesn't look pleased, but he complies nonetheless, inching forward on the couch and spreading his legs apart like a pyramid. He knees one of the waif models in the ribs by accident, and she lets out an unfortunate yelp. I know it shouldn't, but it gives me the strangest sense of satisfaction.

Chad gets down from the antique chair and wipes his nose, crossing the room to retrieve Granger's guitar. He sets it down in Granger's lap, who sighs and curls his large hands around the strings.

"It's called 'No Witness' and for any members of the media in the room, please remember that you heard it here first." Chad steps aside and allows Granger to light up the room.

*You tell me I'm misled / that it's all in my head / when you
climb into bed
You can do no wrong / spinning your lies / it's no surprise / that you'll
be my demise
You always pick the truth that's good for you / you take it
and twist it / leave behind no witness, to your sickness
Your words mean nothing to me / so tired of shoveling your
bullshit around / buried deep in the ground / I'm sinking
down
You always pick the truth / that's good for you / you take it
and twist it / leave behind no witness to your sickness
I'm drowning in what's left of you / your shallow pool / a
wolf in sheepskin / don't know where you've been / so wipe
off that fucking grin*

He sounds good—too good—as if the words slipping from his lips exist at a higher plane of being than Granger himself. The raw gravel of his voice wraps around each verse like smoke. I'm surprised by how melodic the song sounds, though it's an acoustic version; who knows what the thrasher version sounds like in comparison. Perhaps it's not my kind of music, but it's impossible to deny how talented Granger is as an artist. His voice is just the right balance of rough and raw. Watching him belt out the heart-wrenching lyrics with his eyes closed makes me feel like I've stumbled into something very private, as if he's playing his diary onstage. His voice pulls me in like gravity and is almost too much for me to handle.

The crowd falls silent when he finishes the song and their reaction makes it obvious that it wasn't what they were expecting. Granger's song was beautiful and heartfelt, but he wasn't the upbeat, enigmatic rock star they'd hoped to glimpse tonight. The crowd is hungry and here for their pound of flesh. One of the groupies starts feebly clapping and some lazy supporters follow suit. Granger's eyes are still closed though, as if he's trying to make the room disappear. Soon enough, Chad steps in to distill the tension.

"I hope you all enjoyed the preview! Just wait until you hear the heavy beats to accompany those deadly lyrics. That single is headed for triple platinum—now on your feet and let's get this fucking party started!"

Chad's enthusiasm earns a few cheers and the crowd disperses. Even the sofa-riding waifs give up—it's clear that the rock God isn't biting tonight. Someone grabs the last glass off my tray, so I head back to the wet bar for a refill. I'm rounding the corner when I hear Mandy's pleading voice.

"Please, I have a boyfriend."

"It doesn't matter to me."

I immediately recognize the guy's bald spot—that, along with his too tight dress shirt and sloppy posture reveals that it's Chad.

"I need to go back into the living room," Mandy whispers.

I step forward for a better look, but it's clear that she's shaken up. This is perfectly understandable, whether she's nineteen or ninety-nine, because Chad has her backed up against the wall with his grimy paws encircling her waist.

I march over and extricate Mandy from his hold, shooting a death glare at Chad in the process, before handing her my empty tray.

"Mandeep, do you mind taking over champagne duty for a while? Chad and I need to talk."

"Of course." Her voice wavers as she curls her delicate fingers around my tray. "Thank you," she whispers, before rushing off without another sound.

Chad straightens his shoulders and glares at me. "Who are you, her mother?"

"You're lucky I'm not," I snap. "She's a teenager, for God's sake!"

"She's old enough to have a little fun."

"You're disgusting."

"And you're a bitch."

I roll my eyes at the insult. "That's original."

"Whatever, slag."

He elbows me in the ribs as he brushes by, but I don't flinch; I won't give him the satisfaction. After he's gone, I sigh and look around for Mandy's tray, knowing that Richard will try to charge her for losing it, the asshole. I find it teetering on the edge of the hallway table, but I snatch it up and head for the small refrigerator to refill with canapés. I'm thinking about Mandy on route from the kitchen, so I don't notice the woman approaching me until it's too late. It's one of the models. I fail to avoid her and we crash into each other instead, my tray of smoked salmon slamming into her bony chest before crashing to the floor.

She screams as if she's deathly allergic to salmon. "What is your problem?!"

I stifle a giggle at the sight of her wiping the cream-cheese-laden toast points off her clavicle. "I am so sorry, Miss." It's impossible not to stare at the cluster of scallions stuck to her neck; the woman is like walking-talking sushi.

"You fat bitch!"

I shake my head, but not because I'm upset—I just can't believe she went there. The room goes silent as Granger appears beside us, as if from nowhere.

"Easy, bee stings," I say, in a placating tone. "It was an accident."

"*You* are an accident." She sounds all of thirteen years old. "This dress is one-hundred percent raw silk and you're going to pay for it!"

I raise my hands in surrender. "You know, the hotel has a wonderful dry-cleaning service and we'd be honoured to launder your scrap of fabric any time."

She snarls before whirling around to bark at Granger. "Are you going to let some waitress talk to me like this?"

Granger glances between us with a goofy smirk on his face. "I have absolutely no control over this one."

She still hasn't wiped the scallions and cream cheese from her neck, and the flushed red color from her cheeks is now creeping downwards. I'm about to defend myself when Chad steps in to intervene. "I'm going to have to ask you to leave," he says—to me. "I am so sorry, Michaela. I guess this is the help we should expect in Canada." Michaela laughs a tad too excitedly, and I count to ten to stop myself from saying the wrong thing. I need this job—that is, if I haven't already lost it.

"Consider me gone," I announce while bending down to retrieve my tray. "And Michaela? Nice necklace, by the way." I drill my eyes at her food-smeared skin, as snickers ripple across the room. "Enjoy your oh-so-fabulous party!" Mandy stands by the fireplace with both eyes on the exchange, so I give her a wave. She smiles and waves back—my only fan in town.

I march towards the elevator with my head held high, letting my shoulders sag only once the doors are sealed behind me. I'm grateful that the lifestyle I witnessed tonight is peripheral to my own existence and that, in a few weeks, Granger Ellis and his crew will leave. I yawn into my palm and check myself out in the mirrored doors of the elevator. My hair is a giant mess, and I have a small stain on my shirt that appears to be red wine.

My face looks tired, but I'm still me. I smile at the thought, because there's no one I'd rather be. I can't wait to get myself home and showered, snuggling up with Toto on the couch and watching the nature documentary I have recorded. Maybe I'll even make myself something to eat. Strangely, I have a sudden and overwhelming craving for salmon.

Chapter Three

"Look What the Cat Dragged In"

Granger

Man, it took three tries and one autographed copy of my last studio album, but I got the name of the pub where Stevie works. The valet wouldn't fess up about her address, but it's all good. Making music has taught me to work with what I've got.

It's eight o'clock in the evening, but the sun is gonzo, blocked by the big-ass mountains instead. The bar patio is crammed with tourists, huddled under the yellow patio umbrellas like it's raining or something. A group of overdressed women take a line of shots from a carved-up ski—called a shot-ski, or so I've been told. Judging by their matching t-shirts, one of these lovely ladies is heading for the altar.

I asked about the pub at the front desk of my hotel. It was some famous Whistler spot, which opened thirty years ago. Guess that means it's more famous than me. The pub doesn't get me excited, but the view is something else. I've been trekking around for months with my bandmates, but the valleys of Whistler allow my brain to reset—at least the hemisphere that feeds on riffs and chords.

Stevie is nowhere to be seen, so I nod at Chad to head indoors. The crowd inside is whatever, with just a few groups staking out the high-top tables. A DJ sets up shop in the corner, the carpet with its crazy cow designs as his stage. The biggest crowd is by the bar though. Two spots open up and Chad grabs the nearest stool. He's a pain in the ass but less of a burden than having my security team wait outside. Coming here solo would make me desperate as fuck anyways. Though that would be true. I'm ridiculously desperate to spend time with the smart-mouthed waitress who hates my music— venture even more than she hates me.

I'm about to find out that she's not a waitress tonight at all—she's a bartender. Just then, she sees me. Her eyes scan the bar and settle on me and my jackass manager. Her mouth tightens. The stiffness in her lips mimics the stiffness in my crotch. God knows that I love a challenge. She's definitely easy on the eyes, what with that creamy skin, full pink lips, and golden curls like the roaring MGM Lion.

Full disclosure: she's not really my type. She's way taller, curvier, and fairer than my regular groupies. First time for everything though, right? I'm into all the little things about her—that smart mouth, for instance, or that sexy dusting of freckles on her nose. She hit me like a freight train when I saw her standing by the pool, but blimey if I know why. My interest goes far beyond the physical. That's my only explanation right now.

She takes her sweet time heading our way, smiling though it looks painful. "Welcome to Longhorn's, what can I get you?"

I had prepared a smooth opening in my head on my way here, but one look into her big, whiskey-brown eyes and I am completely tongue-tied.

"Hi," I croak, but it comes out all garbled and strange. Her eyes flit from me to Chad, and that lovely smile disappears like I venture she wants to do herself.

"What'll it be?" Man, she really wants to get away from us. Fuck, why did I even bring Chad with me?

"I'll have a whiskey. Scotch," Chad says.

She braces both arms on the counter. "So is it a whiskey or a scotch?"

"Same thing."

An old man hanging out at a nearby stool waves his hand at Chad, whistling through his teeth. "You're gonna' wish you didn't say that, sonny."

"I'll go easy on him, Joe." Stevie smiles and continues her banter with Chad. "Actually, they're not all the same, not at all, and I'm surprised that a Scotsman doesn't already know that. For example, the main differences are geographic conditions and the method of distilling.”

I have a feeling that we’re about to get schooled, but it’s a lesson that Chad deserves. As a Scotsman, I’m embarrassed for him. When it comes to scotch and whiskey, I get the differences, but it’s crazy satisfying to watch someone like Chad get knocked down a few notches—especially by a girl like Stevie.

“Scotch is whiskey made in Scotland and aged in oak barrels for at least three years. All scotch is whiskey, but not all whiskey is scotch.” Stevie’s knowledge in this department reminds me of a Wikipedia page improvising an epic onstage solo.

“Bourbon is Kentucky whiskey; rye is Canadian whiskey, and of course there’s Irish whiskey—not to mention the Japanese, who are doing some very exciting things with whiskey. Scotch is made mostly from malted barley while bourbon is distilled from corn. Add to that the additives plus how long it has been aged, and suddenly a plethora of differences between scotch and whiskey reveal themselves. So, which one will it be?”

I check out Chad, whose mouth hangs open like a ski-jump. He stays in said stunned state for a good minute before speaking a single world. “Fuck, Canadians are weird. Just give me a drink of whatever.”

“Canadians are what now?” The old man, Joe, pipes up again. Stevie mouths something to him immediately, like apparently the fun is over and he should shut-up.

“Relax, grandpa, that’s not your business,” Chad snarls, but it’s a foolish move.

“How about I take you outside and make it my business?” This young guy with hockey hair appears behind the old man and cracks his knuckles.

“Christ, I thought you people were supposed to be all nice and peaceful, like pacifists or something?” Chad shakes his head, the same way he does when shouldering a bad hangover.

"Sure, sonny," Joe mutters, "and James right behind me here is about to pass his fist up where the sun don't shine—and not just any sun, your sun, *sonny*."

As hilarious as this whole thing is, I gotta' intervene. So I step in front of *his-highness-with-the-hockey-hair* before Chad can say another lousy word.

"I apologize for my friend," I whisper to the old guy. "He doesn't get out much. Honestly, we're just here for the view." I nod my head in Stevie's direction, but she has already abandoned the drama to pour more drinks. Yeah, smart girl.

"You and everyone else seated at this bar, buddy." Hockey-hair talks to me like I'm the last guy to some party where no music is even being played. Still, he cools off and backs away to reclaim his stool. I return my focus to Stevie working the bar, watching like a stalker (or I figure that's how it looks).

Her skin-tight jeans cup her round arse like the friggin' moon, with her long shapely legs adding a sway to her hips. Her thighs brush together where they make a V between her legs, but there's something about this woman that I find dead sexy. When she reaches up to grab a whiskey bottle from the top shelf, her shirt rides up, showing off a strip of creamy snow-white flesh. She's curvier than the models I know, but I love that extra meat on a woman; her hourglass figure has me dreaming in all the right ways.

When she turns around, my eyes cling to the black *Def Leppard* tank top knotted up under her breasts. Maybe a weird fashion choice, but she looks damn hot in that thing. I check out her goldilocks curls, piled high atop her head, picturing running one hand along the back of her neck and feeling my dick twitch in my pants.

She slides Chad's glass down the counter, but apparently I forgot to order anything. Chad picks up his drink and mutters something to himself, heading off in the direction of the dance floor. Only a few people occupy the space and Chad is not one to bust a move, but the risk of getting his face bashed in by Hockey-Hair is much less over there.

I pick up the glass Stevie swiftly sets down in front of me and sip at the amber-colored liquid, savouring it on my tongue like piss of the gods. Above all else, this girl has good taste in scotch.

"Good choice. Glenmorangie Nectar D'Or?"

"Good pallet," she shoots back, impressed but not happy about it.

"I'm sure Chad will appreciate your good taste."

She snorts. "Chad got some Alberta Springs rye that I found in the back."

I choke on my next sip, wheezing out laughter as I work to catch my breath. "Wow, you really don't like him."

"Not even a little bit. Why do you bother with him?"

"I have my reasons. Why don't you like him? Other than my party last night—is there any other reason?"

"Isn't that enough of a reason?" She raises one eyebrow; the move is so sexy that I feel a shudder pass through my body.

"What are you doing here, Granger? You kicked me out of your party, remember? Or have you forgotten that little detail?" She wipes down the counter, which makes her cleavage pop and her breasts knock. This time my dick does more than just twitch.

"I want to take you out."

"Why?"

"Because I want to get to know you."

"But why?"

"Because I like you."

"How can you like me if you don't even know me?"

"That's what I'm trying to do—get to know you. God, you're a frustrating little thing, aren't you?"

She rolls her eyes. "Who are you calling little?"

Clearly she'll never be a groupie—thank God.

"Go out with me," I repeat.

"No."

"Why not?"

"I don't want to."

"But I think you do."

"This isn't me being coy, Mr. Ellis, I'm not interested."

"So it's Mr. Ellis now, is it?" I push my empty glass in her direction, and Stevie stares at the thing with lasers in her eyes.

"The bar seats are for paying customers—order, or move on."

"Right then, I'll take a shot of tequila."

She bends down to reach the lower shelf, giving me a straight-on view of her spectacular arse. Then she slams the shot glass down like a gavel, pouring the tequila before my very eyes and throwing back the whole thing herself.

"That'll be eight dollars," she chimes.

Ok, I'm up for this challenge. I place one fifty on the counter and order another shot, watching her repeat the process.

"What has nine arms and sucks?" I tease, gesturing to her shirt.

"Like I've never heard that one before."

"Def Leppard seriously does suck, though."

"Well, that's your opinion."

I've hit a nerve, maybe, so I change the subject. "Why do you bartend here?"

"That's a weird question."

"Does the hotel not pay you enough?"

"That's hardly any of your business, but for your information, I like working at the hotel. I've been there for years."

"You certainly fill out the uniform well here though—*if* that's the uniform." If *Def Leppard* is sponsoring bars in Whistler now, well, *Actuator* just got way cooler. "Are you aware that I sold more records last year than Def Leppard has sold over their entire career?"

"Good for you." She sounds bored as fuck. "But as you'll remember from last night, I'm not familiar with your music. 'Pour Some Sugar on me' however..." She stretches back to remove the elastic band from her hair, shaking out her impressive mane. Dick twitch number three.

"'Last Chance Again'? 'Nail it in'? 'Consumed'? You've heard none of these songs?" It's not like the whole world has to like our music, in fact, I know that our style isn't for everyone—but I'd legit be surprised if she hadn't heard something of ours.

"Nope."

"So it's really only hair bands for you, then?"

She nods and wipes down the counter. "Extreme, Nazareth, Scorpions, Heart..." She shrugs, throwing the rag over her shoulder. "I like them."

"I get it, I get it—power ballads only. You really are something."

"*Mmmhmm...*" she hums, looking past me with a wave. I glance over my shoulder and notice the DJ waving back. He mouths something to Stevie and grins—just as quickly, a new song plays over the sound system.

"This classic is for my girl, Stevie. It won't come as a surprise to you regulars, but I'll ask the tourists in the room to be patient with us."

The Mr. Big song, "Be with You," comes blaring over the speakers. There's a few groans from the crowd and then a round of cheers.

Hold on little girl
Show me what he's done to you
Stand up little girl
A broken heart can't be that bad
When it's through, it's through
Fate will twist the both of you
So come on baby, come on over
Let me be the one to show you

Stevie belts out the lyrics, without a care in her gorgeous little mind. I can't stop grinning at the performance, at her swaying back and forth behind the bar. Her voice isn't that terrible. The DJ lets the chorus play once before bleeding the track into an up-tempo pop song.

"At least he played some of it," she sighs.

"And who is *he* exactly?" I don't like the way he smiled at Stevie one bit, not to mention the look on his tanned pretty-boy face.

"Kit."

"And Kit is?"

"The DJ."

"And you're shagging the DJ then?"

"Are you serious right now?"

Just my luck, Chad picks this exact moment to appear at the bar. Stevie turns her attention to my band manager, like he's a new channel on television.

"Another scotch for you?" she asks. "Or was it whiskey?"

"Come on, man, let's go. Fuck her."

"I intend to." I give Stevie a brazen wink.

"Yeah, good luck with that, asshole," Stevie snorts and it's hot as hell.

"I don't believe in luck, beautiful, but I can guarantee that we'll see each other again."

I make eyes at her before following my manager out the front door—as if we both have somewhere better to be, with a more important crowd. But we don't, 'cuz Stevie is working right here.

Chapter Four

"Nothin' But A Good Time"

Stevie

I wake up after eleven because of my late shift last night, having tossed and turned all night, thinking about Granger's appearance in the bar. Every time I closed my eyes, I saw his ridiculous smirk and wink. Of course, I'm hardly an idiot—after completing a four-year university degree in just three years and skipping two whole grades in high school, I firmly sit several levels above idiot.

With men like him, it's all about the chase. A millionaire rock star, used to getting anything he wants, is bound to respond to the one woman in town who doesn't want him. I just wish my mind and body could get on the same page about the "not wanting" part. Yawning, I take another sip of my coffee before dumping the rest into the sink. My hair is still wet from the shower but I can't be bothered to blow-dry. Instead, I pull it back into a ponytail and retreat into the garage to work on my motorcycle.

I gaze at my cream and chrome beauty with a deep sigh; looking at my gal is like looking at a dream. The throttle gets stuck sometimes and I need to find a solution for that today. I haven't had time to work on it in weeks, but I have my knitting group to attend and dinner with Kit later. I've been into riding ever since I was sixteen years old, thanks to my four older brothers.

I love my hog more than anything else *sans* heartbeat. She's an Indian Scout Sixty, a balanced and lightweight bike that suits me to a T. For an hour, I troubleshoot my problem, which leaves me just enough time to drop by the local library for my knitting circle. Our group is called the 'Wizards of Wool' and we meet every Thursday in the back community room.

Upon arriving, I park my motorcycle on the curb and head inside to find everyone else already seated and working. There are five of us in total. If I exclude myself, the average age is about seventy-five, which is my favourite part of the group. Second to riding, knitting relaxes me like nothing else in the world (not even sex can take the title) and my knitting pals are a big part of that.

"Good afternoon, Betty." I greet our self-appointed leader, who frowns at me and peers over the reading glasses slipping down her nose.

"You're late. Put a toonie in the pot please."

"I thought that was the swear jar?"

Betty grunts at my protest, so I fish around in the pocket of my shorts for a two-dollar coin, dropping it into the mason jar and taking my seat. I've donated generously to the swear jar over the past couple of years, but it either goes towards supplies or our annual Christmas party, so I don't mind. With the plastic chairs arranged in a circle, we chat and face each other while knitting, and I focus on a particularly difficult mattress stitch in the sweater.

"So, tell us how it went with the devil worshipper?" Joe (the lone male in our group, a regular at the bar, and my favourite knitting companion) breaks the silence.

I roll my eyes. "He's a rocker, Joe, not a devil worshipper." At least, I don't think he's a devil worshipper.

Joe is a tiny man with wiry-white hair and a splotchy-red face which has seen plenty of wear and tear. He's fit for a man of eighty-five but perpetually complains about everything: his back, his knees, the weather, the government—even the free coffee at the library.

"You bought a new rocker?" Betty pipes up, tapping her hearing aid.

"No, you old coot, she didn't buy a chair. Our girlie here met a rock musician."

"A rock star," I clarify. "He plays in a famous heavy-metal band. But I didn't meet him per se...I just served him at the hotel."

"And?" Joe presses.

"He's full of himself and drinks girly beverages."

"That's not very *juicy* at all." Joe sounds very disappointed. "You'll have to do better next time."

"Well…" I clear my throat. "He did manage to track me down at the bar the following day."

"That's better! What did he want?" Irene finally joins in on the conversation.

I shrug off her question. "Sex, I think."

"Ha!" Joe cackles and slaps his knee. "It's true! I saw it with my own two eyes, but she shot him down good. Our girlie here knows better than to mess with one of those rockers, don't you?"

Joe insists on calling me girlie despite having known me for years. The nickname has grown on me though, which goes to show how women can get used to anything. Nonetheless, I learned a long time ago that "can" is different than "should."

"I have a strong sense of self-preservation, Joe. But tell me, what specifically do you have against musicians?" I take a little sip from my lukewarm coffee.

"Herpes!"

Just like that, I spit the bitter liquid all over my sweatshirt. "Sorry?"

"You will be sorry, if you let one of them devil worshippers into your pants. They're full of herpes—all of them." Joe nods, seemingly satisfied with his point.

"Is it your belief then that all musicians have herpes?" I summarize, unable to contain my amusement re: his wildly irrational thesis.

"Not musicians, girlie, rockers. There's a difference."

"True, there is," I concede.

"What do you know about herpes, Joe?" chimes Jean, the quietest member of our group.

"I was in the war, Jean! Of course I know about herpes!" He shouts loud enough that even the toddlers in the children's section swivel their heads. This obviously isn't a conversation I want to delve into any deeper, so I attempt to change the subject.

"Neither herpes nor rock stars will be an issue for me. I sent Granger on his merry way. Now can someone please help me with my sweater? It's a disaster!" I hold the evidence above my head like an umbrella.

"Did you test your swatch?" Irene asks.

"You really have to measure your gauge more seriously." Betty clicks her tongue in disapproval. "Knitting is a fine art."

"You can reknit on different needles if necessary," Jean adds, helpful as always.

Having successfully diverted the conversation, we spend the remaining time discussing the cost of groceries, followed by Betty's newest grandson. Pretty soon everything goes back to normal. I'm already packing up my things when Joe asks what I'm doing for the rest of the day.

"I'm meeting Kit for dinner in Whistler."

"Poor kid," Joe says, shaking his head. "That boy's got it bad for you."

"He's my best friend, Joe." It must be the hundredth time I've told him this.

"You've *friend-zoned* him." Joe lets go of a big sigh, as if Kit is some younger version of himself.

I can't help but laugh, with Joe clothed in every shade of adorable before me. "How do you even know that term?"

"I'm a modern man, girlie, I have Twitter."

"Okay, Joe." I giggle and shake my head, watching him return to the group. I wave goodbye to the ladies before grabbing my bag and heading for the door. The hinge creaks as I swing open the frame and Joe shouts after me.

"Remember about the herpes, girlie!" He announces the last part so loud that a few horrified mothers gawk at me. Even the librarian gives me a look.

"Mom, what are herpes?" I hear this one little boy whisper to his mom by the water fountain, and my face heats with embarrassment.

I give Joe a backwards salute farewell and rush out of the building like it's on fire.

➤

Kit and I sit smack-dab in the centre of Whistler Village, just outside the Amsterdam Café, in good company with the mountain bikers and celery-salted Caesars—i.e. the Bloody Mary(s) of the Great White North.

"Ah man, I love that guy!" He wipes tears from his eyes, doubled over in laughter upon hearing Joe's position on herpes.

"He's a fan of yours, too."

"Yeah, how so?"

"Long story." I let out a completely un-ladylike breath. The herpes anecdote was better kept secret, as Joe's comments are seldom easy to explain. I don't want this conversation to enter "friend-zone" territory anytime soon. Kit is too important of a presence in my life to mess things up. Of course he's attractive, but I'm not attracted to him personally. I've seen his type and it's not for me.

Sure, when we first met, my mind considered the possibility. He probably thought about it, too, but my thoughts came from a place of curiosity rather than actual desire. Herein lies the dilemma with close relationships between two people: the thought of your relationship becoming something more always crosses your mind, but you likely abandon the possibility the moment that you dream it up. After all, platonic relationships offer substance and comfort, and they're hard to come by sometimes.

I dig into the enormous plate of nachos that we're sharing and stuff my face with *guac*. Meanwhile, Kit peppers me with questions about last night.

"So what exactly was he doing at Longhorn's?"

"Not sure," I shrug. "Apparently Carl, the valet, told him where I work."

"Carl is a dick. I'll have a talk with him." Kit doesn't sound like he's kidding. In fact, he sounds pissed.

"Don't bother—it's not like my working there is some big secret."

"So he just wanted to see where you worked?"

"No, he wanted to take me out. Oh, and fuck me, but I'm not sure in what order."

Kit releases an uncomfortable-sounding cough. "Uh, what a pig."

"I guess so."

"You guess so?" He raises both eyebrows in unison, and his forehead practically pops out of his face.

"He seems harmless." I try to shrug off the harsh vibe coming from my dearest friend.

"It's offensive *and* an invasion of your personal space."

"You feel pretty strongly about this, don't you?"

"Damn right I do," he growls, stuffing a big nacho in his mouth.

I'm weirdly jealous that he stole such a cheesy bite. I love everything about nachos, but especially how the cheese hardens and sticks to everything. I try to pick some off the plate, feeling him watching my every move.

"Are you interested in him?" The hesitation in his voice is impossible to miss.

"No! At least, I don't think so. I don't know." I don't know what's making me ramble so much right now.

"Stevie, you know he's only here for a few weeks, then it's back to LA or Europe or wherever the hell he lives."

"I know, okay?" I manage to successfully free one strip of cheese and pop into my mouth like a prize. "I'm not stupid, Kit. But I am horny."

He rears back for a moment, smothering his face with both hands and letting out a groan. "Don't tell me shit like that, please."

"Why?" I snicker, wiggling my eyebrows. "Are you grossed out?"

"On the contrary. More like hard."

"Shut up, Kit!" I squeal, leaning forward to whack his arm. I assume he's teasing me and not sporting a rod.

"Well, now you've gone and done it," he jokes. "I'll need to find some relief tonight. What do you say to Buffalo Bill's after this?"

I give him a look. "Oh, I'm sorry. I didn't realize that congratulations were in order!"

"Congratulations?"

"Yes, congratulations on your nuptials. You must be getting married, therefore in dire need of a stag party, because I see no other reason for wanting to visit Bill's."

Buffalo Bill's is one of Whistler's premier clubs, known for attracting a healthy number of tourists in search of their last gasp. What happens in Whistler, stays in Whistler (insert appropriate clichés here), am I right? The music at Bill's is decent and the dancing is upbeat, but it's not somewhere locals flock to these days.

"Babe, you got me all riled up. I need to find some poor unsuspecting girl to unleash on now. Pretty please, help me find a gal wearing a plastic crown and a *bride-to-be* sash who's dying to experience her last night of freedom?" He bats his eyes like an adorable cartoon character.

"Fine," I sigh. "But I'm not staying long."

"That's a good girl." He grins, as if that was precisely what he wanted to hear.

We settle the bill and wander through Whistler Village, alternating between window shopping and people watching before heading to Bill's. The club tends to draw a large crowd and a lineup has already formed outside, but Kit recognizes the doorman who waves us inside, as if we are the *real* rock stars in town.

On our way downstairs, this one girl bonks my head with a giant pink-inflatable penis. "Hey!" I swat it away and she gives me a glassy-eyed, "sorry" before disappearing onto the dance floor.

"Jeez," I say, nudging Kit. "It's not even ten o'clock."

Kit makes a beeline for the front bar as I hang back and scan the room. The club doesn't get much busier than this, but the area near the back bar is also roped off. A crowd of people holding iPhones like flashlights cluster around the area, as more bodies stream inside. I tire of being jostled by the crowd and join Kit at the bar.

"Friend, remind me what we're doing here again?" I sidle up beside him as if we're undercover cops having a top-secret chat.

"Are you kidding? A room full of horny ladies, all fueled by shots and increased need for sexual validation? It's like heaven!"

Right on cue, this cute little blonde—a bride-to-be in a tutu and a tiara—collides with me like a wayward snowboarder merging out of the trees. "Sorry," she slurs, swiveling around in a circle before heading off in the opposite direction.

"Christmas has come," Kit whispers, and I snort aloud.

"Focus, perv, I'm thirsty. Have you even ordered yet?" My eyes hunt for the bartender and find Matt, who I used to work with at the hotel. I give him a wave and he abandons the guy who's waving a fifty-dollar bill in his face in order to serve us.

"Hey guys." He leans across the bar, shaking Kit's hand and kissing my cheek. "The usual?"

"Do you have any decent scotch today?" I ask, watching him pour Kit's usual rum and coke.

"I do, but I can only give you the first one for free, Stevie. The new manager's measuring shit."

"Thanks, Matt. One is probably enough for me tonight." He retrieves the bottle from the top shelf and pours me a double. Just as I'm lifting the glass to my lips, someone bumps into me from behind and sends the amber liquid right up my nose. Kit whacks me on the back until I stop coughing and find my breath at last.

"Busy enough in here?" I manage to spit out.

"Granger Ellis is supposed to be here tonight. It was just a rumour...until he showed up."

"Your boyfriend is here?" Kit acts like this is somehow my fault, so I shoot him a dirty look.

"Where did you hear that?" I ask, turning back to Matt.

"One of the band members made the mistake of striking up a conversation with his driver, and you know how the rest goes." Matt shrugs. "Anyway, I better get back to it. Have fun, guys."

Matt rushes away to serve the growing line of people crowded around *Actuator*'s end the bar. The very last person I want to see tonight is Granger Ellis. "Maybe we should just go?" I ask Kit, who removes the straw from his drink and tosses it aside.

"We're not going. Women engaging in their last night of debauchery, remember?"

"Yeah." I roll my eyes—this is like talking to my brother. "I remember."

We finish our drinks and spill onto the dance floor. They play the usual touristy Top-40 mix, but I cross my fingers that they'll break out the Bon Jovi soon. After all, "It's My Life" always seems to get the crowd going. The dance floor is packed shoulder to shoulder and I keep getting separated from Kit, who eventually cradles my waist and pulls me into his body. We dance to another song before some commotion breaks out in back, emptying half the dance floor. It doesn't take a genius to understand that *Ellis is in the building,* between the female shrieks and flashing camera phones.

Kit leans in to whisper in my ear. "Want to go say hello?"

"Don't tease me."

"I'm not," he says, sighing. "You said you wanted to get laid! Whatever you need, I'm here for you all the way."

I try not to read into his comment, but I do another shoulder-check nonetheless. The crowd parts to reveal Granger zigzagging across the dance floor. Three exceptionally large "men in black" surround him like riot police, scanning the crowd and holding out their arms to keep the fans at bay.

I duck my head as Granger passes me, but he catches my eye anyways and tempts me with a wink. I notice an unfamiliar tightness in his smile, though the gesture is playful. It's like he's trying not to look pissed off. Who knows what his problem is—I mean, he might be a rock star, but I'm not into mind games with powerful men.

He circles the dance floor, waving at fans and signing autographs before his security guards lead him back to the roped-off area. Most of the crowd moves with him, shouting his name and waving their hands as if he's about to throw the bouquet.

"This could really kill your bride mojo," I muse.

"Nothing kills my mojo, babe, you know that."

We bust a move for another two songs on the now nearly empty dance floor, before hitting the bar for a second round. I order a beer and Kit orders another rum and coke. From where I'm standing, I have a clear line of sight to the VIP table, and I feel Granger's eyes on me like a million tiny magnets attracting every inch of my skin. The corner of his lips tug into a smirk, and he mouths something that looks like *fuck me* (or maybe he's saying *fuck you*; it's hard to tell from this distance).

"He really is staring at you," Kit says.

"Is that so hard to believe?"

"Of course not. I just—I thought you were exaggerating the whole thing."

"Thanks for the vote of confidence," I scoff, though I don't mean it. I'm just as baffled as Kit.

"You've never been the self-deprecating type, Stevie. You've got more confidence than every woman in this bar combined, which is about the sexiest thing in a woman. I only meant that Granger Ellis has his pick of the litter on a daily basis, so why waste time when you're clearly not interested?"

"Maybe *I am* interested," I hedge.

"Yeah? Since when?" Kit challenges. "It sure didn't sound like that at the restaurant."

"Since now. I mean, what so wrong with me getting a little action? He's obviously the non-committal type and just here for a short time. It could be exactly what I need."

I don't know if I believe my own words, but I'm smarting from Kit's comment about Granger having his pick of the litter on a daily basis. Who knows how I'd react if he offered me a one-night stand on a silver platter.

"Dear God, you're starting to sound like me." Kit slams his empty glass down on the counter. "I need to dance this nonsense right out of your head!"

Already the dance floor is filling up again, as the novelty of Granger's presence wears off, but Kit drags me back under the strobe lights anyways. We dance to a few more songs, including "It's My Life" which finally makes its customary appearance.

For a rare moment, I feel like I'm on top of the world—so lost in the music that I don't even notice when the security guard approaches us beneath the disco ball. Not until he's towering over my body, blocking my view of Kit like a total solar eclipse, do I notice the two hundred and fifty pound hunk of trouble strolling into my night.

Chapter Five

"Tease Me Please Me"

Granger

She knows I'm here. I even winked at her on the dance floor. She must know, yet she hasn't come to see me. I would be lying if I pretended to be looking for her here, though it crossed my mind that she might be out tonight. As it turns out, Chad planned the radio-station promo at Bill's a while back and I had no idea. Seeing Stevie is a total coincidence, but I couldn't be happier about it.

I watch as the club fills up by the minute, thinking that it doesn't really seem like her kind of place. But then again, I don't really know her, at least not yet. After Longhorn's last night, I went back to the hotel and jacked off in the shower to the image of those pretty pink lips of hers sucking down tequila shots—so I sort of feel like I already do know her, in a way, but I want to know her in all the ways.

At my command, my security team ushers away a group of fans to get me a better view. Her back is to me, and while it provides an excellent line of sight to that plump perfect arse, it's her face that I really want to see. She's with the pretty-boy DJ from last night. The way he's smiling at her is irritating as fuck. The guy is so obviously into her that she'd be blind not to notice. Or maybe she likes leading him on sometimes. The thought both pisses me off and makes me hard at the same time.

Pretty Boy grabs her drink and sets it down, leading her by the elbow to the dance floor. Fuck, if his touching her doesn't make my fists pulse. I keep my eyes glued to his hand, but when he slides it around her waist, I lose it. I gesture for our section waitress to bring me another drink. Tonight I'm drinking Jack and Coke, but it doesn't taste good, rather like bourbon from the well and flat soda. I'm just too tired and pissed off to care.

I tap the security guy and mumble a request in his ear. He looks confused but doesn't argue. I track him across the dance floor, watching like a bald eagle (no joke, I've seen three of those fine birds just this week) and stepping between Stevie and *Pretty-Boy.* Just my fucking luck though, because she rolls her eyes and waves him off. She seriously said *no* to joining me in the VIP area, if only for free drinks and comfortable seats? But more importantly, she said no to me *again*. Who does this girl think she is? Most, if not all of these chicks, even some of the guys, would kill to be back here.

The waitress sets down my Jack and Coke and I down it in one big gulp, ordering myself another before she jets off. Blimey, we've been here for an hour and I dunno' what drink I'm on anymore. My fourth? Or maybe my fifth? *Pretty boy* flashes Stevie a dimpled smile and whispers something in her ear. The way his nose presses against her hair, ready to pounce with his lips on her neck, immediately makes me want to leap over the velvet ropes and throw him into a headlock.

As soon as the waitress drops off my next drink, I order another round. Chad wanders out of the bathroom, looking a smidge brighter and twitchier than five minutes ago, and sits down beside me. "Having a good time?"

"Not really, Chad. You've got to warn me in advance about these things."

"I did warn you."

"Yeah, about two hours ago."

"What's the problem, Granger? The tour was a massive success. The stellar reviews keep rolling in every day. We have your next single lined up, which means a follow-up tour next summer. You're surrounded by fans that literally *all* want to blow you. You have more beautiful women and free-flowing booze than you do air. You're on vacation, man, so relax and enjoy it."

"I can't relax with fifty cameras flashing in my face and that station host breathing down my neck every five minutes."

"He's just excited to meet you. The bloke has an *Actuator* tattoo on his arm, for God's sake, so show a little respect. Besides, it's not like you're not used to the camera."

I set my empty glass down on the table and pick up my next drink. "Don't you ever get tired of this scene, old friend?" The way he looks at me, it's like I've forsaken the world.

"Never."

I glance at Jayne busying herself with some male fans. Ravi chose to stay at the hotel and meditate. Chad was pissed but didn't push it. Lucky him. The dance floor is packed. Stevie throws up her arms and swings them around to the familiar tune of Warrant's "Cherry Pie." She's truly a puzzle, but she doesn't give two fucks about what anyone else thinks. I love that in a woman. Maybe I'm even a little jealous of her.

Chad snorts when he sees who I'm watching. "Seriously Granger, *her* again? What the fuck is with this girl? I mean, she's not even that hot. There are way hotter girls in here tonight."

"Not to me," I bite back. When I say the words aloud, I know that they're true. Shit, now I'm really fucked. I'm crazy attracted to her, in this way that I can't even explain. Not since grammar school have things worked out like this for me, but back then I couldn't get hard anyways.

Chad leans forward and snaps his fingers in my face. "You need to get laid, man. Let me get one of these beautiful girls to blow you in the bathroom."

"Pass." I down the rest of my Jack and Coke and the waitress replaces it, without me even asking. The next one goes down even faster. Chad starts to look a blurry around the edges.

The radio station host joins us next. I answer his pointless questions with the same canned responses as always, trying (and failing) not to slur. During the entire interview, my eyes stay fixed on Stevie's hips, rocking out on the dance floor. I get to my feet and immediately stumble when Chad signals that we're finished. My security guy steadies me and I claim that I have to go to the bathroom, so they clear a pathway for me across the dance floor. I chuckle, because it makes me think of Moses parting the Red Sea; except instead of Moses, I'm nothing but a useless half-cut asshole passing through.

People cheer, but I don't smile or wave. Flanked by huge men in black on all sides, I know to keep my head down. My guards have already cleared the bathroom by the time I'm inside. The bathroom is typical of a nightclub—a waterlogged sink and paper towels like snow on the floor. The first stall that I enter has piss on the seat, but I push through the cowboy-style doors next door and relieve myself at last. There's a phone number scrawled on the wall with the saying:

THE PROBLEM IS NOT THE PROBLEM. THE PROBLEM IS YOUR ATTITUDE ABOUT THE PROBLEM. GOT THAT?

The bathroom poetry gives me an idea. With my next move in mind, nothing can stop me. I poke my head outside to find an empty hall. One of my guys is blocking the pathway to the bathroom, while the rest of them hold people back.

"Hello?" I call, and one of the security guards turns around. "I think someone is still in here."

He scans the bar in panic then ducks into the bathroom behind me. I disappear right away. The hallway leads to a set of doors, which lead to a staircase, which leads outside. I get spat out on the other side of the bar by some restaurant. I light a smoke and lean against the stone wall, planning my next move.

I duck around the corner like a dumb-ass spy, but the paparazzi is lined up three rows deep out front. Waiting, waiting, waiting. Always fucking lying in wait. I laugh before losing my footing and doing a face plant. My cigarette sparks across the pavement and into a puddle. The evening air is clean and refreshing, but I'm so fucking cold, even colder now that I'm face down on the ground. The feeling of gravel and stone against my face is too familiar. It brings me right back to my days in foster homes. I spent a lot of time getting in fights and eating dirt then.

Still laughing, I roll onto my back. The sky glows with millions of white pinpricks. Pricks. I'm a prick. Stars. I can't seem to remember where I am. I'm cold and want to go to sleep. The bright flash of a camera rouses me awake and I see a young girl hovering above me, iPhone poised and ready.

"You're Granger Ellis, right? I'm a huge fan!"

My lips come together to make words, but there's no sound. For some reason, I find this all very funny. I'm laughing like a maniac now.

"Leave now, please." I hear Stevie's sweet voice just seconds before seeing her, but then she's above me. Stevie, with her creamy-white skin and those big beautiful tits. Oh God, those tits.

The random girl whines, "Why is he on the ground?"

"We're secretly shooting scenes for a video. So you can't be here," says Stevie, my Canadian *angel*.

"I don't see any cameras," the girl mutters. "Why should I believe you?"

"They're hidden to ensure authenticity. That's how Granger works, but being such a huge fan, I'm sure you already knew that."

She's fast on her feet, my angel. I hear the click-clack of the young girl's heels retreating, getting dragged upright by my angel. The motion is too much for me. I lurch forward and puke up my Jack and Cokes, wiping gunk from my mouth and admiring my chunks on the street.

"Where are we going now, beautiful?" I close one eye and squint with the other. She's almost fully wedged under my arm. I can literally smell her shampoo, like coconut and sunshine. It reminds me of a Caribbean song, which I then decide to sing. *Brother bought a coconut he bought it for a dime and I said doctor, is there nothing I can take, I said doctor...*

"Focus, please. We're getting you home, rock star, but you need to take a few steps forward." She grunts and lifts me up by my armpits, at least she tries. I put one foot in front of the other, tackling a mountain of stairs. "Just a bit farther. A taxi will be waiting for us at the top."

I might be drunk, but my angel is very out of breath. She grunts as we summit the staircase, tossing me onto the bench and gasping for more air. She braces both hands on her knees, with her tits looking at me through that glorious crack in her cleavage. This woman is the most gorgeous motherfucking creature I've ever seen, and I have no problem telling her so.

"You are the most gorgeous motherfucking creature I've ever seen."

When I announce my love, she barks at me. "Is that supposed to be a compliment? Swearing at me?"

I must have offended her, so I try again. This time, I talk about her ass and those perfect tits and whiskey-coloured eyes. I go on about how her thighs brush together and how much I want those bubble gum pink lips wrapped around my cock.

I try to continue, but milady interrupts me. "Come on, *lover boy*, the cab is here."

At the mention of *Loverboy*, I start singing again, this time to a song that I know she'll appreciate:

> *Everybody's working for the weekend*
> *Everybody wants a little romance*
> *Everybody's goin' off the deep end*
> *Everybody needs a second chance, oh...*

"I'm sure this isn't something you hear regularly," she groans, "but do you think you could stop singing?"

"You don't like my covers?"

"Not when you slur the words."

If my angel doesn't care about the music in me, I'll just have to find a way to play the music in her. Not right now though. Right now I'm drunk. I close my eyes inside the cab and lose track of time. The next thing I know, she's shaking me awake.

"We're here, but you need to wake up and help me. We're doing this by ourselves."

I don't know what she's going on about now; I have *people* for times like these. The taxi comes to a halt but I don't recognize where we are. I don't remember the hotel being this dark.

"We're at the service entrance," Stevie explains. "There's access to your suite from the staff elevator. I'll take you up without the lobby's eyes on us, because I'm sure that's the last thing you need right now."

She lets me go, hunting through her purse. I slump against her body and bury my nose in her neck. "You smell fucking amazing."

"Better than you." She leans forward and speaks to the driver, but I can't hear a thing. I flop the full weight of my skull against the window, checking out the pitch-black night. I can make out the shadow of the mountains silhouetted in the distance. They look tragic and beautiful at the same time.

I hear one of the car doors slam and mine swings open next. I'm pulled from the vehicle by *my angel*. Stevie wraps her coconut-sunshine arms around my hips and drags me across the sidewalk. I try to help out, but my legs feel shaky, like setting Jell-O. I lick my dry lips and wish for another Jack and Coke to ease the pain.

"Do I have Jack in the room?" I wonder aloud, but Stevie laughs at me. "I guess I can always call for more."

"Alright, Captain Sparrow."

The night is still beautiful and I don't want it to be over. "Come upstairs with me," I whisper.

Stevie snorts and laughs. "I think that's inevitable."

She leads us inside to a bank of elevators. The upstairs hallway is scattered with beverage carts, catering equipment, and dining chairs stacked like pint glasses. This is kind of my natural environment. My suite looked the same after my party a few nights ago.

"Bee stings," I mutter, then laugh.

"What?" She sounds out of breath again, because I'm pretty muscular. She's tall enough, but I've got a good five inches on her still. No surprise that she feels winded. I try my best to walk forwards, but I'll be flat on my ass if she lets go.

"You called her bee stings," I repeat.

"I know," she sighs. "It was a low moment for me, but it was true. I've never understood the North American obsession with the super skinny form. There are many shapes and sizes in the world for a reason. To me it would feel like hugging a bag of bones."

"You're not a bag of bones."

"You don't have to rub it in."

"It's a compliment. You're exactly my type."

She laughs, and harshly. "I have the Internet, so we both know that I'm not."

"Go out with me," I try.

"No."

"Why are you so stubborn?"

"You're drunk; you smell like vomit; you just insulted my weight, and now you're asking why I won't go out with you?" She heaves me into the elevator and presses the button for the penthouse. "I'll get you to your bed safely. Then I'm leaving."

One minute later, the elevator pings and the doors open. I'm confused until realizing that we're at the opposite end of the hallway as my suite. I didn't even know that this elevator was here. She drags me down the corridor, stopping in front of my suite door and swiveling around with a look that stings.

"Key?" she snaps. I rummage around in my back pocket, relieved as hell when I find my key, since my security guys usually hold it for me.

Stevie snatches it up and inserts it in the slot. As soon as the light flashes green, she shoves me through the entrance.

"Have a drink with me," I try again.

"The last thing you need is another drink."

I flash her my well practiced stage smile, or what I like to call: my irresistible secret-weapon. "I'm fine, love." I shoot her what I think is a sexy wink, right before the whole room goes black.

Chapter Six

"Bad Medicine"

Granger

When I open my eyes, the first thing I see are legs—long legs, black and hairy. There are eight of them in total. I groan like a god-forsaken avalanche, which makes the spider scurry across the floor, startled by my outburst. My view of the porcelain throne sits at an angle, so I assume that I'm lying on the floor. It's surprisingly comfortable, actually. When I twist my neck around, my face comes into contact with the softness of the pillow beneath my head. *Blimey,* I think, *how did that get there?*

I roll onto my back and stare at the ceiling, stretching my arms up over my head. This isn't the first time that I've woken up on the bathroom floor, but it's the first time that I've woken up here covered in the duvet from my bed. I brace myself on both elbows and try to sit up, met instead with the wickedest headache imaginable. I squint my eyes and wonder what the hell I drank last night.

Judging by my magnitude-one-million headache, I'm guessing it was Jack Daniel's. Liquid amber always does me in, not vodka, rum, or gin—those make for a cleaner morning-after. But Jack always comes right back around to kick me in the arse, as if to say, *Hey Wanker, remember me? We had a great time and now you're going to pay for it.*

I face the massive gilded mirror and survey the damage. I'm shirtless (and in my underwear) with red-rimmed eyes and a five o'clock shadow. It's a look I'm familiar with these days—the look of waste and tragedy. I am the waste and the tragedy. A cramp yanks at my stomach, and suddenly I'm dry heaving into the sink. Thank God nothing comes up, but the smell of vomit is my only cologne right now. My toothbrush is MIA, so I squeeze a glob of thick paste onto my finger and scrounge it around in my mouth.

Mid-scrub, I hear someone sigh in the bathroom corner. So, I stop with my ridiculous "brushing" and do a perimeter check. It's a massive bathroom with two sinks, one walk-in shower, and a jetted bathtub that accommodates four topless models—a fact that I personally know to be true. I head in the direction of the tub and find Stevie snuggling the shower head with a sweatshirt bunched under her own head.

I take a step closer, and she sighs again, releasing a soft snore. I step back and scratch my head. Again, not the first time that I've woken up on a bathroom floor with a hot, random woman, but in my experience, it's usually all tangled limbs and flesh on flesh—not ten feet away from each other while she takes a waterless bath.

"Hello?" My voice is full of rocks—not to mention, it tastes like I just smoked a whole pack of Marlborough cigarettes. No thanks to my toothpaste brushing. I try to say good morning, but a coughing fit knocks me out and I hack into my hand instead (okay, maybe my breath tastes more like a *whole carton* of Marbs').

"What?!" She thrashes around like a vampire escort in a lousy coffin. She even holds up both arms to block out the sun through the skylight window, which is exactly what a vampire would do.

"What the..." she repeats, totally disoriented.

I stay silent, hoping that she can explain the situation, because I sure as hell cannot. The seconds tick by and she just lies there. Eventually, I give in. "You're in my bathtub."

"Well hell," she mutters, rubbing the sleep from her eyes. "Your bathtub is incredibly uncomfortable."

"I'll be sure to tell the concierge. I'll add it to my complaint about spiders."

"What do you have against spiders?" The woman makes no move to step out of the tub. Yeah, this is easily one of the strangest conversations I've ever had. That's saying a lot, given all the drug-using musicians I hang out with these days.

"I just saw one—a spider—on the floor."

"And?" she fires back.

"*And* this is a three thousand dollar per night penthouse suite."

"So?" Man, she is relentless.

"So I'm paying a lot of money for it. I think it should be clean."

"Too rich for insects, are we?"

"That's not the point."

"It kind of is."

I sigh, grazing my hand against the shaved side of my head. "It walked right by me on the floor."

"Maybe you shouldn't be sleeping on the floor."

"Well, that's just it. I was hoping you could fill in the details regarding how exactly I got there. But first, I'd appreciate if you'd get out of my bathtub." I hold my hand out to help, but Stevie ignores me. She climbs out like my very own Cleopatra, fresh off a dream.

Her long legs are clad in tight jeans, plus the top I recognize from last night, but otherwise she's barefoot. I've never seen a frizzier mess than those curls. Her eyes are rimmed with charcoal from day-old mascara, but still, she is absolutely stunning.

"How much of last night do you remember?" she says, trying to tame her hair.

"I remember the bar. You were dancing with some tosser."

"That tosser is my best friend: Kit. Is that what set you off?" She quirks one eyebrow in my direction, but I'm distracted by her body. Her tank top has shifted to give me an eyeful of her lush round breasts, right down to her bra, which is lacy and pink.

"Nothing set me off. I was partying and must have passed out," I mumble, still staring at her tits. "It happens."

"Does it happen a lot?"

"What are you, my mother? No, for your information, it doesn't. I don't do drugs, and I can go months without drinking. "It's just that when I do drink, I go a little mad."

"You blacked out," she explains. "I think that's called binge drinking."

Her face is all frown, but I know she has other expressions with which to grace me.

"That's a little extreme, don't you think?"

"You tried to tip the cab driver a thousand dollars. You threw your judgement out the window!"

"So what? I can afford it. I have loads of money."

"That's not the point. I didn't let him take it, by the way."

"You shouldn't have tip-blocked me and I don't need a babysitter. I was having a good time."

"Well, you were having such a *good time* last night that I found you wandering around alone in the cold. You could barely say your own name. This town is full of tourists with smart phones, so I brought you back here before you did something stupid."

"How did you bring me back?" I'm surprised, because I'm not used to going anywhere without my security guards.

She shrugs. "I carried you into a cab."

"You carried me?"

"Yes, I carried you. You were really out of it, and the valets are douche bags who don't keep their mouths shut. I had the taxi drop us off at the service entrance. Oh, and I brought you into the elevator on my own. Well, I guess I kind of dragged you into the elevator, but same thing."

"Why am I half-naked? And why do I stink?"

"You threw up on your clothes outside the bar, so I took off your shirt and pants. They're in a garbage bag by the front door."

"And the bathroom?" I ask the question, but at this point I'm not sure if I really want to know.

"I brought you in here in case you needed to puke again, but then you passed out. I couldn't wake you up at all. You were shivering so much, I thought you were hypothermic."

"That's ridiculous," I snort.

"It's actually physiology. When you drink past a certain point, your body can't regulate its temperature anymore," she starts, but I cut her off.

"Not really in the mood for a science lesson right now."

"Regardless, I wasn't about to carry you up that fancy penthouse staircase, so I made you as comfortable as possible here instead. Sorry about the comforter; it ripped when I was bringing it your way. Kind of looks expensive—must have an eight-thousand thread count or something..." She rambles on, as if she just lost control of her pretty little head. "Flimsy things, my flannel sheets are much sturdier."

"I don't care about the duvet—I'll buy the hotel another one." I wave my hand in one big swoop. "In fact, I'll buy ten."

"You do that, high roller."

I choose to ignore her little jibe. "So that explains what I'm doing in the bathroom, but what about you? What are you doing in the bathtub?" I meet her gaze but she averts her eyes in a flash.

"You were out cold," she whispers. "I was worried. What if you choked on your own vomit? It's not that uncommon."

"So, it's not because you're a big fan, then?"

She scrunches up her nose. "I hate your music, remember?"

"Do you want breakfast or something?" My brain is too foggy to think of a wittier response.

"No thanks," she yawns out, "the food here is overrated anyways."

"Well, I guess I should say thank you."

She nods once. "You should."

"I'd appreciate if we could keep this whole thing between us."

"Of course, that's why I brought you in via the service entrance."

"Thank you," I expel a huge breath. "I'll make it worth your while. Just let me find my wallet."

The second that the words leave my mouth, I wish I could take them back—she looks horrified. "You want to pay me to stay quiet? What kind of person do you think I am?"

"No, it's not that, I just figured that you'd want something for your efforts..." I trail off, completely aware of the hole I'm digging.

"You know what I have to say to that comment, Mr. Rock-Star Granger Ellis? I say that you can just go right ahead and fuck yourself!" She bends down to grab her heels and stomps away like an Ice Queen, slamming the bathroom door, probably pretending it's my face.

>

Okay, so I fucked up. I get that. I went out and partied and woke up again with that familiar panic—followed by the usual ball of anxiety and regret in the pit of my stomach. But I figure it's not too late to come back from last night at Buffalo Bill's. She took care of me when she didn't have to, after all. She protected me from the prying eyes of the media and opportunists who wanted to exploit a story, not asking for anything in return. That has to mean something, right?

I tried tracking her down at the hotel and the bar but that didn't work, so I need to look at the bigger picture. How do I convince her that going out with me is the right thing to do? I've tried impressing her with my lifestyle and bank account, which usually make women trip on their own shoes. I've given her a solid idea of my music, my fame, my access—but Stevie isn't like the rest. She's different, more down-to-earth, and I need to switch tactics for my luck with her to change.

Maybe I'll try humility, as painful as that sounds. One of the servers from the hotel lounge told me that I could find her at the library on Thursdays—a detail that only cost me two hundred dollars plus the promise of a poster signed by our band. The server, Mandy, didn't tell me much else, other than saying she's part of some group.

I drive my rental car to the library, wondering what kind of group she belongs to in the community. Maybe a church group? Hopefully nothing too cult-like. I'm glad that I stopped at the grocery store just outside of Whistler to buy some snacks as a goodwill gesture. I mean, fuck, I don't know what one brings to something like this. I settled on some mini chocolate croissants and glazed donuts in the end. Hopefully that does the trick.

The truth is, I'd love to shake off this broad and be done with it, but I can't get her out of my head. Her smell, her smile, all of it drives me crazy. It seems like a long-ass drive to get where I'm going to. The hotel offered a car but I wanted to drive myself, not wanting any witnesses, in the event she shoots me down again.

I arrive to find that it's not a church group at all, but some kind of strange sewing circle. I slip in through the back door and watch for a while to get my bearings. Stevie is by far the youngest among the "grey-hairs" but she somehow seems to fit right in. That's just her way, I guess. She's the type of girl who can fit in anywhere. It's the same casual confidence that knocked me off balance from the start. I clear my throat as I approach, and her head snaps up.

"You have got to be kidding me," she says, scowling.

"I brought treats." I hand the pastry boxes to one of the old biddies, who practically salivates at the sight.

"Do not touch those!" Stevie barks, glaring at the cardboard boxes. "The *Wizards of Wool* cannot be bought with treats!"

"Oh, hush now, girlie. I'm starving and my blood sugar is getting dangerously low." I recognize the old man from Longhorn's before he turns to address me. "Yer' that rock star, aren't you?"

"What kind of songs do you sing?" a larger lady asks me.

"It's a combination of hard rock and alternative metal," I explain, but the old man cuts me off.

"Say what now?"

"It's music with a lot of bass and heavy aggressive riffs," I explain, louder this time.

Another group member gives me the hairy eyeball. "Anything I might have heard before?"

"Maybe you've heard of 'Safer Before' or 'Sewn Shut'?"

"Do you know any Glenn Miller?" interjects the larger woman.

"Sorry?" I claim one of the empty plastic chairs for myself. I wasn't expecting this much of an interrogation, especially from the nursing home brigade.

"Do you play any of the classics? Anything like 'Moonlight Sonata'?"

I would laugh, if the whole thing weren't so absurd. "Yes, I'm familiar with Glenn Miller, but unfortunately we're just a three-piece band, and no one in the group plays trombone."

"That rock music of yours is devil's music anyway!" the old man shouts.

"I promise you it's not." I take one of the chocolate croissants now being passed around the circle.

"You bite the heads off chickens!" he shrieks.

"That wasn't me nor a chicken—it was Ozzie Osborne and a bat. It was also thirty-five years ago. He was on drugs and thought the bat was fake."

"That doesn't explain the herpes!" the old coot chimes. This time I do laugh, at the same time that Stevie groans.

"Please stop talking about herpes, Joe." Stevie sounds exasperated as hell.

"Fine, if it's not the devil's music, prove it by singing something for us!"

I almost choke on my pastry at the challenge. "I really don't think that's necessary."

"If you want to court our girlie here, it is."

"Yeah, prove that you are worth it," one of the old ladies pipes up. "Sing us something nice."

"Nice?" I shake my head. "My songs aren't known for being nice."

"Then sing us something we've heard before. Something from the old country, like 'Danny Boy,'" Joe adds.

I get down on one knee and turn my attention to Stevie. "If I do this, will you please let me take you out tomorrow?"

"I work tomorrow."

"You don't."

"I do."

"You don't have to," I try, but she just snorts.

"I'm not changing my schedule around for you."

"Oh, go out with him, dear," one of the old ladies says, and I appreciate the vote of confidence. "He's clearly trying so hard."

Stevie sighs like a hurricane. "Fine, I'll think about it."

"That's all I ask." I get to my feet and take a deep breath, working to recall the lyrics to "Danny Boy."

Oh Danny Boy, the pipes the pipes are calling
From glen to glen and down the mountainside
The summer's gone and all the flowers are dying
'Tis you 'tis you must go and I must bide

I watch Stevie as I sing. Her eyes lock with mine, her lips part halfway, and she looks a little dazed. My voice must be doing the trick. It damn well better since I'm running out of ideas. Her pupils dilate and the blush of pink across her skin has a mesmerizing edge as I belt out the words. The old biddies clap and cheer when I finish the tune, swarming me before I can get to Stevie.

"Take a picture with me," one old broad says. "I'm going to snap chat it."

"You don't even know what Snapchat is, Betty," Joe argues.

"You bet I do. My grandson set me up and now I have stories."

"You've got stories alright," he mutters.

"Is the video on?" Betty says, waving her phone in my face. "Did I take a video?"

"The donuts you brought are stale, by the way," Joe informs me, right as another lady wraps her arms around my waist.

"Tweet this, Betty!" she says, and Betty cackles.

"Yes, Joe, I have Twitter too. You're not the only one, you know."

They're buzzing around me like vultures with a fresh kill, so it's no surprise that I miss her when she slips out the back door. After fifteen more minutes of mindless chatter and photo-taking, I return to my rental car, no closer to my goal. Most men would have given up by now, but I am not most men. She may have won this round, but this girl has never met stamina like mine.

The next morning, I track her down at home, but my mouth goes dry upon glimpsing her poised at a forty-five-degree angle over her gleaming white motorcycle. Her perfectly round ass sticks up in the air, encased in form-fitting yoga shorts. Her hair is pulled high on her head, save for the fallen tendrils sticking to the wet nape of her neck.

I swallow hard before clearing my throat. To my surprise, she doesn't turn around. "Stevie?" My voice sounds more like a croak. Damn if it isn't way too hot in this garage. "Stevie!"

She rights herself and twirls around like a record player, removing a massive pair of headphones. I can't help but laugh upon noticing that they're hooked up to an actual, real-deal Discman CD player. I stare at her for a moment, until she steps forward and snaps her fingers in my face.

"*What-the-phylum* are you doing here?!"

"Um, what's a phylum?" Her version of *what-the-fuck* is very new to me.

"Seriously? You don't know about King Phillip Coming Over For Great Sex?"

"Who the hell is King Phillip?" I ask, thinking that if some wanker named Phillip is on his way over for sex with Stevie then he's about to be a dead man.

She grins and twirls her finger in the air, like she's casting spells all over the place. "You know...Kingdom, Phylum, Class, Order, Family, Genus, Species."

It's like her voice bounces on every word. I give her a blank stare and watch her face fall a thousand feet. "I'm a musician, not a code cracker, Stevie."

"Oh my God, did you even attend high school?"

I chuckle at the question. "Not really. I mean, yeah, sometimes. Foster kid and all."

"Huh..." She bends back over her bike, cranking a bolt real tight. Man, I'd really love to crank some of her bolts sometime. "Are you going to tell me why you're here, or not?"

"I came to see you."

"How did you find out where I lived?"

I stuff my hands in my pockets, rolling back on my heels with a pathetic shrug. "I bribed the valet at the hotel."

Her eyes narrow into slits. "That's a huge invasion of my privacy."

"Worth it though, to see you bent over that bike."

"You are a chauvinistic pig."

"Relax, love, I didn't mean anything by it."

"I'm not your love, Granger, nor your doll, nor your sweetheart." As she speaks, she whacks me in the chest with her wrench. It fucking hurts.

"This isn't going the way I planned."

"How did you expect it to go?" she huffs out. "You show up at my house like some stalker and then ogle me in the garage when I'm working on my bike?"

I sigh and throw up my hands in surrender. "I'm sorry, you're right. I should've just asked where you lived and if I could swing by, but I didn't, because honestly...you scare the crap out of me."

"I scare you?" She looks at me like I'm a dog that just spoke.

"You intimidate the fucking hell out of me, Stevie. Even more so, now that I know that along with everything else, you're a grease monkey."

"More stereotypes." I notice her mouth twitch this time. "Fine, since you're here, you might as well help."

"Happy to, but what exactly are we doing?"

"We're bleeding the brakes on the bike."

"Come again?"

She rolls her eyes like it should be obvious. "The brakes? We're bleeding them to get the air out and ensuring that no bubbles are trapped."

"Okay?"

She shoots me another look. "Nobody wants squishy breaks."

"Is that the technical term?" I tease, but she gives it right back.

"Are you sure you should be teasing me about technical terms? Have you even held a wrench before? How is that even possible with a band name like *Actuator*?"

When I don't answer the question, she gestures for me to approach the bike. "I need you to balance the handlebars for me, keeping the bike nice and level."

"Don't I get to use that wrench you've been talking about?" I'm only teasing her; in fact, I have absolutely no intention of touching any tools.

"Not likely. Now if you can reach it, grab that old bucket behind you."

I pass her the bucket and let her walk me through the steps. "I'm removing the cover on the master cylinder and attaching the bleed hose to the top. The other end goes into the bucket."

I try my best to keep the bike steady, watching her work in the process. She is so goddamn sexy that I feel myself start to swell. I'm in desperate need of an adjustment down below but I don't want to drop the bike and screw up her handiwork.

Instead I do my best to focus. "Why are we doing this exactly?"

"Why? If there's too much air in the brakes, it takes longer to stop and messes with the ride. Okay, now I need you to pump the brakes continuously while I crack open the bleed screw to let out the fluid-mixed air."

I follow her instructions and fluid spills into the bucket below. "Once the bubbles stop showing up in the bucket, we know the air is out of the system."

She taps the hose a few times while I do nothing but squeeze the brakes. "I've never felt so emasculated." Actually, I've never felt so horny, but I have to laugh it off. Otherwise I'll drop this hunk of metal and press her against the nearest wall.

"There's a first time for everything," she quips.

"I think I'm in love."

Stevie shakes her head real fast. "I highly doubt that." She balances the bike on the stand, screwing on the caps before removing the bucket. I take a step back and survey her long, tanned legs, both glistening with sweat. I'm still staring when she hits me with an *Actuator* question. "So where does your band name come from?"

My mouth twitches as I suppress my smile, or try to. "The dictionary."

She wipes her hands on the greasy rag. "What do you mean?"

"We picked the band name out of the dictionary. Well, technically, Chad did. We wanted something that started with an *A*."

She snorts. "I hope that's not the story you tell the media."

"Now that I've told the truth and helped you out, you have to do something for me."

"Do I now?" She laughs. "I hate to break it to you, but all you did was hold up the bike."

"And pumped the brakes. Besides, four hands are always better than two."

"You really are impossible."

"I'm motivated."

"By what exactly?" I raise both eyebrows like David Bowie.

"What do you think? That gorgeous arse of yours, for starters."

"Just when you were ahead..." she mutters.

"Wait...I was ahead?" I shoot her a wink. "Come on, doll. Please let me take you out. Just one date, love, and if you still aren't convinced that I'm your man, sweetheart, I'll leave you and that fine arse of yours alone forever. Cross my black heart."

This time she full on grins, and my heart beats faster at the sight. "Fine, you win, but only one date. Then we're done."

"We'll see about that."

She tosses me an oil-stained rag, which I snag and tuck into my pocket. "Hey, that's mine!"

"Nah, love, it's like the modern day version of your handkerchief. I'll keep it."

"You're weird," she giggles. "I like weird." She flutters those big whiskey-brown eyes my way. I love how they're framed with the darkest of lashes. For a moment, I'm plain speechless. When I do recover, I give her a big grin of my own.

"I'll pick you up tomorrow morning at nine."

"A day date? Why?"

"I have something special in mind."

"Aren't you at least going to help me clean up?" She gestures to the giant mess on the floor.

"I did my part, love. I just held the bike, remember?"

I shoot her one last wink, and her mouth drops open, sending me chuckling right out the front door.

Chapter Seven

"Love Don't Come Easy"

Stevie

'm already dressed and waiting out front when the black stretch limo comes rolling through my townhouse complex like the royal mountain parade. Just kidding, there's no royal mountain parade in Pemberton. I glance down at my khaki shorts and tank-top, certain now that I've underdressed. Like, what does one wear on a date with a rock star these days anyways?

The limo comes to a stop and the back window glides down to reveal Granger's smiling face. "Good morning, love."

I mumble good morning right back before climbing inside. The driver, who comes rushing around the car to intercept me, looks horrified that I've opened my own door, so I give him a half-smile.

"Don't worry, I can handle doors." I must sound ridiculous, but I'm such a ball of nerves that I don't even mind. Once inside the sleek car, I inch my butt across the leather seats until I'm directly across from Granger. I'm uncomfortably aware of his eyes on me the whole time. His gaze falls to my chest when I settle into the seat, as the tops of my breasts are peeking out from the scooped neck of my tank top. I clear my throat and cross my arms, but that only seems to make it worse.

"You look good." His voice is thick, and I don't miss the dilation of his pupils.

"Thanks." By this point, I'm dying to slip on my new cardigan, but now my motivation seems too obvious. It's weird, because I'm normally not this conscious of how I look. Who knows what's wrong with me today—maybe it's the weather, or my rock-star company— you know, *environmental influences.*

"Where are we going?" I ask, accepting a glass of orange juice and taking a sip (*correction:* orange juice *and* champagne).

"Somewhere you haven't been before."

"How do you know that I haven't?" I challenge, raising an eyebrow.

"I guess I don't, but I'm hopeful."

"I'm not big on surprises," I mutter, and he laughs as if he's on TV.

"Why am I not surprised that you're not big on surprises?" He slides across the seat until his jean-clad thigh presses right up against mine.

I shift my weight away from him out of habit. "So you're really not going to tell me?"

Our eyes lock together, and it's like his gaze holds the master set of keys to mine. "Why tell you when I can show you?" He slides on his sunglasses with a big grin.

We sip our mimosas in comfortable silence during the twenty-minute ride. The limo pulls into a heavily wooded area which feels unfamiliar to me. A helicopter waits for us outside with the pilot standing at attention beneath the rotor. I have to resist the urge to jump up and down, because I've always wanted to ride in a helicopter. That being said, it's mostly a tourist thing and definitely outside my budget.

Granger takes my hand and leads me to the pilot, who introduces himself as Greg. Greg looks about my age. He's kind of cute, but his demeanour is all business. He ushers us into the helicopter and leans forward to strap me in safe and sound, but Granger shoves a tattooed arm between us before he can touch my harness.

"I think I've got this."

Greg nods like a robot going haywire, looking a little chastised, before climbing into the front. Granger takes his sweet time belting me into the seat, letting his calloused fingers rest on the bare skin of my arms. A shiver of pleasure runs through me as his hands skim my waist; if his smug smile is any indication, he definitely notices. The rotors spin faster until I can't make out each individual rotor anymore. They become a cartoonish blur of gray against the brilliant blue sky. Greg signals for us to put on our headphones, which doesn't totally cut the sound, but the microphones allow us to have a conversation.

We float up into the air, swaying side to side as the helicopter takes flight. I sit back against my seat to relax, taking in the sharp peaks and lush green treetops soaring above the mountain valley. The landscape looks more rugged from up high, punctuated by crystal-clear lakes and the deep blue ocean following the coastline. Greg points things out now and then but for the most part he's quiet, letting the stunning vistas speak for themselves.

Even though we have the headsets, Granger and I don't speak. He lets me take it all in at my own tempo. In no time, we're making our descent and landing beside a glacier so bright and blue that the colour almost hurts my eyes. Safe on land, Greg unloads a picnic for us to enjoy before making himself scarce. I stare at the red-checkered blanket, wicker basket, and iced bottle of white wine, spewing out the first thing that comes to mind.

"I feel like I'm on *The Bachelor*."

Granger seems caught in the headlights for a second, but he's laughing again in a heartbeat. "Is that a good thing?"

Apparently I'm so funny that he has to wipe tears from his eyes. I look at him as if I'm in the CIA. "I'm not sure yet."

"Well, I had to pull out all the stops, of course. What better place than beside this twelve thousand-year-old glacier?" He motions to the view in the distance.

"It's beautiful," I concede.

"Care for an early lunch?" He gestures to the picnic basket and sits down cross-legged, with no problem folding his long legs under his seat. I try for the more graceful side sit but end up in this weird half-squat position instead. My thighs look enormous, so I give up and mimic his pose.

Granger pours us each a glass of wine and flips open the basket. "There is cheese, crackers, prosciutto, olives…"

"Yes," I interrupt before he's even finished. "All of the above, please."

We eat in amicable silence until the food is mostly gone. "How am I doing so far?" he soon asks.

"Full marks. You could do a dissertation in wooing," I tease, but he catches my slip.

"I take it from the comment that you did yours?"

I can feel my face turning red as I formulate a response in my head. This has never been my favourite subject. "Yes, I did my Masters."

"And?" he presses.

I bite into the last olive, navigating around the pit. "And my PhD."

"That's it? That's really all you're gonna' give me? Stevie, tell me, in what subject did you complete your Masters and PhD?"

"Molecular biology," I mumble, and he spits out a mouthful of wine.

"Shit." He wipes wine from his sleeve. "To be honest, I'm not even sure what that is."

"It's the scientific study of biological activity at the molecular level. Essentially, molecular biology is centered around biomolecules inside various systems of a cell, including how to understand the interaction between DNA, RNA, and proteins." Pretty soon, I see that all too familiar glassy look creeping into his eyes, so I bite down on my tongue to stop myself.

"Sorry, I tend to get a little carried away with the topic. I'm boring you…"

"You're not boring me." He shakes his head. "Actually, you're making me feel a little insecure. I'm still trying to wrap my head around your having a PhD—what are you, about twenty-five?"

"Twenty-six," I correct him. "I did an accelerated undergraduate program, completing four years of studies in three, and I skipped two grades in high school."

He chokes on another sip of wine. "Fuck me, you must be smart."

"I just liked school a lot." I shrug. "Biology always made sense to me."

"So, why are you working at the hotel? Sure, the economy has its ups and downs, but I'd assume that your level of education would open some doors?"

I swirl my wine around in my glass before continuing, unable to stop thinking about the activity of the fermented molecules. "I worked in a research lab in Vancouver for a year, but it wasn't for me. Much of the work done in molecular bio is quantitative and mine was focused on medical research and drug development. Specifically, I was working on molecular cloning in the pharmaceutical industry, studying the activity of new drugs against proteins."

"Sounds like important work, no?"

"It *is* important work, but the corporate-political side was hard to wrap my head around. I came home and bought my townhouse to get closer to nature and my own roots. Anyways, I made the change and the rest is history. Besides, I genuinely love what I do up here. I consider it the study of human interaction, except that I do it in one of the most beautiful places in the world. I have a lot to be grateful for in my life."

He's quiet for a moment, but the look he gives me is intense— and hungry. "Well, I shouldn't complain, since your work placed you directly in my path."

"That's true." I set down my glass and lean back on the blanket.

"It is so peaceful here." You can always count on men to change the subject, though I'm glad it's moving along. "My life is never this quiet."

"I'd imagine not," I respond. "But it could be."

"How so?"

"We all make choices, Granger. Part of my heritage is First Nations. There's a word, *Ka'til'a*, which means *stop and listen deeply*. It reminds us to seek spaces of stillness and quietness amidst the busyness of our lives. Things don't just happen to us—we aren't idle passengers on this ride. I chose to leave the lab and move home and work at the hotel. I chose to come to this amazing glacier with you. If you want silence in your life, choose it. If you don't, celebrate and be grateful."

"You pretty much say whatever pops into that gorgeous head of yours, don't you?"

"I do."

"Good, don't stop."

"I wasn't planning on it."

We both fall silent, gazing over the glacier like a fine work of art, which isn't a bad way to describe it. Granger inches closer to me until our shoulders touch. When I glance over to glimpse his profile, he's obviously watching me from the corner of his eye. His chest starts to rise and fall more rapidly as I stare, and a thick vein throbs in his neck.

"Stevie?" I watch his Adam's apple bob up and down as he swallows. "Stop staring at me like that, or else I'll have you on your back and topless before you can say *molecular biology*."

I let out an involuntary squeal of surprise and squeeze my legs together to dam the rush of liquid rising to the surface.

"Want to hear a biology joke?" At this point, I'll say anything to ease the tension, but I know it's working when he chuckles. "Sure."

"What did the conservatively-minded biologist say to his teenage daughter?"

"What?" I mean, at least he's humouring me.

"The only cleavage I want to see is at the cellular level!" My voice comes out shaky and my eyes cling to his bouncing leg.

"I quite literally have no idea what that means, but you're way too cute for that to matter." He stands up quickly and extends his hand to help me. "Should we be off then?"

I nod in agreement and he waves over Greg. I offer to help the pilot tidy up the picnic, but he orders me away to wait by the helicopter while Granger wanders into the center of the glacier. I watch him stand with his head cocked to the side and his hands on both hips. Even from behind, one thing is clear, he is a truly magnificent force.

➤

It's after three in the afternoon when we land back in Pemberton. I assume that our date is over, at least until Granger informs me that he's picking me up for dinner later, after I've had a moment to change my clothes.

"What if I'm working?" I protest.

"You're not."

"And you know this because…"

"I have my ways, Stevie. Look, I just want to take you to dinner, so please don't fight me on this."

When we arrive at my apartment complex, Granger walks me to the front door and kisses me on the cheek before ushering me inside. "I'll be back at seven."

He doesn't give me a chance to argue, descending the front steps two at a time and hopping inside the limo. I shut the door and slip off my shoes before racing upstairs to call Kit.

He picks up on the first ring, sounding kind of smug. "You're back early."

"The date isn't over yet. We're going out for dinner, apparently." My breath escapes in an excited gust. "The big question is—what do I wear?"

"That's why you're calling me? For fashion advice?"

"Come on, Kit," I moan. "I don't have a ton of girlfriends to rely on—you know that."

"What about Kate or Becca?" Kate and Becca are my old acquaintances from high school.

"Kate has a four-month-old baby and hasn't dated in over ten years. Becca is traveling through South America. Please, please, pretty please?"

"Fine," he grumbles. "Lucky for you, I happen to be nearby. I'll be there in five minutes."

Kit lives in Whistler. I'm surprised that he's close by, but as they say, never look a gift horse in the mouth. I race downstairs to unlock the front door before climbing two flights to my bedroom closet. I throw open the closet door and evaluate its contents. Jeans, jeans, and more jeans. Eventually I pluck out a handful of sparkly club tops from my university days, laying them flat on the bed. Kit's footsteps sound on the stairs the moment I try on the first top.

"I'm in here!" I shout back, without taking my eyes off the bed. Kit comes up behind me and I feel his breath tickling the back of my neck.

"You smell like sunscreen." I hear him suck in a big breath, then I spin around to face him.

"We went for a picnic up on the glacier," I explain.

"You look flushed." He studies me. "Are you drunk?"

"What? No! We just had some champagne—and a little bit of wine."

He sighs and glances between me and the bed. "No to those glittery tops. You're going to want a dress."

"A dress? Why?"

He sighs again, as if I'm impossible. "Because he's a rock star worth millions of bucks, who seems desperate to get you into bed. If I were him, I'd be pulling out all the stops. We'd be having the most expensive, over-the-top dinner imaginable."

"You think so?"

"I know so." He nods. "Now, let's see what else we've got here."

Kit combs through my entire wardrobe before landing on a fitted knee-length dress, lacy and nude in style, which I haven't worn in years. I order Kit from my room and slide into the little number—it's tighter around the middle than I remember, but otherwise it fits. I swivel my hips in the mirror and honestly cannot believe how good I look.

Encouraged, I dig out my strappy nude heels. Ages have past since I last wore them. There's mud caked against the left stiletto, presumably from stumbling home through the grass after a party. I wash them off in the kitchen sink, observing Kit hanging out on the couch and cuddling Toto with both hands. When he sees my outfit, he whistles like the wind between the mountain peaks.

"Your tits look awesome in that dress."

"Awe, don't you have such a way with words, Kristopher Jones."

"Just saying." He sets down Toto and joins me at the breakfast bar. "So you like him then?"

"I'm still deciding."

"Are you going to fuck him?"

"Jesus, Kit! I shout, dropping my stiletto on the floor.

"What?" He lifts both hands in surrender. "I tell you about my adventures with *the sheilas* all the time."

"Exactly—you tell me—I don't ask. I certainly don't look for details."

He inches his hands across the counter until his fingers grasp mine. "I just want you to make the right decision for yourself."

"I'm not making any decision, Kit. I'm going out for dinner, and I still have to shower and get ready, so unless you want to do my hair and makeup, you should probably get going." I tear my hand away and he leans away from the counter.

"Fine, I'll go." He pushes the stool backwards and gets to his feet. "But is it ok if I watch TV with Toto until your date arrives?"

I come around the counter to wrap my arms around his waist. "Of course it's okay. I'm sorry if I'm moody. I'm just a little nervous. Thank you for helping me with the dress. I don't know why I'm making such a big deal of this."

After a beat, his arms come around my shoulders in a tight squeeze. "It *is* a big deal, Stevie. You rarely ever date, so it has to mean something, right?" He releases me from his hold and spins me around before smacking me in the butt. "Get in there and scrub up."

I head for the shower and hear him opening the fridge door in the background. Bottles clink like bells as he shouts out, "I'm having a beer!"

I shake my head—he's over here so often, I should start charging him for groceries. "Leave a tip then!"

It only takes me forty-five minutes to shower, dry my hair, and don my makeup, dedicating most of my time to taming the insanely thick curls tangled atop my head. When I re-emerge, I still have another hour to kill, so I join Kit for a beer on the sofa. We watch an old episode of *The Bachelor* which reminds me of this morning's events, thus I tell him about my date.

"A helicopter?" he groans. "Really? It's guys like him and shows like that which give women such unrealistic expectations in the first place."

I take a sip of my beer and feel the bubbly liquid sliding down my throat. "You don't know what you're talking about. I have no expectations."

"That's why I love you."

"Because I have low standards?" I snort.

"Because you're real. You'd be amazed at how hard that is to find these days."

"Back at you," I say.

When the doorbell rings, Toto darts under the couch. I set my beer down and grab my shoes, but Kit is already halfway to the door.

"Wait!" I shout after him, but he either doesn't hear or doesn't listen. I fumble with the straps on my heels, racing along just in time to see the door swing open.

"Evening, mate." Kit greets Granger as I'm staring at the back of my best friend's head. We're almost the same height, so I can see over his shoulder no problem, but I wish that I hadn't peeked.

Granger waits across the threshold, trying his very best not to appear pissed off, but the muscle jumping in his cheek tells a different story. "Are you ready to go?" His voice is gruff, and he totally ignores Kit's greeting.

I nod and grab my purse from the hall table. Granger is already headed down the stairs when I give Kit a quick hug goodbye. "Call me tomorrow," he says, and I can't help but notice the troubled look in his eyes.

"I will," I promise, as we mouth each other goodbye. With the pace Granger sets, I have to jog to catch up and that's no easy feat in heels. We reach the limousine and I climb in behind him, feeling the knots form in my stomach.

"You look nice," I chime as we start moving. I mean it, too. He wears a perfectly fitted navy blue suit paired with a sharp white dress shirt, which is unbuttoned enough for me to glimpse a hint of the tattoo on his chest. He opted for no tie, with his hair gelled up to reveal the close-shaved sides. I think it might be freshly shaven, like, as of this afternoon. I consider running my hand across the smooth skin but soon remember that he's mad at me for some reason.

"Granger?" I ask, because he's yet to acknowledge me. He's been staring out the front window and when he does turn to face me, his expression is unreadable.

"I said that you look nice."

"You look...well, *nice* probably isn't the right word." His eyes flare as they hunt across my body. "You're gorgeous."

I give him a wide smile. "Thank you, Granger."

"Well, that was easy," he chuckles. "Usually with women, it's this insecure back and forth, but you go right ahead and take the compliment."

"That's the way it should be." I shrug and give him a wink. "I know I clean up well."

He scrubs his chin with a hoarse sigh. "I'm sorry about how I reacted back there. But we were together just a few hours ago, and then when I arrive there's another man at your place."

"He's not a man—that's Kit."

"Still a man, love. A *red-blooded* man in close personal proximity to *all* of this." He waves his hand up and down my body for emphasis. "Look, can we start over?"

I roll my eyes to the ceiling and pretend to consider his offer. "Let me see...for one thing, we are actually *blue-blooded* creatures. The red pigmentation of our blood is actually from contact with oxygen and thus visible only when blood leaves the body."

"You're a smart one, then, aren't you?" He shakes his head and links his fingers through mine. The contact makes me gasp, as if even the slightest touch from Granger resonates all the way into my toes. He leans forward and brushes his lips against mine, so softly that it could be a dream, before pulling back with a half-moon smile. "Did you have fun today?"

"It was beautiful, but it was a lot. You don't have to go all out like that for me. I'm not like that."

"That's exactly why I want to treat you like a princess. So, I'll pre-warn you: for dinner, just keep an open mind and go with it."

The limo pulls up to the restaurant and Granger helps me onto the sidewalk. I recognize the Barefoot Bistro right away, but I've only been inside once in my life. Granger holds my hand as we walk up the stairs, greeted by the maître d' like the stars of a classic Hollywood movie. I glance around and notice that the space is completely empty of customers, despite the full complement of wait-staff lined up against the back wall. *Strange,* I think, before realizing that this might be normal behaviour for a rock star.

"Have you been here before?" he asks.

"Only once, for the oyster happy hour—otherwise it's a little out of my price range."

"So you've never done the vodka tasting room?"

"Definitely not." I shake my head, wondering if anyone who actually lives and works in Whistler could afford the vodka tasting room. One of the waiters greets us before leading us down the hallway, where a closet full of down-stuffed Arctic Canada Goose jackets awaits us.

"These are actual military-grade parkas suitable for thirty degrees below zero," I announce to the hallway. "They're used by explorers on trans-Antarctic expeditions as well as by workers at high-Arctic observatories, and they'd suitable for some of the most extreme and challenging environments in the world."

Granger chuckles and gives me a look, just as the waiter steps forward to help me put on the jacket. "I think I can take it from here," Granger tells him.

The waiter, who doesn't look older than twenty, becomes totally flustered. "Of course, Mr. Ellis. Just so you know, I'm a big fan. I love all of your music but especially your last album. *Black Lung* totally rocked."

"Thank you, I appreciate that. What's your name?"

The waiter, who's now sporting a goofy star-struck grin, is happy to answer. "Brandon."

"I appreciate that, Brandon. *Black Lung* meant a lot to me."

With that, Granger manoeuvres me closer to his chest, zipping up the enormous coat falling far past my knees. I play with the fur-lined hood as he does up his own jacket before following Brandon into the ice room. It's a small, narrow space with divots carved into the walls, all holding rows of premium liquor. The air is warmer than I expected, probably because it's a dry cold. The lighting is dim and the ice casts everything an eerie blue glow.

Brandon lines up four shot glasses for me and four for Granger, proceeding to have us select from the bottles on the wall. I choose two flavoured vodkas to start and Granger doesn't protest. When Brandon offers to pour Granger's third and fourth selections, I wave them away because two shots of anything is more than enough for me. I can still feel the tingly burn all the way down the back of my throat. Granger downs his remaining shots along with mine while Brandon gives us the background on the origins, ages, and distilling processes.

Not until we're back in the lobby do I realize how cold I am. My nose is numb and my fingers burn like the sun. I rub them together to re-establish circulation as Granger helps me out of my coat. When he puts his hand on the small of my back, a cool shudder reaches all the way through my spine. His hand feels icy through my dress fabric, but his touch has me burning from the inside. I bite down on my bottom lip, stifling the moan now threatening to break loose from my body as he leads me back into the restaurant, which is still completely empty.

A new waiter greets us and leads us down another flight of stairs to the wine cellar, where a small table is set up by candlelight. I take a seat and Granger waits to push my chair in like a proper gentleman. He's obviously well rehearsed at the gesture, which I didn't exactly expect with his rock-star reputation.

Two more waiters join us, one of them holding up a champagne bottle while the other sports a large knife. It reminds me of the knives my brothers once used to clean fresh-caught salmon and carve the holiday turkeys. I watch in fascination as they sabre off the top of the bottle, releasing some of the frothy liquid onto the floor. A third waiter appears to pour the remaining liquid into flutes and Granger hands me one before holding his own up for a toast.

"Here's to you and that incredibly sexy dress."

"I'll drink to that," I say, which for some reason makes him snort.

"You're damn cute, but you already know that, don't you?"

I ignore his question and change the subject. "Can I ask you something?"

"Sure."

"Did you rent out the entire restaurant?"

He cocks his head and quirks his brow. "I did."

"Why? Especially if we're down in the cellar anyway."

"I like my privacy," he shrugs.

"It seems like a waste of money."

"Stop worrying already and enjoy yourself. You promised to keep an open mind."

I'm about to speak when yet another waiter appears to fill us in on the specials.

"Madame, our appetizer options tonight include veal, foie gras, or beef wagyu in a balsamic reduction…"

Granger must read the look on my face, because he immediately interrupts. "What's the matter?"

"It's not a big deal." I shake my head, but still he persists, searching my eyes as if they hold crystalline codes for everything that I am.

"Stevie...tell me what's wrong."

"It's just...umm...I'm wondering if you have any cruelty-free appetizers?"

For a moment, the waiter looks horrified. "I'm so sorry, Madame, I didn't realize that you were a vegetarian," he begins, but I shake my head to stop him.

"I'm not, I just don't believe in torturing my food before I consume it."

"Very well, let me check with the chef in regards to alternative options." He scurries off and already I feel bad for raising a stink, though not bad enough to chow down on a baby cow or some animal that they force-fed to death. Meanwhile, Granger watches me with an amused smile playing on his lips.

"What?" I snap. "Do you even know how they make foie gras, or how it's banned all over Europe in its traditional form?" We just haven't caught up yet in North America."

"I'm not arguing—you just never fail to surprise me. Beneath that tough exterior, you do have a soft heart."

"Well, I'm definitely soft in a lot of places," I joke, but something besides laughter flashes through his eyes.

"Mmm...I look forward to finding out."

The waiter returns with some very accommodating options. I settle on some local smoked black cod, followed by a salad and an entrée of free-range tenderloin. I consume two glasses of the most delicious wine and feel totally at ease with both the intimate setting and Granger's easy conversation.

"So have you always been an activist?" I can tell he's teasing me now, but I shake it off.

"I'm far from an activist, but part of my heritage is Lil'Wat First Nation. My ancestors have a special relationship with the land. We believe that *nothing should be done that hurts the children,* the children of Mother Earth, that is, which includes the trees and rivers and insects and animals. Still, the circle of life is necessary. We should all be grateful for the animals that sustain us, instead of inventing creative ways to prolong suffering in pursuit of some bourgeois fantasy."

He laughs aloud at the last part. "You are the first woman I've ever dated to use the word *bourgeois* in a sentence."

"I'm probably the first woman you've ever dated who uses proper sentences at all," I tease back, and again he snorts.

"That's not jealousy I hear, is it now?"

I take a big bite of the chocolate mousse waiting in front of me and sigh out my answer. "Maybe just a little bit."

After dessert, Granger leads me back upstairs and into the waiting limo. He doesn't even pay the bill, but I figure he's got some kind of rock-star arrangement going on.

"Thank you for a perfect evening."

He surprises me by looking a little deflated. "Is it over?"

"I guess it depends on what you had in mind," I answer. His face flushes and I'm shocked to find that he looks a little embarrassed. "I may have also rented out the pool area at the hotel."

"The place where we first met...smooth." I laugh. "But I don't have my bathing suit with me."

"I have one for you," he pipes up right away.

"I hope it fits."

"I hope it doesn't." He smirks. "So what do you say? Are you up for a swim?"

➢

Turns out the suit doesn't fit—like, at all. I pluck at the tight fabric and study myself in the changing-room mirror. He opted for a sea-green two piece. The bottoms are okay, higher cut than I usually wear, but workable. The top, however, is a string bikini made for someone with far less chest. I sigh and tug at the small triangles, willing them to grow with the motion. Eventually I give up and throw a fluffy white pool towel around my neck instead.

Granger isn't in the indoor pool section when I exit, so I wander onto the outer deck to look for him there. Steam is rising from all three hot tubs with Granger situated in the one nearest to me. It's lit up from beneath us and the jets are completely off, so I can see every angular line of his perfect, tattooed form. The usually quiet, piped-in music is cranked up loud and Motley Crüe's 'You're All I Need' plays over the stereo. Yeah, he definitely has thought of everything.

"You coming in?" he asks, scanning me from head to toe.

I drop my purse and phone onto the nearest deck chair before my hands drift to the towel around my neck in hesitation. I'm not a shy person, but this bikini top definitely pushes the boundaries of decency. I consider wading in with the towel still around my neck but decide that would be even stranger than simply taking the plunge. I turn my back to him and place the towel on the closest lawn chair, proceeding to cross my arms over my chest and turn to face him. I scamper into the hot tub as if the pool deck is made of hot coals, settling into the spot right across from Granger.

"Are you cold?" he asks, giving me the strangest look of the night.

"No." I shake my head while locking my arms in place.

"Then get over here." Without warning, he grabs my hand and tugs, causing both arms to fall away. When he takes in the bathing suit, his eyes widen in appreciation.

"Fuck me sideways."

"Uh…no?" I answer, though rationally I know that it's not a question.

"I am a lucky son of a bitch."

Before I can ask what he even means, he's on top of me. His lips imprint themselves into mine, his hands run through my hair—he is everywhere. We are all tongues and gnashing teeth. He slides his rough, calloused fingers around the back of my neck and a moan rattles from his chest when I press my breasts against him.

Granger pulls back and sucks in a deep breath. "You truly are something, Stevie," he whispers. "I'm still rock hard, despite this *gawd*-awful music."

I answer him with a playful shove, sending a splash of blue-chlorine water at his face.

"Literally, fucking terrible. How anyone had sex in the eighties is beyond me."

His thumbs skim the bottom of my breasts, as he nudges up the tiny-triangle top. At first he doesn't kiss me, instead staring at me in this way that ignites a pang of need between my thighs. It feels almost painful. I reach around to unknot the ties on my bikini top and my breasts spill into his waiting hands. He releases a raspy growl along with a noise that sounds like *fuuuck*.

"They're just as incredible as I imagined they'd be."

"You've seen breasts before—lots of them, I'm sure." I'm a big mess of nerves, but I manage to spit out the words.

"Not like these." He stares at my chest, as if he's looking God in the eye, before bending down to pull one of my wet nipples into his mouth and sucking hard. I whimper as he swirls his tongue around the hardened pea before moving on to give the other one some attention. Back and forth, he sucks at my nipples—pressing them together with his rough calloused hands, lavishing both with attention in unison.

"Granger," I moan his name out like a question, but I don't know exactly what I'm asking for yet. He answers by bringing his mouth back up to mine, his breath hot against my lips as his tongue overtakes mine. His kisses are almost ruthless as he explores and devours every corner of my mouth.

I squirm against the erection straining through his swim trunks, hearing him groan as his fingers slip beneath my bikini bottom. One hand finds my centre and he thrusts two fingers into my wet heat, his other hand rounding my back to squeeze and caress my ass.

"Do you know how much I want this, Stevie? How patiently I've been waiting?" His voice sounds a little unhinged, but the doors swing loose inside me too.

"I guess you and I have different definitions of patient." My voice comes out uneven, so I follow the joke with a low wanting moan.

"I can't wait any longer, love. I need to get you upstairs and sink myself into you *now*."

Visions of him doing just that—all night—dance across my vision just as my phone rings on the nearby lawn chair. *Alas*, I think, *iOS interruptus.*

"Don't answer it," he demands. It stops ringing but starts again just a few seconds later. Granger latches his mouth against the sensitive flesh on my neck and traces the patch of skin just below my ear. "Stevie, please don't answer it."

"Granger, stop," I moan out. "I have to."

He pulls back a tad but doesn't release me. Instead he nips and licks up the column of my neck as I reach to pick up the phone. I can barely hear the voice on the other end, but after a few seconds, I determine that it must be Joe. It sounds as if he has been crying.

"Slow down, I can barely understand you. Where are you?"

Granger stops kissing my neck and gives me a worried look.

"Are you hurt? Are you bleeding? Stay safe and I'll be right there."

I listen as he rambles on incoherently, but I manage to get his location. I hang up the phone and turn to Granger, who's already out of the hot tub and drying off with a towel.

"That was Joe. He's been in an accident and seems confused. I have to find him."

He nods and throws the towel over his shoulders. "Then I'm coming with you."

Despite knowing that it's not his problem, I'm secretly relieved to have Granger's help. Joe is like family to me, and I can't imagine anything happening to him. My hands are shaking as I step out of the hot tub and locate my own towel. Granger leads me inside to change and all the while I do my best not to think the worst. Joe is like my honorary grandfather; if something terrible happened to him on the same night that my heart picked up speed for a rock star, that might close the slopes for me and Granger forever.

Chapter Eight

"Open Arms"

Granger

Me and him have only met twice before tonight, but I could pick Joe out of crowd anywhere. His hair sticks up in every direction—the old dude looks like Einstein—and his pants are way too big. There's even a hole in one of his shoes. He stands in the middle of the road, looking massively out of sorts.

"Joe!" Stevie cries, launching her lovely body from the passenger seat. Man, she nearly gives me a heart attack upon rushing to meet Joe in the middle of the road. We're on a dark stretch of highway, and as with most of the roads along the Sea to Sky Highway, this one is nothing but hairpin turns and rockslide hazards.

"Get out of the road!" My voice is louder than I expected, but hey, they both listen. I wander over to Joe's car, which is crumpled against the cliffside, to inspect the damage. The front end is wrapped around a utility pole like bloody hell, and black smoke thunders out from the engine.

"It was dark—I didn't see it," Joe's voice rattles like mad. His eyes are rimmed red, as if he's been crying. I imagine that's something he wouldn't want Stevie to witness. I may not know the old man, but you don't have to be a genius to see someone's pride.

He looks to be in okay shape overall though. Suffering from a case of shock maybe, but that's all. Stevie wants to call an ambulance but he shuts her down real fast, insisting that he's fine. I ask about a tow truck, but the old man shakes his head. Man, he reminds me of a sad house-dog.

"Don't have the money for that, sonny."

Not that the car is worth towing anyways, between the paint-stripped hood and broken taillights, which probably arose from an unrepaired accident at some other time. I mean, maybe this dude shouldn't even be driving.

"Do you want me to call ICBC for you?" Stevie asks, but I have no idea what she's talking about anymore.

"What's the point?" Joe sighs. "I only have the basic anyway. I couldn't afford the collision comprehensive."

Only then do I realize that they're talking about insurance.

"We can't just leave it here, Joe!"

"Honestly, girlie, I think that's all we can do at this time."

I agree with Joe, because otherwise they'll fight about it all night in the middle of the goddamn highway. This way, Joe saves face and I get to herd them into my car. We drop off Joe first. I'm going to call Chad to take care of the tow, but I just want my girl off the street right now. The thought of anything happening to Stevie makes my chest feel like a prison. The ride to Joe's front door takes about thirty minutes. He says thank you and exits the car. Stevie is silent after he's gone, so I fill in the empty space for us both.

"You care a lot for him."

"I do. He's like a grandfather to me," she explains with a sigh. "His wife died about five years ago. I never met her, but the ladies of the *Wizards of Wool* say that he's been a little lost without her." She sighs again and looks my way.

"I like Joe, of course I do. But I think my need to protect him also has something to do with his loss. The idea of being with someone for over forty years and then *boom,* they're gone, just like that? I can't fathom that kind of loneliness."

I steal a glance at my girl in the passenger seat, with her beautiful features lit up green in the dashboard light. Again my chest constricts. I want to tell this girl that I've felt that kind of loneliness for most of my life, right up until the day that I met her, pretty much. But I don't. I tug her hand across the center console and kiss her knuckles one by one. Only in that moment do I realize that I might be falling in love with Stevie. I know it's insane—we haven't even shagged yet—but it's fucking true.

"Let's get you home," I growl.

"But what about the hot tub?" She juts out her bottom lip and fuck me if she isn't adorable. My cock twitches in my jeans and I remember how close we came to shagging. I know I have her hooked. It'd be so easy to drive her back to my hotel, or even a roadside motel.

"Another time." My cock gets bigger when I see the look on her face—milady is crestfallen. She wants me just as much as I want her. Hell, it makes dropping her off feel awful.

"Why?" She sends her big curls tumbling over her shoulder with a tilt of her head.

"Because you have your friend on your mind, and I'm not that big of a bastard."

She sighs but doesn't argue. I'm a little disappointed that she didn't fight harder for us tonight, but waiting is the right move. I want this girl more than a million fans screaming my name, but I can wait for her. Good things come to rock stars who wait.

"Let me take you out again."

"No."

My heart twists when she cuts me off. "No?"

She turns around to face me. "I want to take *you* out."

"Isn't that what I just said?"

"Look, Granger, today was beautiful, really. From the helicopter ride, to the limo, the exquisite food, and the private pool, it probably ranks as one of the most memorable experiences of my life, but it feels like a fantasy life—one that I had an opportunity to glimpse for a night. It was extravagant, excessive, and ultimately not me."

"It was just dinner, Stevie, and a picnic on a glacier."

"It was far more than what you say. Today was a beautiful gesture and I am grateful for every minute. Now let me make a gesture of my own. Let me take you out and I'll show you the real me."

It's been a shitty three days without her, but I'm good at miserable. My last five years were packed with an impressive web of groupies, and Chad escorting them home before sunrise. Sure, some have stuck around—as company to find release with after a long tour, or yet another recording session—but I've never given them much thought. With her though...with her it's been constant.

I thought about her again this morning, mid-jacking off in the shower. I thought about her during yesterday's press interviews and radio spots. I considered calling but figured that would be overkill. Fuck, I don't want to scare her away. It's no surprise that my palms are sweating by the time I pull up to her townhouse. I mean, I'm a grown man—why am I acting like this?

The garage door is wide open when my taxi arrives. I catch a glimpse of Stevie's fine yoga-pant ass, sticking straight up in the air yet again. She's hunched over her motorcycle gripping a wrench. I toss a few bills at the driver and hop onto the curb. The anticipation of seeing her is killing me. When I slam the taxi door, she stands up and turns around, like a bonnie ballerina on ice.

"Hey, rock star." She gives me a big grin, which I swear makes my heart skip a beat, in the most cliché way possible.

"Hello, beautiful. Need me to hold the bike again?"

"I think I'll probably manage," she deadpans. I figure that she's probably right. I've never met someone as independent as Stevie, male or female. "Well, I hope you got your celebrity rest, since it's going to be a full day."

I stuff both hands in my pockets. "What do you have planned for us?"

"Something that won't work in skinny jeans. Do you have a change of clothes?" She tilts her head in that familiar way that I've come to love.

"I don't." When she said *dress comfortably*, I thought that she meant skinny jeans.

"I may have a pair of Kit's track pants upstairs, if you want to try?"

I clench my fists, preventing myself from saying the wrong thing, but the idea of another guy's pants anywhere near her house makes me want to howl at the moon.

"I'm not wearing another guy's pants. Besides, I'm a foot taller than him."

"That might be an exaggeration." She immediately rolls her eyes. "But okay, it's your funeral."

Stevie goes inside to fetch herself a zip-up sweatshirt, motioning to the bike when she returns. "Are you okay if we take this?"

"Of course, but I'm driving."

"I don't think so, rock star," she laughs out. "Nobody drives my baby but me."

Without letting me respond, Stevie throws one leg over the bike. My dick twitches as I picture the action in a way different context. She wriggles her hips, getting me to straddle her waist. Yeah, clearly today will be all about keeping my shit together. In five minutes, we're at the café she picked for breakfast. It looks more like a country store than a restaurant though. There's even an old dog drooling on the front patio—the mutt reminds me of Chad when he passes out.

"Welcome to *The Pony*." She removes her helmet and shakes out her hair. Her huge, messy curls fall around her face and I have to count backwards from ten again. Otherwise, I'll end up launching at her like a mountain lion.

The inside of the restaurant is *intimate* in the worst way— actually, packed might be a better word. But we snag the last free table by the window.

"So what's good here?" I ask, picking up the menu.

"Everything," she sighs. "They use a lot of seasonal and locally produced food, so it's all amazing. But I'm going for eggs and bacon."

The waitress appears and I order Stevie her eggs-and-bacon, plus a coffee, along with a hamburger and a Bloody Mary for myself. I'm about to press Stevie about the rest of our day when someone butts into our conversation.

"Stevie?" There's some yuppie-looking freak making eyes at my girl. I look at Stevie and realize that her face is deathly pale.

"I thought that was you," he continues.

"Duncan," she chokes out, gripping the menu so hard that her knuckles turn white.

"It's been awhile." His hand lands on the back of her chair. I want to yank it from its socket, but I don't know what role this guy plays in her life. Hopefully not a very important one, judging by the sleazy look to him. I mean, sure, women might find him handsome—that big dimpled smile, Ken-doll hair, and high-school football physique, but there's something else there too, a streak of something much worse.

Stevie doesn't answer, which weirdly doesn't seem to faze him. "I wanted to say that I am sorry—about how it all went down with your brother—but you must know that I wasn't in the wrong."

When she doesn't speak, I take my cue to get this fucker away from us ASAP. I lean forward and lay one right on her lips. I'm planning on a quick kiss to send a message, but it morphs into an intense dance of soft moans and tangled tongues as I attack her hot little mouth. When I finally pull away, Ken-doll looks shocked.

"I didn't know you were seeing someone." He shifts his attention to me and recognizes my face right away. It's like I can see our music playing in his eyes.

"She's more than seeing someone." I turn and face him head on. "Isn't my woman a smoke show?" His face morphs from surprise into anger. "Is this guy bothering you, love?" I rub circles into Stevie's palms with my thumbs.

"You're dating Granger Ellis?" Ken-doll demands, looking like some dick who just sucked a lemon.

"Please, Duncan, just leave us alone." She doesn't meet his eyes. Her meek demeanor is such a contrast to the feisty Stevie I've been getting to know. It makes me want to kill this bloke.

Thankfully, the waitress arrives with our drinks and that alone breaks the tension. Ken-doll finally seems to get the message. He wanders back to his seat, mumbling something like *see you around* as he disappears into the restaurant crowd. What the hell was that? Stevie bores holes into the table with her eyes. I'm dying to speak, but figure I'm better off waiting for her to explain. We sit in silence for a solid few minutes before she speaks up.

"Duncan and I drove past his house together one time—that's the only reason I knew where he lived. He said that we couldn't go inside because the cleaners were working and couldn't be disturbed. I don't think he intended to show me where he lived, but arrogance got the best of him. At the time, I remember finding it weird that we couldn't go inside. I should've trusted my judgment, but it's amazing how much a woman overlooks in the pursuit of ass."

I choke on my last sip of beer. "I'm sorry, did you just say *pursuit of ass*?"

She shrugs off my comment. "I did."

"Ass? Really?"

"Now, surely you're not one of those men who believes that women are motivated solely by love and marriage. He was hot—what other reason would there be for blatantly accepting obvious false truths?"

I take another sip of my Bloody Mary, thinking hard before answering, in case I'm walking into a trap. "I've just always thought that women were more sensible when it came to love."

"Ok, and I just threw up in my mouth a little. Anyway, you should probably get out of here; your time machine back to Victorian England just arrived." She snickers like she is the funniest girl in the whole world—although to me, she kind of is.

"Come again, love?"

"Believe me, I wish that I could come all night." I know she's kidding, but I feel my face getting hot regardless. My fingers tighten around my frosty glass of vodka and Clamato juice—which is like tomato juice except made with clams. I've been told that it sets the

Bloody Mary apart from the Caesar, but I'm still getting used to calling them that up here. For now, my breakfast drink is a necessary distraction. I don't want to think about this beautiful creature fucking anybody else—ever. It's an interesting sensation for me, to say the least.

"Anyway." She sighs before continuing with her story. "You don't seriously believe that women everywhere go on tolerating the *fucktardery-that-is-man* all because of some misaligned belief that they'll be swept off her feet by a white knight?"

"*Fucktardery*?" I repeat, just making sure that I heard her right.

"I accepted Duncan's half-truths because he was attractive and uncomplicated—at least I thought so—not to mention decent in bed. I never expected anything more from him, but I also didn't expect the wife, and that was the major deal breaker for me. But no, I didn't think us calling each other a few times a week and meeting up for dinner meant that he wanted my hand in marriage – I just thought we were having fun. Men should really wake up to this new reality and stop romanticizing about settling down with some demure lady-in-waiting."

"I take it that this is a subject you feel quite strongly about." I clear my throat and force a lump down my throat.

"Honestly? It just irritates me when men want to mess around on Tinder as if it's freshman-year Spring Break, but they still want a nice girl waiting with a bouquet of shitty flowers and rice in her hair. Seriously *fucktards,* no one will be there if you haven't put in the time and effort. Besides, I want someone who makes me feel like the bridge of a Guns and Roses song and can make me come on loop."

"And that's why you're not together? Because he wouldn't take you to his house?" I press, knowing that there's more to this story.

"No, we're not together because my brother Spencer beat the shit out of him; therefore, Duncan had him arrested."

"Your brother beat him up because it didn't work out? I mean, I get that you're his sister, but that seems a little harsh."

"You don't know my brothers." She rolls her eyes. "They would've just scared him, if not for the black eye he gave me."

"He gave you a black eye?" I have to tamp down on my instinct to kick over the table and pound his face into the linoleum floor.

"Honestly, it was really more of a red eye—like a handprint bruise. Not like it sounds, and obviously I kicked him in the balls afterwards. It was just a knee-jerk reaction to having me confront him."

"Confront him about what?"

"I came by his house with Thai food once, plus a beautiful bottle of Okanagan Riesling. It was a surprise, but his wife answered the door. She was so pretty and thin, between her peaches-and-cream complexion and not one stray hair. Two little blond babies poked their heads out from behind her knees afterwards, and I knew then that I couldn't tell her the truth. So I pretended that I had the wrong house. When I told him what happened, he slapped me, hard. My brother, Spencer, got a suspended sentence and the lawyer cost my mom her entire retirement fund, so you can understand why I'm cautious about dating now. That whole situation was on me."

Breakfast arrives. I wolf down my burger as Stevie picks at her food. It makes me feel shitty, because I saw how excited she was when we arrived. After she wraps up her story, I push my chair back and scan the restaurant to find Duncan. I don't know what I plan to do once I find him, but I have to do something, for Stevie. I want to do something. Unfortunately for me though, he's already long gone. I don't want to ruin our date by getting arrested myself.

The cheque arrives and I dig around in my pockets for my wallet, but instead she holds up her hand. "My date, my rules, and one of my rules is that whomever asks the person out pays." When she extracts her own wallet and frees a red fifty-dollar bill, my laughter booms through the restaurant.

"No," I say, shaking my head. "You're not paying, love."

"I am," she protests. A blue and white card falls on the table mid tug-of-war for her wallet, which I turn over carefully in my hands. It has a barcode and her full name, Steven Tyler, plus an expiry date and the word MENSA scrawled across the top. I squint to read the caption below the word MENSA.

"*The High IQ Society.* Is this yours?"

"It is. So what?" She grabs for the card like a worked-up kid.

"I figured that you were smart, but who knew you were an *official* genius."

"I am not a genius. It's an international society in which members come together to provide each other with a stimulating and inclusive social environment," she recites.

"Inclusive if you're a genius, right?"

"I am not a genius." She pouts. "True geniuses are people like Albert Einstein or Stephen Hawking, both of whom scored over one-hundred-and-sixty. The highest score ever recorded is over two hundred. I promise you that is not me."

"What would you call yourself then?" I tease.

"Gifted, I guess? I've been a Mensa member since age eleven, when they tested me in school."

"So what's your score?"

"I was always taught that it's rude to share."

"That means it is high," I challenge.

She rubs her forehead in frustration. "Look, I'm going to go to the bathroom. When I return, we're going to talk about something else."

She disappears into the back of the restaurant, but I Google the minimum Mensa score the moment she's out of sight. Not a genius my ass. In truth, part of me—a big part of me—is hugely intimidated. I barely finished high school and would've flunked out without Chad. Now I'm dating someone with a PhD in molecular biology. A girl who ranks among the top two percent of the population in brainpower. Yeah, I may have pleaded ignorance to Stevie, but I know exactly what Mensa is, making for one more thing about Stevie that scares the ever-loving hell out of me.

She returns from the bathroom and the cheque arrives. I go ahead and let her pay, provided that she promises to let me treat her next time. We leave the restaurant and haul ass onto her bike. She still won't tell me where we're going. We wind down the highway and get lost in the scenery. This Pemberton place is amazing, from its snow-capped mountains, low strung clouds, and hordes of Arbutus trees, which are the colour of fire. It's like the part of Scotland where I grew up—well, at least the area where I was born. We moved around plenty back then. We pull into the parking lot about half an hour later. The sign reads: *Joffre Lake Provincial Park.*

"Are we going camping?" I joke.

"Close," she mumbles over her shoulder. "We're going hiking."

My stomach plummets the very moment that she says those words, because I haven't been hiking once in my whole life. I finally see what she meant by the skinny jeans.

"How long is this hike?"

"Eleven kilometres," she answers, matter-of-factly.

"That'll take hours!" I shout, but Stevie just nods.

"About five, roundtrip, to be exact."

The look on my face must be pretty far out there, I figure, because Stevie is laughing and rolling her lovely eyes.

"Relax, rock star, we don't have to do the whole thing."

"I don't exactly have the right gear."

She flips open the saddle bag on her motorbike to show me a folded backpack, bottled water, and some snacks.

"See? All you need is the shoes on your feet."

Not having another option, I follow her to the trailhead, checking out the other hikers on the way. They all seem geared up with hiking boots and big packs on their shoulders, which means that I'm fucking screwed.

"How hard is it?" I ask, but Stevie just snorts.

"I think that's supposed to be my line."

"Stevie..." I groan out, "please don't make a sex joke before we hike to our death."

"It won't be grueling—it's rated intermediate."

Clearly, Canada's definition of intermediate is quite different from my own. It takes me about twenty minutes to figure this out. The elevation is far too steep; for chrissakes, we even need to scale rocks in some sections.

"Intermediate, my arse," I mutter under my breath. She hears me up ahead, but *milady* doesn't bother to respond. My one saving grace from this position is taking in the full view of her swaying hips and round behind, which happens to look perfect in the tight black yoga pants she wears. Eventually we reach a field of boulders that insist on being scaled, followed by a few steep rocks and some switchbacks.

The trees open to a small bridge with a trail curving along the shoreline like the Loch-Ness-Monster. I'd heard that this area was home to a similar supernatural beast: the Cadborosaurus. Tourist books described the thing as a giant snake with a horse's head and something resembling dreadlocks. It's drop-dead stunning, but the key part of the route is the glacier high up on the mountain. The view is enough to make a man hard. It's surreal as hell, like a famous painting that would never fit in a museum. The glacier-fed lake is a light shade of turquoise, which I can't even describe, it just "is." Not much just "is" today. Our hike was worth the trek though, I have to admit, despite the swamp-ass in my jeans and chafing in all the worst places.

"So what do you think?" I'd have to be a snowman to miss the excitement in her voice.

"I've never seen anything like it. It's stunning—song-inspiring, in fact."

"That's what I thought! You're an artist, so I figured that you'd appreciate natural beauty."

"You know that I do." I slowly stalk towards her body, sliding my arms around her waist and pressing my lips against Stevie's. Her skin is salt and sweat, and her mouth tastes like mint gum, but still I want to throw her on the forest floor and sink myself inside her body. It's way more than just wanting sex. Every moment with this woman feels like a religious experience. I want to be with her lightness and energy all of the time.

"Thank you for sharing this with me," I murmur against her lips.

"Will you make it back okay, rock star?"

"As long as I'm behind you, I'll have the proper motivation." I give her a wink.

My girl rolls her eyes and pulls away, I guess to unzip her bag. "Fine, but when we fuck, we look each other in the eyes."

After drinking most of the water and eating all of the snacks she brought up the mountain—fuck, I probably should have carried the snacks—we decide to head back down. I can barely move my legs by the time we reach the parking lot, and it's not like Stevie doesn't notice.

"Poor baby," she coos. "Why don't we head back to my place, and I'll massage all those sore spots for you?"

Just like that, I'm standing at attention once again—and I mean that in more ways than one.

➤

Stevie keeps her word, having me relax on the bed as she runs the shower. I strip down to my boxers because my clothes are stiff from the dried sweat and natural grime. Still, I have attention only for her legs. Her fucking killer legs. Long, shapely, and muscular—though not too muscular, with smooth calves and a hint of ass cheek peeking out from beneath her pajama shorts. I can feel the swell beneath my jeans getting tighter just from looking at her.

"What?" She eyes me over her shoulder with an impossible look in her eyes.

"You." The word comes out like a growl, but I can't help myself. I stalk forward and snake my arms around her waist, thrusting my hardness against her backside. She stands upright and I use the opportunity to spin her around and move her backwards toward the wall. "You're driving me insane."

"What did I do?" She heaves in a big breath while I thrust myself between the apex of her thighs, watching with satisfaction as her eyes grow drowsy with lust.

"What *didn't* you do?" I answer back. "As punishment for strutting around in those tiny shorts, I'll be stripping you naked and fucking you harder than you've ever been fucked." I don't know what has come over me, honestly, other than my burning need to be buried deep inside her, but she surprises me with her response.

"Is that a promise?"

I push my hips up and plunge my tongue into her hot little mouth. She rewards me with the sweetest sounding little keen. Just when I think that I have the go ahead though, she stops me in my tracks.

"You're filthy, Granger."

She pulls away to give me the once-over.

"You have no idea, love."

Stevie pushes me away with a heart-stopping laugh and disappears into the bathroom. She reappears soon enough though, with an armful of towels, plopping them down on the bed with a look at my face. "You really are sore, aren't you?"

"Is it that obvious?" I chuckle. She sits down behind me and kneads my shoulders with both hands. It feels so good that I moan out loud.

"Keep doing that, love."

"You should take a shower," she mutters. "It will make you feel better."

"You make me feel better," I mumble, but I still hop off the bed. She leads the way to her attached bathroom, which is much warmer and more inviting than most bathrooms I've been in, and I've been in some of the nicest bathrooms in the world. Without waiting for her to leave, I shuck off my boxers and step into the shower stall, which smells just like her coconut scent and immediately has me hard. When I run my hand down the length of my cock, she gasps.

"I'll just leave you alone, then," she says, but I don't miss the blush creeping across her cheeks.

"No you won't." I grab her hand and pull her inside fully clothed, all the way into the shower. The door still hangs open, with steam floating out and water splashing all over the floor, but I really don't care. I'll build her a new bathroom if I that's what I have to do, but right now I just want her pressed against me.

First I back her against the tile wall. Second I devour her face like a demon falling hard into love. Her tank top and shorts soak through to the bone. I thought she would protest, but she submits all the way. I read the gleam in her eyes though and know that she wants this just as much as me. So I let the water rush down my back, washing me clean while I strip off her wet top layers. Her sports bra is the hardest, like some medieval chastity belt for boobs, but once it falls away, there's no turning back. Her skin is pink and rosy from the warm water, and her full breasts fall into my hands like no tomorrow. I feel like they're made for me specifically. I pull one of her perfect, slippery nipples into my mouth and suck like a baby, all the while noticing her knees buckle beneath me.

"The bed, Granger," she croaks out, but I don't need a second invitation.

We abandon the shower with the water still running. My hands scramble around her body, tugging those wet shorts down her legs followed by her white cotton panties, both of which she kicks into the corner. Unable to help myself, I devour her perfectly symmetrical, cream-white breasts, meanwhile teasing her caramel nipples with my teeth. I simultaneously thrust myself against her mostly naked form, but it's almost too much to take. I'm going to cum real soon if I don't ease off, which isn't my usual. After years on the road, getting myself off with fake groupies takes longer and longer, but the woman in my arms is one hundred percent real.

Her fingers bite into the meat of my biceps as a rattle passes through her frame, signalling that she's near to climaxing. My fingers find her folds, slick and ready for me, and I plunge into her silkiness.

Meanwhile she slams her head against the wall and moans like the mountain wind. My thumb presses into her clit and she comes apart screaming in my arms. I take great satisfaction in her being a screamer, because whimpers and yelps will not do between me and her. The thought invites such a wave of jealous possession into my mind that I cannot begin to understand the feeling, so I push it aside and instead carry her to bed. After laying her on the bed, I stand back to watch the rise and fall of her luscious breasts.

"Granger, that was..."

I cut her off before she can speak another word. "Just the preview, sweetheart." I keep my eyes locked with hers, stroking my cock and watching her eyes widen at the sight. Women have often told me that my cock is something to be proud of and whether or not that's true, I haven't gotten any complaints in the orgasm department.

With Stevie though, it feels different. I'm too horny to see straight but also anxious for the first time in my life, because there's something about her that I can't explain. I have to bring her pleasure and really rock her world, if I'm going to wipe out the memory of any-and-all wankers who got to her first, and if I am to make her fully and completely mine.

She pants breathlessly as I hover above her spread bald-eagle form, thumbing her bottom lip before brushing my mouth against hers. She tastes like cherry lip gloss. I want to take my time exploring her beautiful mouth, but first I have to taste the rest of her. When I slide down her body, her breathing picks up and I tease her with my tongue for a while, letting her beg before I reach my destination.

"Granger, please." She circles her hips around to bring her centre close to my nose. I love that she's not shy at all. Most girls get so self-conscious about oral, but the way she squirms around now tells me that she loves my fingers. She's so ready for me and I know it, and that's fucking hot.

"You taste like honey, love." My dick pulses like it has a heartbeat, which I guess it does. If I don't give myself relief soon, my cock will rocket right off. Still, I remind myself that this all about her. Man, I need her to come again. My fingers join my mouth as she releases a low, pained moan.

"I can't—" she mutters, "I can't come again."

"Just let go." I slip another finger inside her, circling my tongue around her clit. She clenches against my fingers as another scream, equally impressive as the last, tears from her mouth like a runaway mountain biker heading down the mountain into Whistler Village. The vibration of her wild release and shaking figure sends a bolt of arousal zinging through my bloodstream. Before she can even formulate words, I'm on my feet and tearing open a package from my jeans before sheathing myself entirely.

I plunge inside her and swear that my sight goes black for a moment from the sensation. She fits me perfectly. I learn just how true that statement is as I start moving inside her. I cage her head between my arms and attack her mouth as my thrusts pick up speed. My head is pounding, my dick is throbbing, and I can feel the pressure like a thermometer about to shatter, cum and feelings spilling everywhere. "Come once more for me, love."

"I can't." She thrashes her head from side to side, with both eyes squeezed shut. "It's too much."

"You can and you will," I demand, feeling her spine stiffen before she cries out yet again.

"Fuck Granger!" I love that she's cursing my name. I'm all about how her body quivers in my arms. I lean back and place my hands on her beautifully-rounded hips, studying her face while I pound into all corners of her sexiness. Her mouth hangs open, her eyes are half mast, and her sweet sultry grin has me exploding inside of her in seconds. As I pump my release, I surrender my own strangled cry before collapsing onto her in breasts in a giant heap.

I'm breathing heavily and probably squishing her with all my weight, but she doesn't complain—thank God, because I'm not ready to let go yet. This woman has totally and completely blown my mind. The way I'm feeling right now has me terrified. Somehow, this creature beneath me has managed to make me dangerously unhinged.

After a beat, I scoot up alongside her body and sling one arm over her waist. I've never been an overly affectionate person—probably something to do with my upbringing—but I can't keep my hands to myself with Stevie. It feels different with her after today, as if we got to know each other better, like kids around town with nothing to do. It has nothing to do with sex (no doubt we'll have plenty more of that) and everything to do with how much she shared with me.

Somehow, she convinced me to hike. I met her cunt of an ex-boyfriend and discovered yet another reason (Mensa) why Stevie is totally out of my league. Thankfully for me, she doesn't seem to realize that dozens of IQ points set us apart. I can close that gap anyways with a little extra creativity. Even if I have to serenade her with a musical rendition of her very own dissertation, I'll do whatever it takes to make her mine.

Chapter Nine

"Kiss Me Deadly"

Stevie

The sun is out full force, with record-breaking temperatures baking the village in Vitamin-D for the long weekend. In turn, the bar is shoulder-to-shoulder busy. We already have a thirty-minute wait for the patio and it's barely past noon. I can't fill the drink orders fast enough as the tourists pile in for bullfrog margaritas and buckets of ice-cold beer.

The smell of deep-fried hot wings and world-class poutine floats out from the kitchen and floods the bar, causing my stomach to rumble like thunder over the Peak of Whistler. I should be hungry after skipping breakfast, but my appetite has gone on hiatus these past few days. I've been far too consumed by him to even think about consuming *food.*

I've only been here for an hour, tops, but already I feel run off my feet. My exhaustion is only made worse by the fact that I miss Granger. He's been in Vancouver for meetings and other than one hurried phone call, we've hardly been in touch over the last few days. Ironic, since it's only been a few days and I myself used to make fun of girlfriends for pining over men. Lovesickness always seemed just that—a sickness, but from the way he's stuck in my head, I might've accidently joined the lovesick club.

I mean, I've been attracted to a lot of men in the past, and I've fallen *in lust* with more than a few. Even with Duncan, the douche, I thought we might be heading for love. But none of them made me feel the way I do with Granger. Every time I see him, my stomach leaps into my throat and my skin tingles all over, so it's no surprise that my throat gets thick and my body seems to thrum when he suddenly appears beside me. I glance from side to side and see that besides the black-clad security guards flanking either end of the bar, he's alone.

"Granger." I wipe my sweaty palms off on my jean cut offs. "Fancy seeing you here."

He's wearing a ball cap pulled down over his eyes, dressed casually in a tank top, shorts, and flip flops, which is out of character. His tattoos are on full display, but these days it seems that almost everyone in our age group is inked, so he doesn't stand out in the crowd. His eyes immediately drop to my chest and scan my too tight tank top—it's one that I've worn deliberately to encourage more tips on a busy day like today.

"I like your top." Now there's that rough, gravelly voice that I've come to crave.

"So do I, man, so do I," a guy on the stool next to him says, whistling through his teeth.

Granger looks at him, then me, before calmly leaning over to whisper in his ear. I can't hear what he says, but I watch as the young guy's face blanches right before my eyes. He lurches upright as if some invisible force just flash froze his stool.

"I'm sorry, miss," he mutters before disappearing into the crowd. Granger slides onto the stool he vacated, evidently not flash-frozen after all, and gives me a knowing little smirk.

I tilt my head to the side in this way that always makes him melt a bit, or so it seems. "What did you say to him?"

"That's between him, me, and the good Lord. Now if you aren't too busy, love, could I grab a Corona?"

I study him for a second before bending down to retrieve the bottle from the fridge. I place the beer on the bar top before speaking. "Sometimes you are too much, Granger, you know that, right?"

I slide the sweating bottle across the counter and he slams half of it back in one fluid motion. Then he leans forward and gestures for me to do the same. When I do, he takes my chin in his palm and whispers softly in my ear. "I know this may seem like I'm overstepping, but you, Steven Tyler, are mine now. And those gorgeous show-stopping tits of yours are mine. And those silky-soft nipples I see puckering under your shirt are also mine. Mine, mine, mine. So fuck that guy and his wandering eyes. Got it?"

I pull back and quickly nod, while plucking at my shirt to hide the current state of my arousal. He follows the movement with his eyes as I watch, mesmerized, as his full lips wrap around the neck of the bottle and swig back the cold liquid. I can't help but imagine those lips between my legs, or the tip of his tongue giving my nipples some much needed relief. I can see the outline of his nipple rings through his fitted tank top and my mouth goes dry at the thought of sucking them between my own lips, tracing circles around his nipples and exploring every gloriously inked inch of his body.

I let out a tiny little moan and he answers with a smug smile. "Hey, bartender," he calls out, adding, "you look a little overheated. Maybe it's time for a break?" The mention of a break pulls me back to reality and I glance over at the server stand, only to see three very pissed-off waitresses congregated there.

"Shit," I mumble, before rushing back over to fill the orders piling up. A tray of shots, four glasses of white wine, three Bellinis, and two Caesars later, I've finally caught up. I'm mixing up a mojito when my eyes travel back to Granger's now empty seat.

I instantly feel deflated since he came all the way down here to see me and I barely had time to flirt. The good news for him is that this place is so busy, he went mostly undetected. Other than the young guy that he scared away, no one really seemed to take notice of his presence and there weren't any requests for pictures or autographs in the short time that he graced us with his presence.

"I'm taking fifteen!" I shout across the bar to my co-worker Tammy, tossing the damp rag I'm holding into the sink before heading to the back room. Back in the staff area, I grab a bottle of ice-cold water from the fridge and press it against my neck in an effort to cool myself down. It's stuffy out front and the lack of airflow is compounded by all the bodies packed into the place. I'm about to unscrew the top of the bottle for an ice-cold sip when two big hands suddenly pluck it from my grasp.

"Let me take care of that for you, love."

"Granger!" I turn around to face him. "You can't be in here!"

"Sure I can." He cracks open the plastic bottle and presses it to my lips. "Drink."

I gulp down a few mouthfuls before pushing it away. "I thought you left."

"There's no chance of that. Not when those sweet little buds of yours so desperately need relief." He removes his baseball cap and tosses it in the corner before grabbing a handful of my tank top in his hands. He uses the fabric to pull me closer before peeling the whole thing over my head.

My skin is slick from the heat so my bra slides up no problem after he pushes it askew, latching his mouth onto one of my aching nipples. I swear to God that I see stars when his teeth graze my sensitive flesh. He sucks hard on one nipple while using his other hand to tweak and massage my breast. He lavishes attention on both in the end, until my legs feel shaky and I'm about to come right there in the back room. He glances up at me and his eyes are practically on fire as he traces the swell of my breasts with his tongue.

"W-what if someone comes in?"

"Relax, love. My security team is at the door. I promise you that no one is coming except for you."

At that he drops to his knees, unzipping my shorts and sliding them off with my underwear in the process. My eyes roll back into my head and I almost lose it from the rush of cool air touching me right where I'm exposed, but the feeling is quickly replaced by the heat of Granger's mouth between my legs.

"Oohh…" I moan, grabbing the back of my chair to steady myself. He gently bites the insides of my thighs and licks a path towards my apex before gazing at me with those gorgeous green eyes.

"You have a spectacular pussy."

His tongue circles my clit as his fingers join the party to bring me to the brink. I know it won't be long now. "Oh my God…I'm so close," I manage to groan out.

"Just let go, love. Let me take care of you." He buries his face between my legs again, and I take his advice and let go as the waves of orgasm crash over me. My already unsteady legs shake as my body convulses and I'm surprised that I don't lose balance. As if sensing this, Granger spins the chair around from behind me and guides me down to recover before tugging my underwear and shorts back up my legs. He kisses me with my sweet and musky taste still on his lips, and I find it incredibly erotic. I fasten my shorts and tug my bra back into place as he locates my shirt on the floor.

"Uh, but what about your situation?" I point to the noticeable bulge in his shorts, and he laughs in his usual rock-star way.

"This was about you, Stevie. My situation is nothing that can't be fixed by me jerking off in the shower to the memory of your tits and that beautiful pussy."

"But I could—" I start to say, but he just holds up his hand to silence me.

"Your break is officially over, Miss Tyler—and I won't be the one to get you in trouble."

I get to my feet and cross the room to slide my arms around his neck. He slips my shirt back on my body and slides his hands down my arms before planting a sweet kiss on my lips.

I nibble a bit at his bottom lip. "Thank you."

"No, thank you," he sighs out. "I'm not usually such a possessive asshole, and I know better than to bother you at work. I can't explain any of this with anything besides I missed you."

"I know what you mean. I feel the same," I say. "I missed you too, and I'm glad you came." He laughs at the last part and I feel myself blushing.

"I mean, I know you didn't come but—" I stutter and he silences me with another kiss. "Trust me, love, watching you come and being the man responsible for it was well worth the trip. In fact, I look forward to seeing more of the same, just as soon as you get off."

This time it's my turn to laugh at the innuendo and his face reddens adorably. "In any case, you know what I mean. So I'll see you tonight?"

"Definitely. I look forward to returning the favor."

He bends down to scoop his hat off the floor and heads out the front entrance. Before he opens it though, he turns around for one last word.

"And Stevie?"

"Yes?"

"I'll do my best not to play the part of jealous boyfriend if you do one thing for me?"

"Sure, Granger, what is it?"

"Can you attempt to find a different shirt to wear to work?"

I glance down at my *boobalicious* tank top and smile. "What? No way. Do you even realize the kind of tips these babies bring in on a busy weekend like this?"

He looks at the ceiling and I swear if I didn't know any better, I'd think that he was counting to ten. "Just think about it, okay? I hear that turtlenecks are making a fashion comeback," he deadpans, and I laugh so loud that it makes him jump.

"For the record, I despise turtlenecks—and you are lucky that you're cute, Granger Ellis." I push past him as he opens the door, grumbling to himself all the way to the front exit with his bodyguards in tow. I swear, if I didn't know any better, I'd believe he was raised by mountain lions, ones that Raven-the-Trickster taught to play rock n' roll.

Chapter Ten

"Back for More"

Granger

The sky is dark when she meets me back at the hotel after her shift. I'm tired after an afternoon of meetings with the band, and she's bagged from a full day on her feet, so we make love slowly in my bed and fall asleep in each others' arms. I wake up sometime later in a panic, because she's not with me anymore. I can't feel her warm body beside me in the bed, so I stretch out and pat around for an arm, a leg, anything.

I scrub one hand down my face and groan, doing by best not to overreact, but I've been here many times. Story of my life, in fact—just when things are getting good, someone runs away. I force myself out of bed and head downstairs, expelling a breath when I hear the TV blaring. There I find Stevie on the sofa, watching music videos.

Reaching the bottom of the stairs, she starts belting out the lines to some god-awful eighties' song, and I can't contain my smile. She gets to her knees and sings even louder, this time with her eyes closed and arms spread wide. I listen for a few more seconds before clearing my throat. She whirls around and almost topples over the sofa when she sees me, but right away it becomes clear that she's not embarrassed. In fact, she gives me this huge, face-splitting grin; and just like that I'm a goner.

"What's this crap?" I ask, coming around the sofa to sit down beside her.

"It's not crap—it's *Whitesnake*."

My eyes travel to the fifty-inch flat screen, where a woman is writhing around on the hood of a car. I cock my head to the side and stare at the television. "She looks like a tranny."

"That's not nice."

"It's true."

"It's not. If you look hard enough you'll find beauty in every person."

"That's horse shite. What about a serial killer?"

"Beauty is relative—subjective—and you create beauty in the world by recognizing it in others."

"That's naïve."

"You're just jaded."

I shrug. "Well I am a rock star."

"Eye roll."

A deep chuckle leaves my chest. "Did you just say *eye roll* out loud?"

"I did, because your misanthropy is showing and I'll let you in on a little secret—it's not attractive." She furrows her brows like a real pro.

"Why is she wearing a nightgown and doing the splits?"

"That's Tawny Kitaen—eighties' video vixen and queen. GOING DOWN THE ONLY ROAD I'LL EVER KNOW… LIKE A TWISTER I WAS BORN TO WALK ALONE…" she belts out, slightly off-key. "Anyway, I wish my life was like an eighties' video."

"Thriving on the hood of a car with big hair?" I ask. "Your life can be that way if you want."

"Doubtful."

"Why not?"

"I'd probably dent the hood," she answers with a giggle.

"Now you're putting yourself down, what about that whole, *beauty is in everyone* comment that you made?"

"I'm not putting myself down; it's factual, and I have no issue with me denting it—I'm proud of this ass." She giggles again and it almost kills me.

"I'm proud of it too." I give her ass a good slap before running my hand down her smooth, toned leg. The way that her bare thigh feels under my palm has me ready to throw her down and wrestle into her yet again, but just as my fantasies take flight, there`s a knock on the door.

"Expecting someone?" She quirks one eyebrow at me, acting cute as fuck. I just shake my head at the performance.

"No one, so it better be room service with a snack, or else I'm not letting them inside."

"Ooh...ice cream, please." She smacks her lips, lacking all shame.

However, it's not room service at the door after all—instead it's Chad. He rolls in like he owns the place, grabbing two beers from the bar fridge before sitting down in the chair opposite the sofa. He tosses one of the beers in my direction and gives Stevie the once-over.

"I didn't interrupt anything important, did I?" He directs the question my way, in a challenging tone that I'm not used to hearing.

"Actually mate, you did." My cock and I have no problem shutting him down. "What do you need, Chad?"

He really makes himself at home, sinking into the club chair and throwing one arm over its backside. "The MGM Grand called. They have a slot for next week. They want you guys to fill it." He casually explains, taking a long pull from his can.

"We're not some second-choice backup band, Chad. It's too short of notice."

"That's exactly what I said," he hedges. "But they've offered to triple the appearance fee and they plan to pitch it as an exclusive event. They even promised to have the venue sold out in twenty-four hours."

"Why us?" I mean, we're good; I know we are, but triple the appearance fee is pretty unheard of these days.

He shrugs. "You drew a huge crowd last year. Vegas likes you."

"When?"

"Next week."

"It's too soon."

"The band's already on board," he finally announces.

"You went to Ravi and Jayne first?"

"Don't be mad, man. It's a solid gig, and the slot's only available because some pop star princess they booked found God and cancelled the remainder of her tour."

Shit. It actually does sound like a pretty good opportunity and we'd garner some pretty big media attention in advance of next year's tour. I could probably even play a few songs from the album we're working on right now.

"Fine," I sigh, "but I want heavy media and social on it. Promote it as a surprise pop-up event. I don't want people thinking that we're sloppy seconds to Rihanna or Taylor Swift or whomever the fuck just cancelled on them."

"You know it." Chad is grinning like a madman. He swigs back the rest of his beer in one big gulp. I've barely touched mine, which is unusual for me, but my stomach doesn't feel quite right. Perhaps because Stevie has gone eerily quiet in the corner. I'm worried about how she's taking the news, since it cuts our time together short.

Chad crushes his empty can and tosses it onto the coffee table before getting to his feet. "Vegas, baby!" He claps his hands together. "I'll call that club promoter and set up the same venue for the after party. That VIP area was *siiick*." He walks by Stevie, without acknowledging her presence. "And sorry I interrupted whatever this was." He rudely gestures between us, slamming the door before I can call him out for the comment.

"Ignore him." I shake my head without taking my eyes off the now closed door.

"It's kind of hard to ignore him when he's everywhere," she whispers.

I cross the room and pull her into my arms. "Hey, look at me." She complies and lifts those big, beautiful amber eyes to meet mine. "It's just you and me here—no one else. I'm sorry for the way that he just acted. He was rude and ignorant and I will talk to him."

"He either acts like he hates me or as if I don't even exist. To be honest, I'm not sure which one I prefer." I can see the raw hurt in her eyes, and it kills me that my jackass friend put it there.

"I know, Chad's a difficult one to explain. His life has been just as hard as mine, if not harder. I'm not making excuses for him. It's just that he doesn't trust people easily. But he'll come around." I swipe my thumb across her soft, full lips before leaning forward to kiss her senseless. She tastes like cherry lip balm and mint toothpaste, and her hair smells like coconut oil—cold-pressed but not at all extra-virgin. I want to devour and drown in her body all at once, and I have no idea how we reached this point so fast. I've never been one to smell a woman's hair, and I've never given a shit about someone's eye colour, never mind the fullness of their lips.

Stevie is different though—she's special—and the thought of being away from her already drives me so crazy that my brain goes wild thinking about eloping together in the mountains—no joke. Maybe Big Foot will fill in as the best man at our wedding. *Actuator*'s fans sure as hell would love to see that, though on second thought, Stevie would not. I bet she has rules about hanging out with supernatural beasts, just like she does about foie gras and baby cows.

Chapter Eleven
"Miles Away"

Stevie

I'm on shift in the lounge when Granger comes rushing inside, sliding right up to the table and butting in mid-order. He's smiling wider than a festive drum and meanwhile holding something in his hands.

"Can you talk?"

I clear my throat and give the table my most apologetic smile. "I'm a little busy right now, Granger."

One of the men at the table perks up at his name. "You're Granger Ellis!"

Granger nods his head. "I am, and I just need to borrow my girl for a minute if that's alright."

"Sure, sure." The man bobs his head up and down as Granger pulls me away from the table.

"Seriously!" I huff out. "What is so important that you're interrupting me at work?" I glance around at my tables and take note of the half-empty glasses.

"Vegas," he intones, and my eyes land back on him.

"What?"

He thrusts a piece of paper into my hand. "You and I are going to Vegas."

"No. What? Why?" I'm so confused, not to mention tired, from staying up late with him last night.

"I want you to come and see my show in Vegas."

"But I thought the tour was over."

"It's that special appearance Chad was talking about. I want you there."

"When is it exactly?"

"Tomorrow night."

"Granger! I can't just drop everything and come with you. I work, remember?"

"I've already arranged for the time off with your Manager." He sounds super proud about this.

"You can't just do things like this!" I shout loud enough that a few heads turn our way. "You can't go on interfering with my life like that on a whim." When I finish, I can see that he's a little deflated.

"But I want you there. I want to show you what I do and why it means so much to me."

I let my shoulders sag as I turn the paper over in my hands. It's a print out of my flight information.

"How long are we going for?" His smile returns just like that.

"Only two nights. The first night is the show, but I thought that we could stay one extra night to see the sights."

"I guess it's only two days." He lets out a loud whoop when I relent, drawing even more attention our way.

I notice my manager, Richard, hovering by the bar. He does not look happy, but I forget all about him when Granger pulls me into his arms and kisses me, as if for the first time. His kiss has my toes curling in my shoes, and I actually feel a little lightheaded when he pulls away.

"Thank you for saying yes. You won't regret it." He plants another one on my nose. "I'm leaving tonight to get set up, but I've arranged for a car to drive you to the airport in the morning. All you have to do is get on the plane and everything else will be arranged."

"I've never been to Vegas before."

"Really?" He looks surprised. "Then I'll have to make it that much more special for you."

"I'm going to see you live in concert, Mr. Ellis, I doubt that's something I'll ever forget."

I'll admit, I might be a Mensa member and a proud bearer of multiple degrees, but I didn't expect my studies in molecular biology to land me with front row seats to the show of my life—complete with the one-and-only rock star that I plan on inviting into my bed.

Chapter Twelve

"Nobody's Fool"

Stevie

McLaren Airport in Vegas bears a striking resemblance to my Aunt Debbie's living room, straight from the nineties' with its disco-ball ceiling and dusty rose-pink tiles. Luckily, I am the first one off the plane, thanks to my first-class ticket and general lack of luggage. I figure the carry-on tucked under my arm should be more than enough for two days in Vegas. I've packed a bathing suit, pajamas, a change of clothes, and a little lingerie (just in case) along with one of those fold-up toothbrushes from the pharmacy. I also shaved everywhere, and by everywhere I mean *everywhere*.

I Googled the Wynn hotel where Granger and I'll be staying, and it seemed fair to assume that they'd probably provide all needed luxuries, such as shampoo and soap. As I head down the escalator, I take in the sponge-painted, peacock-blue carpet waiting for me at the bottom. It appears specifically designed to make hung-over tourists even dizzier upon departure.

Speaking of hangovers, I spot dozens of weary travellers in dark shades who are clearly on their way home, which I find funny juxtaposed with their wide-eyed, smiling character foils stepping fresh off the planes. I head outside to the taxi area, only to find a driver waiting for me in a slick suit. He holds a sign with my name written across it in tiny black writing, so I wander his way and drop my bag at my feet.

"I'm Stevie."

"Welcome to Vegas, Miss Tyler." He retrieves my bag from the ground and opens the limo door. "Mr. Ellis asked that I should take you right to the MGM."

"I thought he was staying at the Wynn?" I pause, halfway in and halfway out of the limo.

"He is, but the concert is at the MGM Grand's Garden area. It's one of the largest venues on the strip. I would've liked to see the show myself, but at the one thousand dollar minimum ticket price, that wasn't happening. Your boyfriend's pretty popular, Miss Tyler."

"He's not really my boyfriend," I mutter, before finally climbing in the rest of the way.

As the taxi pulls away from the curb and weaves into the gridlocked traffic, I stare out the window at the concrete and neon jungle. Even inside the air-conditioned car, it smells like fuel and dust. The landscape along the highway is flat and brown, peppered with palm trees and billboard after billboard of advertisements. The sun is starting to dip below the horizon, sending streaks of brilliant orange and red across the sky.

When we arrive at the towering gold and green glass hotel, I'm taken around the back and escorted to an elevator by another handler in an expensive suit. The only difference is that this one is about twice the size of the driver and wearing an earpiece. We arrive at a closed door marked private just as he thrusts my carry-on bag at me.

"You can change in here."

This is not at all what I expected. I expected to be dropped off at the hotel, so that I could relax and get my bearings before heading to the show, maybe even take a shower. Instead I'm inside a cramped dressing room trying to wiggle into the black bandage dress I brought. Luckily no one is here with me, because I'm likely to take an eye out with all my yanking and gyrating.

Eventually I get the thing on, but there's no mirror so I'll have to assume that it looks good. I step into my black heels and stuff my discarded clothes into the bag. As soon as I'm outside of the little room, my well-dressed handler grabs my duffel and advises that he'll be waiting in the limo for me later. I really don't feel like being shuffled around at the moment, but I'm relieved not to carry my duffel around all night. At least I still have the cute black-clutch purse I bought to tote my ID and lip gloss around town.

My handler leads me down the hallway to another elevator, but he doesn't ride with me, leaning in to hit the button and giving me a brief, efficient smile. "Take a right off the elevator and find suite number three. Your hostess for the evening will be waiting."

It's a short ride and the moment that the doors open, I hustle down the hallway to look for suite number three, assuming it's the one with the open door and sunlight spilling out into the hallway. A ridiculously attractive woman waits at the threshold and greets me with a warm smile.

"Miss Tyler?"

I nod my head and she takes me by the elbow into the suit. When I enter, I see that I'm not the first to arrive. There are another half-dozen people present, including Chad, much to my dismay. I ignore him for the moment and get my bearings. *Luxury suite* is probably an understatement and *sky box* doesn't do it justice either. We're in a large, open space with lots of chrome and gray accents. A row of silver warming trays hold appetizers and one waiter in a tuxedo mans the back bar. Beyond the TV screens and white leather club chairs, I notice a balcony with movie theatre seating that presumably looks over the stadium. The hostess offers me a drink but I politely decline and extract myself from her hold on my arm. I skirt around the leather chairs and head onto the balcony, passing Chad in the process. He gives me a dismissive once-over but doesn't say anything.

It's dark on the balcony because the opening act has already started their performance. The only illumination is the indigo light reflected from the stage. From where I am standing, every seat looks full and the energy in the cavernous space is palpable. Gigantic screens suspended from the ceiling display a close-up view of the band while intermittent shouts and whistles punctuate the music. I take a seat in the first row and try to settle the nervousness in my stomach. I don't know why exactly, but the thought of seeing Granger on stage is almost too much to handle. My knees bounce up and down in anticipation and when Chad comes out and takes the seat next to me, I sigh dramatically and roll my eyes to the ceiling.

"Hi, Chad," I say, quieter than rock music will ever be.

"I can't believe you actually came." He doesn't say hello back, other than criticizing my presence. I figure that's the only acknowledgement I should expect tonight.

"Granger asked me to come."

He shrugs off my comment. "He invites a lot of people to his shows—I wouldn't read much into it."

"I'm not reading into anything. I want to hear him play."

"I don't doubt that. He's an absolute beast on stage. A living legend. Nothing in the world is more important to him than this. You get me?"

I look away, but I do get it. I'm not an idiot; I can read between the lines. Granger is a performer and rock is his first love. What Chad doesn't know is that I totally understand his level of passion. It's the same all-consuming, heart-rate accelerating kind of feeling that molecular biology used to give me—as nerdy and *small town* as that sounds.

"I'm here to see the show, Chad, not to compete with sixteen thousand people."

He deliberately scans the length of my body before giving me a pointed look. "Yeah, that's probably a good thing. The fans win every time."

"Good to know," I answer, turning my attention back to the vacant stage. The house lights come up and the roadies scuttle back and forth between clusters of equipment, feverishly tuning guitars.

"You understand that Vegas is only the tip of the iceberg, right? It's always been this way and that's not about to change. The women, the parties..." he trails off with a cackle. "I wouldn't be surprised if they coined the whole *what happens in Vegas* tagline because of Granger. He wants what he wants, and he gets it."

"Chad, is there any point to this diatribe," I answer with a sigh, "or do you exist only to torture me?"

"Maybe I'm just being a nice guy and offering the good old Canadian waitress a dose of reality. Maybe I'm trying to keep you from torturing yourself, but have it your way, I guess." He stands up without waiting for a response and then disappears back inside the suite.

The house lights go down and the crowd starts chanting. It sounds like they're shouting *Actuator* at first but the chant eventually morphs into Granger's name on repeat. The stage lights flicker on to reveal the band, with Granger in repose at the end of a catwalk. A low fog crawls across the stage while a spectacle of lasers traces patterns across the crowd. The opening notes sound and the crowd devolves into audible shrieking as Granger's heady and rich voice comes over the microphone.

I'm not familiar with the song, but it's a sexy, slow-tempo ballad that has my girl-parts standing at attention. After a few bars, the song speeds up and fire cannons light up the stage as Ravi leads into a drum solo. Granger rushes toward the crowd with his guitar looped around his neck. The way he handles it reminds me of how he handled me, and I have to squeeze my legs together to quell the memory.

He slides back and forth with a subtle swing in his hips, singing the lyrics full tilt with his eyes closed and his head thrown back. The look on his face is euphoric; I hate to admit it, but I see what Chad is talking about. For him, this must be it—that thing—the one that makes everything else make absolute sense; that thing you chase and try to keep for as long as possible before it evades you again.

I have to admit that even Jayne looks good up on stage. The three of them are so natural together, making it all look easier than breathing. I watch the entire concert this way, entirely fixed to my seat. I don't eat, I don't drink—I don't even break for the bathroom. I am glued to my seat and completely enraptured by him. It may not be my type of music; but in every note, in every burning look and nuance, he's made it a little more mine.

The crowd calls for two encores and *Actuator* obliges. After the last one, he thanks the crowd and gives us a wave before disappearing backstage. I stand up and feel my knees buckle, because apparently my legs are half asleep. I spend a few seconds getting my circulation going, massaging my legs and shaking them out before heading back to the suite.

Chad is already gone, as are the majority of guests, but the hostess is there and she's the only one I know anyways. "Is there anything else I can get you, Miss Tyler?"

"I'm fine. If you can just direct me back the way that I came. Is there a ride waiting for me downstairs?"

"Of course." She nods. "Let me lead the way."

Outside the venue, the same limo with my black-suited driver from earlier is waiting. He gives me a brisk nod and holds open the door. Once inside, I ask if we're heading to the hotel now, and he nods. "We are, but I've been asked to drop you off at XS."

"What's XS?"

"It's one of Vegas' best-rated, multi-million dollar nightclubs," he explains, though without really explaining anything else.

"As nice as that sounds, I was hoping to see Granger," I counter, as a nightclub doesn't sound particularly nice right now.

"And that's exactly where you will find him."

Inside the hotel, I'm met by another slick-suited, ear-pieced bodyguard. It's starting to feel like a bit much. I mean, I'm a twenty-six-year-old woman, not some unaccompanied minor who needs to be escorted around town. When he goes to take my arm, I take a step back and give him a look, but he quickly recovers and clears his throat.

"If you'll follow me, Miss Tyler."

We weave through the casino floor until we reach a gold sign that reads XS. As we climb the staircase to the club, I finally get the clever name. "Excess...cute," I mumble to myself, taking in the lavish, gold accented staircase, outlined with heavenly bodies. The interior of the club is even more extravagant, with sparkling gold columns, matching heavy curtains, and an enormous gold chandelier. The space is amazing, with a row of white leather VIP booths facing the glowing pool. A famous DJ spins away by the dance floor, a fact I only know from the poster at the entrance, and the thumping bass makes my teeth rattle in my mouth.

My escort taps his earpiece and speaks into his sleeve before escorting us off to the left. We maneuver shoulder-to-shoulder through the crowd until we reach a roped-off area with plush couches and low tables littered with bottles of every kind of liquor. The mostly female crowd is upscale, and the place obviously must have a pretty strict dress code. I look down at the two hundred dollar black dress that I splurged on for the occasion and feel very out of place amongst the sparkly pink and white dresses.

When I look to the right, I recognize Ravi, sitting on a stool and chatting up an exceptionally beautiful blond. He waves my way then returns to his conversation. I don't see Jayne, but I roll my eyes at Chad surrounded by groupies on one of the far couches. Hardly a surprise. I'm scanning the room for Granger when the crowd parts to reveal the rock star I've come to know. He's sitting directly in front of me on a big, white leather couch, but he's not alone. There's a woman on his lap and they look very friendly.

I try and steel my reaction—to rationalize that perhaps I don't know what I'm seeing. Maybe there's a perfectly good explanation for this. Maybe she won a lap-sitting contest or something. But as hard as I try to remind myself that we're in no way exclusive, the red starts to seep into the sides of my vision. Pretty soon it flashes full red as she leans back and seals her lips over his mouth. I watch in complete shock as they go at it for a few seconds before springing into action myself. I take one step forward, then another, until pretty soon I'm standing right in front of him.

"Granger." My teeth are barred like a dog and Granger's eyes widen when he sees me, but rather than pitching the tiny-waisted troll from his lap, he gives me a lazy rock-star grin.

"Hey love," he half shouts. "Did you enjoy the show?"

It only takes about two seconds of slurred speech before I realize that he's wasted. The girl on his lap giggles and bounces up and down, her cement-like tits hardly moving with her at all, and the movement hikes up her micro-mini skirt another inch.

"I'll give you a show!" she squeals, moving her hips in a circle.

"What the hell is going on, Granger?" I demand, but he just laughs.

"Have you never been to an after party, Stevie?" He shifts around with the same girl sitting in his lap. "Why don't you come and join me and—" he squints at the girl. "What's your name again, doll?"

"Amanda," she giggles. Her complete lack of self-respect is almost enough to make me vomit in my mouth.

"No, thank you." I squeeze my black clutch and bite down on my bottom lip to keep my tears at bay. I'm not a crier by nature, but this situation is completely mortifying.

"Sit down," Granger says, a bit more forcefully this time. "I ordered you a drink, see?" He gestures to a champagne flute on the table, flanked by a bottle of champagne and another bottle of cognac. Beside the bottles lies a jewellery box with a pearl necklace on display.

"I'm not thirsty," I clip.

"It's called a Black Pearl. It comes with jewellery—don't you want jewellery?"

"What I want is to see you stop embarrassing yourself."

Amanda gives me a look and an eye roll. "That's a ten thousand dollar drink. He cares about you, *obvi.*"

"He has a funny way of showing it. I'm not thirsty, and I'm definitely in no mood to waste ten thousand dollars on a cocktail."

"It's my money to waste," Granger pipes up.

I need a minute to make sense of the jumbled words leaving his mouth. "I want to go home," I say, stepping away from the table and crossing my arms. Granger shoves the girl right off his lap and hops to his feet. "Look, Stevie, I'm glad you came, I am, but we just finished a long show and I need to relax. This is my after party and I'm not leaving."

"Fine, stay then, but I'm leaving."

"Find your own goddamn way home then." He flops onto the couch and I wonder in what world this behaviour is acceptable—then I remember how Chad told me that Granger practically coined the phrase *what happens in Vegas*...and my hands shake like tiny earthquakes as I muscle my way through the crowd.

"Wait!" A female voice behind me stops me in my tracks. I turn around to find Amanda with her hand outstretched, offering me the pearl necklace.

"Granger said to give this to you." She looks crazy pissed to deliver this particular message on his behalf, with her lips pursed as if she swallowed something nasty. I give her a once-over before releasing a short laugh.

"You know what? Keep it. You're working pretty hard over there, so consider it payment for services rendered."

It takes her a moment to figure out what I mean, but I know when she does, because her mouth drops open and hangs that way like a tambourine. I whirl back around and continue to fight my way through the crowd, hearing her call after me in a high-pitched voice. "Bitch!" she screeches, but I don't engage. Instead I make a beeline for the entrance, darting down the golden staircase and practically flying out the front door.

I'm still shaking when I finally flag down a taxi outside. Thank God I have my passport and wallet with me, since I have no idea where my bag went anymore! I figure he can keep the dirty plane clothes and travel toiletries, especially if it means never having to look at his lame face again. I ask the driver to drop me off at an affordable hotel. He doesn't ask too many questions, but he's kind in directing me to a Motel 6 right near the strip. It's by the road and therefore loud, but apparently it's also close to the airport, so my trip tomorrow morning will be short.

Upon exiting the taxi, I also notice that the motel is situated right across from the MGM Grand—a terrible omen if there ever was one—but I don't have any more US cash to taxi somewhere else. Besides, the room is only thirty-nine dollars for the night, and it's clean and comfortable enough. Inside I strip off my dress, which smells like Vegas-pumped air, both sickeningly sweet and overly-manufactured. In run a warm shower and scrub myself from head to toe with the chalky bar of hotel soap. Then I climb into bed and try to fall asleep with the TV playing in the background as white noise. The tears taunting my cheeks earlier are long gone now, but that's no surprise. Right now I'm too numb inside to feel much of anything at all.

➤

Bright and early the next morning, I pay ten dollars for a shuttle to the airport. It's a lot less glamorous than the way I arrived, but I try not to think about that for now. In a way, I'm doing the drive of shame, wearing last night's dress with no baggage other than my small purse. I cram myself into the window seat beside an old lady with a dozen shopping bags from the outlet mall. She slides into me some more every time the bus rounds a corner. I sigh and glance out window as the driver announces that we have eight more stops to go. He weaves in and out of traffic like a madman, the shuttle doors letting in plumes of dust and hot air every time we make a stop. A bead of sweat runs down the back of my neck as if mocking the complete lack of air conditioning on board.

Once inside the airport, I find the international counters and purchase an overpriced one-way ticket back to Vancouver. Next I take on customs, trying to ignore the strange looks I receive while simultaneously finding the best way to explain my complete lack of baggage. I bet a woman traveling alone with no baggage is airport screening red-flag number one, but eventually I get through security and find a place near my departure gate to hunker down. I buy a *Fabulous Las Vegas* sweatshirt from the gift shop to cover my dress, but right now that slogan is largely debatable in my mind. Then I slide on my shades and rest on a bench, trying to imagine how I appear to everyone disembarking from the plane. Ironically, I made the same observation yesterday. If I look as rough as I feel, the glances cast my way are no surprise.

I lean my head back and stare at the ceiling, cursing myself for accepting Granger's invite in the first place. I should've known that this might happen. A hard-partying rock-star lifestyle is not something I sign up for willingly. From the first moment I met Granger, I was in way over my head. Now thanks to my horrible decision-making skills and pricey airplane ticket home, I might not have enough to cover my mortgage payment this month. I'll have to ask my mom for help, or beef up on my hotel shifts until I'm back on track. But I'm not playing the victim—all decisions have consequences and I guess these are mine. I just wish it didn't have to hurt so much. I've spent a long time trying to avoid getting hurt, but I feel like every single time I open up, it happens again. Sometimes my heart is like a geyser, with calm water flowing underneath the surface; except for now and then when the ground opens up and the water shoots up like a stream of tears, reaching furiously for sky.

Chapter Thirteen

"The Price"

Granger

I wake up with a start. My eyes jet open, as I rack my brain for clues about last night. At least I'm lucky enough to roll over in an empty bed, but then I remember something important: Stevie was supposed to wake up next to me. Just like that, I'm livid as fuck. I sent her a ticket, got her a suite at the Wynn, and sent my best guys to watch out for her. The least she could've done was show up.

Then I remember—but not all the way—just the worst bloody flashes of my life: Stevie did show up, and I'm a fucking prick. Bile rises in my throat and my heart beats way outta' step. I remember the show. It was a great show, we killed it. I had a few drinks before curtain call to calm my nerves, then a few more afterwards to celebrate. Nothing out of the ordinary. I remember the car driving us to the nightclub. There was champagne and something harder in the limousine. We knocked a few more back on the drive (and who knows how many more after that).

For chrissakes, even the club owner was hammering shots down our throat. Still, I can handle my liquor. The music was loud, I remember that part, and some girl was kissing my neck. I just assumed it was Stevie! But it wasn't—it was off, she was off. The hair was too light; the eyes were the wrong color. And then, the real kick in the nuts, I remember Stevie arriving and looking pure dead brilliant. Her black dress showed off her curves in just the way I like. Man how much I wanted to rip it off. I did rip it off in my head, but the look on her face didn't match mine.

Then I remember more, in painful flashes this time. The things I said to her. I wonder if I actually said them, or if my mind is making stuff up, overcompensating and filling in the blanks. But she left the club, so yeah, I must have said something pretty bad. I remember the other girl again and feel sick to my stomach. Thank God I'm fully dressed. Then my mind goes into overdrive. How the hell do I fix all this? I've done it before—fixed things. I've retraced yesterday's steps, offered apologies, and made amends. I'll do exactly that again. I'll find her and fix this.

I lurch out of bed, looking for my shoes. The booze sloshes in my gut, but at least I find my shoes. I head into the living room and just my luck, there sprawled out, half-naked on the sofa, is the girl from last night. She stares at me like I'm something on the room service menu.

"Good morning, sexy," she purrs. Her legs are bare and drawn beneath her arse. She wears one of my t-shirts and nothing else.

I can't say I'm not confused. My heart speeds up like mad, as I try to wake my memory of last night. "Did we…?"

"No, silly. I was up for whatever you wanted but you kept talking about that fat bitch from the club and how much you loved her. You kept repeating her name and then passed out on the bed. I would've stayed with you, of course, but to be honest, you were snoring like a buzz-saw, so I grabbed one of the shirts from your suitcase and crashed out here. Hope that's okay?"

I smack myself in the forehead and rub chunks of sleep from my eyes. Pretty soon I can barely see in front of me. Everything is blurry. Man, if only I could erase last night. I kissed this vapid little tart? What the fuck was I thinking?

"If you're ready to go now, big boy, so am I…" She whips off her t-shirt, showing me her breasts. But I've rubbed my eyes so hard, even her nipples are blurry.

"Listen, I am sorry for last night, very sorry. It appears that I gave you the wrong impression. But that *fat bitch*, as you call her, happens to be the love of my life, so would you please for the love of God get the fuck out of my room?"

The look on her face quickly switches from coy to catty and pretty soon, she's calling me every fucking name in the book. I've met some fire-breathing groupies in my day, but this one is pure dragon. Rock stars have security entail for a good reason, but I shouldn't need my guys with this peach. She listens when I tell her to get dressed and get out. She calls me a drunk, washed-up asshole when I try to call her a cab, but I figure she might be right.

Once she's gone, I'm on the phone with my security team to track down Stevie. I have to explain what happened in person. She'll be pissed, I know, but we haven't talked about being exclusive yet. I was acting on nerves, adrenaline, and alcohol. I get through to the head of my security team, but the guy goes dead quiet on the line. I need to know Stevie's whereabouts and I make that very clear. Then he delivers the last blow. Apparently he tracked her down last night, right after she bolted from the club. He said she crashed at a motel and fled to the airport this morning. His contacts say she landed at Vancouver International over an hour ago.

He keeps on talking, but I don't really hear him. I stopped listening the moment he told me she was gone—so I hang up on him mid-sentence and launch the phone across the room. It bounces off the floor-to-ceiling window, hitting the carpet with a solid thump, which does in fact make me feel better. I circle the room and rip the landline out with the cord before throwing it with all my strength at the painting above the sofa. The glass shatters and rains down over the plush cushions. The sound is so completely satisfying; I want to hear it again and again.

At this point, I'm screaming at the top of my lungs and kicking my booted foot through the front of the flat screen TV. I rip down the drapes, tear the bedding to shreds, and bite the bedroom pillows until the air is made only of down feathers. I pick up the half-empty bottle of vodka, tossing it so hard that it explodes against the wall. Lucky me, a shard of glass ricochets back to slice through my hand. I curse myself and shout her name aloud like I'm mad, using the metal ice bucket to break the whole lot of mirrors in my suite.

Once the room is gutted, with nothing left to destroy, I give it up to the aftermath of my tantrum, fighting and panting with sweat and tears. My hand oozes blood onto the beige carpet. It's like there's not enough destruction in the world to make me whole. None of this means anything now that she's gone. Now that there's no one left to watch me shatter myself into a million tiny pieces.

Chapter Fourteen
"Heartbreak Station"

Stevie

I try to ignore the meter during my taxi ride from the airport to my apartment, knowing that it's costing me a fortune, probably more than my flight home, given the 168 kilometers drive leading along the Sea-to-Sky Highway from Vancouver International Airport to Pemberton. I left my bike at home because of the stupid limo Granger sent for my flight out, and now I'm paying for it—both figuratively and literally. I could have taken a bus but after my trip to Vegas, I'd rather go bankrupt than board a Greyhound right now.

The cab pulls up to my garage and I hand over my credit card while debating whether or not to send Granger an invoice for my troubles. Once inside, I drop my purse at the door and kick off my heels before heading into the living room to seek out Toto. He's there in his kennel with a fresh pile of romaine lettuce and watercress waiting for him, letting me know that Kit came by already this morning.

I walk into the kitchen and swing open the fridge, staring at the interior like a mysterious galaxy. I'm not at all hungry, nor am I expected back at work until tomorrow, presenting a rare moment in which I have nothing to do. I flick on the TV and surf through the channels, unable to settle down. I'm restless and agitated, kind of like Granger's music. Eventually I head to the bedroom and strip off my Las Vegas sweatshirt, slipping into pajamas. It's just past noon, but I climb into bed anyways. The blinds hang open but I'm much too tired to get up. I pull the covers over my head instead, thinking that I'll deal with the rest of the world tomorrow. For today I'm hiding.

➤

I wake up suddenly upon hearing the key turn in the lock, feeling as if I bashed my head into ice while skiing the Blackcomb Glacier in the thick of winter. I do know that I am back in my bed at home, but I don't know what time it is or for how long I've been asleep. It's dark out though and I assume my day-in-hell hasn't yet turned into tomorrow.

I hear the front door open and leap out of bed to run downstairs. Part of me, a small part, wonders if it might be Granger, but that's obviously irrational because he doesn't have a key. Somehow though, that same small part of me wants it to be him—the same part that wishes I could just erase the past few days like an etch-a-sketch and start again.

I fly around the corner in time to catch Kit taking off his shoes. He yells out when he sees me and falls back against the door. "Bloody hell!"

"Hello to you too," I say, groggily.

"You're home? I thought you weren't coming back until tomorrow morning?"

"It's a long story." I sigh and tug the sleeves of my pajamas over my hands. "Come upstairs and I'll tell you about it."

He follows me to the couch and we cuddle together as I explain the events of the past twenty-four hours. When I tell him about the club (and the girl), he puts his arm around my shoulders and I sag into him like a bag of tears. Kit is literally the only thing holding me up right now.

"I don't know what to say, Stevie."

"There's nothing to say. You were right to warn me about him, but I didn't listen. Why I thought some rich and famous rock star would truly be interested in me, I don't know."

"Don't put yourself down like that. I saw the way he was with you—he was definitely interested. Don't make his indiscretions about yourself, because they never are with guys like him. Trust me when I say this; I know a thing or two about this topic."

I rest my head on his shoulder and wipe away my tears. "You already fed Toto?" I ask, and he nods. "Then why are you back here? Not that I mind. You're always welcome here."

He shifts uncomfortably next to me. "I was going to hang out—maybe crash for the night, so that I was here for you in the morning."

"Why would you need to be here for me?" He moves his arm from around my neck and leans forward. He's not looking at me and his body language is making me nervous.

"Kit, why would you need to be here for me? What aren't you telling me?" I press.

He runs a hand through his blond hair before extracting his cell phone from his pocket. "Have you seen the internet today?"

I give him a sideways look. "You know that I don't do social media. The last time I was on Facebook was like a month ago. Why?"

He swipes right and I inch closer to see the screen. Kit grips the phone in his palm and obviously doesn't want to show me whatever is there.

"I just didn't want you to hear about it from someone else," he explains.

"Hear about what? Seriously, Kit, stop being so cryptic." I snatch the phone from his hand and my stomach drops when I see the article he has open. It's from some gossip news site and has already been shared and liked by the thousands. My eyes scan the headline first before I open it with a click.

ROCK GOD GRANGER ELLIS GETTING COZY WITH A CANADIAN WAITRESS

The article, if you can call it that, is mostly fluff and otherwise accompanied by a few pictures of us leaving the restaurant last week. Granger is holding my hand and looking straight at the camera as I watch the ground. I don't remember anyone taking our picture, but with him, all the shouts, whistles, and stream of cell phones held high in the air have become like white noise during the short time that I've known him.

The article itself is not the bad part—the bad part is the comments. I don't know why I even bother to read them, perhaps for the same reason that cars slow down on the highway to witness a wreck. But I can't stop reading. All the breath leaves my lungs as I absorb hateful word after hateful word.

UGLY, FAT, DITCH PIG, GOLDDIGGER, OGRE, PLAIN JANE, TOO BORING, TOO AVERAGE, TOO CANADIAN, WORTHLESS BITCH, KILL THE SLUT...

And so on. There are a few kind comments peppered in between the derogatory remarks, but they do little to balance out the raw hatred.

"Why would people say things like this?" My voice is like a tree splitting in the woods, and who knows if there's anyone around to hear it after all.

"Because that's what people do now." Kit shrugs. "It's partly the anonymity and partly the so called *New World Order*. The internet is a fucked-up place these days."

"I can't read anymore." I throw the phone down on the couch. "It's not enough that I was humiliated in Vegas; now I have to be humiliated all over the internet." The moan that leaves my chest sounds almost ancient, as if my ancestors are here sighing with me. "What am I going to do now?"

Kit moves closer to rub my back. "Honestly? There's nothing you can do, but people have short attention spans these days, especially trolls, and that's the good news. The articles will blow over in a few days and then everything will be back to normal."

"Articles?" I say. "There are more?"

Kit ignores my question and keeps on rubbing my back. "Deep breaths, Stevie. Let's just handle one thing at a time. I've got you now—you know that, right?"

Chapter Fifteen

"Don't Know What You Got (Till It's Gone)"

Granger

This traffic will be the death of me. My knee hammers up and down in the taxi as the meter passes two hundred dollars. It just keeps on ticking—not that I give a fuck. I slam my head back against the seat and give up. It took less time to charter a plane out of Vegas than to mosey up this damn highway.

"We've been sitting here for at least ten minutes now," I bark at the driver. "Is there another way?"

"There's rush-hour traffic in front of us, ferry traffic behind us, and we're driving up the side of a mountain, so no, there's no other way, okay?"

"This is bullshit."

The dude just shrugs. "Welcome to Vancouver."

We crawl up the narrow pass for another half an hour before it opens up. I make an offer to pay him extra if he'll pick up the bloody pace, but he thinks I'm crazy. Says he'd rather not be scraped off the side of the rocks. But we get to Stevie's eventually. I throw some American cash at him and hop out, but I pay him extra to wait there until I give the signal. Who knows what's in store with Stevie, but God knows that I don't want be stranded on the lousy curb. I didn't bother with luggage. Well, I didn't bother with anything. My mind has been stuck on the same loop since I woke up this morning—find her and fix it—whatever it takes.

Her garage door is closed and who knows if her bike is around. I jog up the steps and bang on the door, shouting her name. I need to see her face—it's the only thing that matters right now. The door flies open, but it's not Stevie.

"What the hell are you doing here?" Kit, the fucking *thorn-in-my-side* best friend of hers barks, just as he walks through the doorway.

"I should ask you the same. Where's Stevie?"

"Why should I tell you anything?"

"Now is not the time, Kit. I need to see Stevie and I need to see her now."

"Well, maybe she doesn't need to see you."

"I swear to God if you don't get out of my way…" Before I can muster any more words, the dude pops me right in the nose.

"What the fuck?" My hand blocks the warm rush of fluid and my fingers get drenched with blood. This is a whole new meaning of the phrase "caught red-handed." I was shit to Stevie and now the world knows it, or at least her best friend does. I squeeze my watering eyes tight, but he hits me again before the sting of tears leaves me the hell alone.

"Fucking stop, Kit!" I shout, but my words do nothing. Soon he's on top of me. He knocks me onto the stoop and we crash down the stairs, hitting the concrete landing. Kit sends hit after hit my way but I block 'em all, hoping Stevie is watching me somewhere. The guy is swearing at me, not that I can make out anything he says. I shove him—hard—and when he's got no more energy to smack me silly, he falls to the ground.

Not for long though. I get to my knees after he finds his feet. He braces himself on his elbows, works to catch his breath, and gives me a shitty look.

"I've never seen her weaker than during the time you've been together. You're making her unravel," he pants.

I can't help but laugh at the guy—pretty harshly too. "It is so obvious that you're fucking in love with Stevie, so why don't you just admit it and stop trying to sabotage us?"

Kit leans forward and braces both hands on his knees. "You think you know me so well."

"Oh, I know you." I give him a look. "I know dozens like you. The proverbial *ladies man* running through a different woman every night, while you lay awake pining for the one you never got to have."

"Never say never," he spits back. It takes everything in me not to tackle him.

"You'll have to get through me first."

"I don't see a problem with that."

"Look, Kit, you got a few shots in—I'll let you have that, because I hurt Stevie and I deserve it. But make no mistake: Stevie is mine and nothing is going to change that."

"I wouldn't be so confident about that, rock star." He sneers at me, like some crap internet troll. "You don't deserve her."

"Maybe I don't, but neither do you. So why don't you get out of my goddamn way and tell me where she is?" I wipe the blood from my nose on my jeans, getting to my feet.

His breath is leveling out, but his shoulders sag and I've never seen a guy so fucking interested in the ground.

"She went to the gym," he whispers.

"Yeah, right. Why the fuck would she do that? She hates the gym."

"I don't know," Kit snarls. "Maybe because every shitty website and garbage celebrity news channel is ripping her to pieces right now?"

My stomach drops. I can taste the bile building in the back of my throat again, because chances are that Kit is telling the truth. It wouldn't be the first time that someone near me has been hurt by all this, and it probably won't be the last.

"What gym?" I don't think Kit even hears me. "Kit, WHAT GYM?"

"The one at the hotel. Employees are allowed to use the gym when it isn't busy."

I head off before he finishes his sentence, not that it helps. He just shouts after me.

"Ellis?!"

"What do you want, man?"

"Maybe I am in love with her. But she's my friend first, and I have her best interests at heart. I want her to be happy, whatever it costs me. I hope that you can say the same."

➤

The taxi costs well over four hundred dollars, and the driver pretty much hates me after witnessing that fight. But he gets me to the hotel. We pull up front and I hand him another wad of cash, slamming the door and running through the lobby, not giving a damn about the excited shouts from guests. My phone buzzes again with another missed text message. I ignore it, as I have the last dozen messages. They're all from the same person. The same person who's calling me again now.

"Damn it," I mutter, pulling my phone from my back pocket. "What?" I shout into the receiver.

"Where the fuck *are* you, Granger?" Chad is on the other end, but that's just as well, because he's even more riled up as me.

"Your publicist has been blowing up my phone for the last four hours! You gotta' give her a statement."

"No comment," I hiss, and he has the nerve to fucking laugh.

"Come on, man. You gotta' go on record and explain that this girl isn't anything to you. You have to admit that it looks bad. A hotel waitress? She'll mess with your rep and make it seem as if you enjoy slumming it."

"You deaf, Chad?" I cut him off. "I said no fucking comment. The only thing I *gotta' do* right now is find my girl. And if you ever, ever refer to Stevie as *slumming it* again, then you and me and all this shit, are over."

He goes quiet as steel. Good, I know that my words have hit home. Chad and I have been together for too long. I've never threatened to fire the guy, but I don't like the shit coming out of his mouth right now. He hangs up before I can beat him to it, which suits me beautifully. My priority right now is Stevie and only Stevie.

I don't have a key card for the pool area. I just slam my fists against the door until an attendant pays me some attention.

"Mr. Ellis…Is there something I can help you with?"

I couldn't care less about the rules right now. I push past him and jog into the gym space. Sure enough, my girl is right there. She runs on one of the treadmills at the back, but there's one other guy there working by the free weights. I tap on his headphones and his eyes get so massive that it's almost funny.

"You're Granger Ellis, right?" He rips out both ear buds. A show of respect, I guess. "I saw you play in Los Angeles last summer. Great show, man."

"Thanks. Look, I hate to be rude, but I need you to leave…now."

"Sorry?" The dude looks at me like I'm speaking Cantonese.

"Me too. Just get the fuck out, please?" He shakes his head. I venture that none of this adds up to his dreams of meeting a rock star, but he's still Canadian. People up here are too polite, and this one heads straight for the change room without another word.

Meanwhile, my girl is drenched in sweat. She wears a hot ponytail and runs faster than I would run myself. In her hand, she clutches the same old black Discman and I wonder if she's listening to the World's Greatest Power Ballads CD or something? As I step closer I can hear the buzz of Nazareth's "Love Hurts." It's the small things, but somehow this girl always gets to me. I'm smiling until I see that she's not. What I thought was sweat is actually tears, and I finally get it: *shot to the heart*—these are more than just words.

"Stevie!" She doesn't hear me through the music, but I can fix that. I hop onto the adjacent treadmill and wave in front of her face. "Stevie!" She gasps so hard upon noticing me; I venture that she almost chokes. Her hands go to the red emergency button, which she slams like a cymbal, jumping onto the side of the belt and staring at me.

"What are you doing here!?"

"What do you think I'm doing here?" Even I catch the exasperation in my voice. "I'm here for you. I love you, Stevie."

"You don't love me," she laughs, pretty bitterly too. "How can you love me when less than twenty-four hours ago, you had your tongue down someone else's throat?"

I step onto the treadmill until we're toe to toe. "I fucked up, big time. I know that I fucked up, but I do love you. You're the only thing that's truly good in my life."

She sighs. "I don't sleep with just anyone, Granger. The last few weeks, they've meant something to me, but clearly they didn't mean the same to you."

"That's not true. I know who you are. I know that you don't just sleep with anyone. You gave that to me; you chose me, and I repaid you with betrayal. I want you to know that nothing else happened with that girl. Fuck, I don't even remember how it started. I was so fucked up."

"I believe that you didn't mean to hurt me," she whispers, "but it doesn't change anything." New tears appear on her face then. She swipes them away with her hands, but I've never seen her cry and it totally guts me now.

I can't help myself. I step forward and lace my arms around her body. I shouldn't be touching her, I'm very aware of that, but what else is there to do? "Why are you here, Stevie?"

"What?" She gulps back another round of tears.

"On the treadmill. In this gym. Why?"

"Maybe because you broke my heart...and I don't know what else to do." Her voices wavers a little, actually, a lot. "Or maybe because I came home to a barrage of hateful feedback. I'm too fat, plain, ugly, poor, and disgusting to ever be with someone like you."

I press my nose into her cheek and inhale deeply, hoping it won't be the last time. "Shhh...you're none of those things. You're beautiful, perfect, and mine."

"I'm not perfect, Granger."

"You're my kind of perfect. The last thing you need to do is run on a treadmill because some lonely fucking troll on Facebook got under your skin. You hate treadmills, remember? You told me once that they're pure evil."

"They are." She sniffs, but a smile edges its way into her voice.

"Let's get rid of them, then. I'll have every single one of these torture devices pulled outside and lit on fire, if it pleases milady." That one finally gets a laugh out of her.

"I'm still so angry with you," she spits at me.

"You have every right to be."

"But mostly I'm hurt. I don't think I've ever felt that degraded in my whole life."

They're probably the hardest words to hear, but I deserve to hear them. "I know."

"You have a problem, Granger."

"I know."

"You need help."

"I know. I know, I do," I repeat this over and over like a chant. "I want help, just please don't leave me. I can't lose you."

"I can't be your crutch."

"You're not—you won't be," I argue. "For the first time in my life, I feel ready to change. I don't want to black out and wake up in hotel rooms not remembering anything about the night. I never want to wake up with that feeling again, especially knowing that you're gone. I trashed my hotel room when I realized that you'd flown home and racked up a twenty thousand dollar bill doing it."

She pulls back and looks at me with fire in her eyes. "Don't you dare put that on me! Haven't you spent enough of your hard-earned money trashing things?"

"Where you're concerned, it'll never be enough." I coax Stevie into my arms, tilting up her chin to stare into those beautiful whiskey-brown eyes. "That's my shit. I just wanted to explain what it feels like for me without you. I've never felt this way about anyone in my life. The feeling is outside my comfort zone, yet I don't want it to stop. I'll do anything for you, Stevie."

She gives me an upside-down smile. "This is the kind of thing you need to do for you, Granger, not me."

"And I will…I will, just stay with me, please…" My lips meet hers in the softest, sweetest kiss, but pretty soon the fire creeps into my bones and I'm about to swallow her whole. Still, she whimpers and rubs herself against me. I'm happy to see that her body still responds to mine—actually, I'm about five seconds away from stripping her naked and *making* her mine on the treadmill.

"I care about you, Granger,' she gasps, pushing me away (or trying and failing). "I won't lie—I want to be with you too, but addiction is a tricky thing. You'll say whatever you think I need to hear. This cannot be about me; it needs to be about you."

"So then make it about me. Tell me what I must do to convince you."

"It's not about convincing me; it's about convincing yourself." She runs her finger down my nose and across my lips. The contact gives me chills. Even the slightest touch from Stevie is too much.

"Then help me convince myself. Because I fucking love you. *I. Love. You.* I can't explain it. I know that it happened quickly and maybe it's irrational, but I fucking do, alright?" She nods cautiously, wisely, as if my girl has a soul older than the mountains.

"Yes, okay. You love me," she concedes.

"Thank fuck." I slump my shoulders as the fight leaves my body. "When you left Vegas like that…I lost my mind. I know that I need help, but not without you."

"Is that wise?" she asks.

"I'm probably not supposed to say this—I'm probably just spouting dysfunctional shit, but you're the reason I want to get right in the first place. So please, stay with me?"

She just shakes her head. "You know that I never really left."

"But you did," I protest.

"I didn't," she shakes her head again. "I left that disgusting display in Vegas. I left that shell of a person you pretend to be sometimes, but not you. Never you." She clears her throat. "This is going to sound crazy, so feel free to say no, but I have an idea that might help. Have you ever heard of a sweat lodge?"

"Is that like an Indian thing?"

"First Nations, yes. They are popular among some tribes as a method of healing. It's not meant as treatment, just a first step towards wellness. A neighbouring band has a program that I'm familiar with up here. It could be meaningful, or it could mean nothing at all, but it's a good start to help you determine what the next step should be."

"Would you be there with me?"

"I could be." She shrugs, opening her hands, like she's offering me the air. "But that would be up to you."

"I'll try it then, if you're there—the whole time." I clutch her hand, while my girl studies me with an expression that I can't figure out.

"Yes, Granger. I'll be there, provided you understand that this needs to be about you—not us. I have no more control over this situation than you do."

"Seriously, love, I am in control. Always have been. Just let me do this and give me a chance to prove myself." I say the last words with conviction; hell, I almost believe myself. "I promise to take care, if it means I get to care for you."

"You know," she sniffs back some tears. "A promise is only necessary when it could otherwise be broken."

I hear her words, but I care more about her eyes—those beautiful fucking eyes. Hers are the forever kind. They appear as if filled with crystals, which I know are actually unshed tears, but somehow they also feel like songs, like messages—how could they not, with the way Stevie looks at me right now.

Chapter Sixteen

"Something to Believe In"

Granger

I don't want to admit that I'm scared.

I mean, I'm not scared of crawling inside the dome-like hut, nor the tribal elder draped in his ceremonial blanket and tending to the fire. Mostly I'm afraid of what will happen if this doesn't work.

Stevie offers me a lovely smile and holds my hand, giving me strength enough to cross the threshold. The hut is made of cedar planks, lashed together with ropes, then covered in canvas blankets. I follow Stevie's lead the whole time. We crawl on our hands and knees, digging our fingers into the rank dirt. It's way hotter than a sauna in this place, and the whole thing smells like burnt sage.

Stevie leans over and whispers in my ear. "We've crawled in sun-wise. Now we need to bow to the Great Spirit."

I don't want to mess any of this up. I straighten up and bow with my girl, falling back to sit cross-legged against the wall. Stevie sits beside me, but not as close as I'd like. Still, it's definitely tight quarters, with five other men and women in the space. One man introduces himself as the sweat leader before saying a few words.

"This is a place of mental and physical healing. We gather here today to ask Mother Earth for her wisdom and power."

He recites a prayer in his native tongue. The fire tender carries the superheated rocks from the sacred fire outside the lodge. He places the red-hot stones into a shallow pit, which sits in the centre of the tent.

"For the next two hours, we welcome good Spirits to cleanse our bodies and minds, as we sweat out our impurities and toxins and remember that impurities and toxins are symbols of things that keep us distanced from Mother Earth herself."

I check out Stevie sitting cross-legged next to me—eyes closed with her lips tipped up into a sexy smile. Her curly hair is frizzy, with strands stuck to her forehead like a helmet. Sweat drips from her chin and lands between her breasts. If I know anything, it's that this girl is perfect. How I deserve any piece of her is beyond me.

He chants another prayer and closes the canvas flaps. The tent becomes total darkness. A voice in my head whispers that I would be wrong to deserve a piece of Stevie, because those pieces belong to nobody, not even her. I'm not even sure what that means, but the heat has made me dizzier than I expected.

I have to strain my eyes to find her, guided by the red glow of the stones, but nothing else. I almost can't make her out, but there's just enough light to see her pouting lips and button nose, even her long eyelashes. Her breath is all peace. From this angle, she looks like salvation.

I inhale the thick steam into my lungs, feeling myself relax. The sweat leader sings a low tune—music really *is* everywhere—which hits me deep in my bones. A slow drum beats in time with the pounding of my own heart, at least it fucking seems that way. The sweat leader finishes his song soon enough. I'm actually kind of disappointed to hear it end. Then the leader tells us a story about Mother Earth, kind of like the bible stories I got told as a kid.

"Friends, this is a place of transformation and purification. We seek to heal the mind and bring forth clarity of purpose. Focus on breathing and meditation."

I slow my breathing, followed by my thoughts, staying present. My mind blanks after a while, and I lose track of time. The next thing I know, the canvas flaps open and we're back outside in the cool mountain air. I lie down on the damp grass, feeling dazed and dizzy, like I'm not yet ready to form words, like speech is foreign. I dressed light, but I came out sweatier than I'm comfortable being around my girl. Someone hands me a bottle of water as if reading my mind and Stevie's voice sounds out from above me.

"So?" Stevie says, pulling me to my feet while taking a few large gulps from her own bottle of water. "What did you think?"

I breath deep before answering. "I might be a songwriter, but I'm all out of words." And it's true—already I feel clearer, sharper—as if the world has been tuned like a guitar.

Stevie nods at me. "It's a good first step."

"First step?"

"On the path to healing." She speaks under her breath, giving me a shyer look than suits her really. What I don't tell her is that I wasn't expecting a path—I kind of thought we'd already reached the end. Looking into my eyes, it's like she can see right through me. "You understand that these are symbolic cleansings, right? Purification ceremonies intended for self-reflection to help send you in the right direction."

"And what direction would that be?" I know my voice sounds stiff, but that only makes me think of scotch and whiskey.

"It's not one and done, Granger. Every alcoholic thinks their self control trumps all others."

"You used the 'A' word." I grind my teeth together to keep my anger in check.

"What would you like me to call it?"

"I drink, Stevie. So do a lot of people—you included, I might add, and I'm not labeling you. Genius or not, the last time I checked, you weren't a medical doctor."

She rubs her forehead hard enough that she leaves a mark. "Fair enough, I shouldn't be using labels. But the genetic basis of alcohol dependence concerns the metabolism and the pathways for reward circuits, and how they interact with dopamine receptors. There is a neurobiology of addiction that cannot be ignored."

"Stevie, for the love of God." I cut her off right there. "Not right now."

"You're right," she relents. "I'm overstepping. I shouldn't be the one showing you the next step, but if you honestly don't think there's another step to be taken, I don't even know what to say."

I'm losing control of the situation, so I blurt out the first thing I can think of on the spot. "I'll go to meetings!"

It's not the reaction I expected. Instead, she presses those beautiful lips together and frowns. "This is supposed to be for you, Granger, not for me. You need to do what's right for you."

I nod, working up the courage to take her hand. "I want to start going to meetings."

She gives me a smile that I can't refuse, and I figure I might be drunk on Stevie. Looking at her beautiful face is like being inches from the sun. It makes me stronger and tougher, and I know one thing for sure: Stevie is the only nightcap I care about anymore.

Chapter Seventeen

"Knock 'Em Dead, Kid"

Stevie

I take Granger to *Lift*, my favourite coffee shop in mountain square. It's cozy, welcoming, and happens to brew the best beans in town. Things have been a little strained between us since the sweat lodge ceremony, but I'm trying my best to give him space to choose his next move. He has extended his vacation by another week, which gives us more time. What comes afterwards is anybody's guess.

Behind the counter I notice Len, a friend of Kit's who hails from the same town in Australia. I met Len at a party and we almost went out on a date—almost, because Kit seemed to have a thousand reasons why we wouldn't be a good match.

"Hey Len!" I greet him brightly and he comes around the side counter to give me a one-armed hug.

"It feels like it's been forever, Stevie. You and Kit staying out of trouble?"

"I can tell you that I am." I roll my eyes and he laughs before returning to his post behind the counter. "What can I get you, beautiful?"

"I'll take a mocha with whip...Granger?"

"Nothing for me," he mutters.

"You sure, mate? I make a killer cappuccino." Len tugs his woolen toque down over his ears and gives Granger a nod.

"I said nothing," Granger snaps back.

I give him a look. "Ignore him, Len. He's having a diva moment."

Len has a great laugh and alongside Granger's black mood, it's nice to hear now. "Well, he's earned one." Glen turns his attention to

Granger. "Your music got me through a lot of hard times, mate. I'm a huge fan."

Granger surprises me when he chooses not to respond. He's usually so gracious with fans, but this time he just grunts and walks away. I give Len an apologetic shrug. We wait inside while Len prepares my coffee, and I carry it out to one of the picnic tables outside. The view from the patio makes for some stellar people watching, as Whistler draws visitors from all over the world, usually seeking out the beauty of nature, or come wintertime, skis and snowshoes.

"Are you okay out here? We might be a little exposed," I ask.

"I'm fine with being exposed, but won't you be cold out here?"

"It's warm enough this morning," I say with a shrug. "Besides, I was starting to feel a little too warm with your overheated ego back there."

"Good." He tugs my hand down until I sit, taking his place beside me and moving in a bit closer.

"What's got you all caveman possessive?"

He places one hand on the back of my head. "I just want your attention."

"You have it."

"So does Kit, and that other guy in there…".

I cut him off. "You're jealous because I know the barista? I live here, remember? It's a tight community."

"I want to be your community. Besides, I can read the interest written all over his face."

"Please." I roll my eyes. "I can't control another person's interest in me."

"What about Kit's interest?" I can barely hear him. He speaks like the stars, which is to say soundlessly, or almost. "You can tell me that I'm crazy about the coffee bloke, but you can't deny your best friend's interest in you."

"It's not a big deal," I mumble, taking a sip of my mocha and sighing as the chocolaty goodness hits my lips. "Kit understands what we are and are not."

"Maybe he understands rationally, but he likely can't stop himself from thinking about you in that way, and I mean *every time* he looks at you."

"And that makes you jealous?"

"Savagely." He chuckles without humour. "I can't help it, but it makes me want to beat my chest and howl at the moon."

"Interesting imagery." I remove his hand from my neck. "So is that what all this PDA is about?"

"No." He's quick to meet my eyes. "*You* are what this PDA is all about."

"Alright, sure." I can't deny the warmth flowing through my veins, knowing that he wants to show off our relationship.

"The more people who see us together the better, I figure—and if that happens to include Kit…"

His sentence is cut short by the camera thrust between us. The flash goes off in my eyes like a light bulb popping. For a moment I'm blinded, until I notice that three plain-clothed security guys—big ones—have surrounded the table. One of them is holding the photographer back like a pinned voodoo doll. I don't know how I didn't notice the security beforehand, since all three men are built bigger than my brothers, and all them are wearing flannel jackets in July. Perhaps it's just some missed attempt to look *Canadian* enough to blend in with their surroundings.

"So, what can you tell us about your new flavour of the month, Granger?" The photographer shouts while continuing to snap pictures. "What happened to Lily St. Clair and the week you spent together in Cannes?"

I curl my fingers around the bottom of the wooden bench to keep myself in check. I'm not much for following celebrities, but I do know that Lily St. Clair is a famous supermodel, like her mother, and thus also a billionaire, like her father. That said, I hadn't heard that Granger had been dating her highness.

"How does Lily feel about your new and very average love interest?"

The security guard yanks the photographer back against his beefy chest and the man lets out an audible *oof*.

"There is *nothing* average about Steven Tyler. I can promise you that." Granger surprises me by leaning back and taking a slow sip from my mocha. I honestly thought we'd be hightailing it out of here as soon as the paparazzi arrived, but it appears that he wants to put on a show. A small crowd gathers outside the café as a few more photographers snap pictures of us from a distance, but none are as brave as the one interrogating us now.

"You're living every girl's dream, honey. Hang on for as long as it lasts." The photographer shrugs loose from *beefcake's* hold, dropping his business card on the table near my arm.

"When it's all said and done, call me if you want to dish. I promise to make it worth your while."

"Okay, I think we've humoured you long enough. It's time to give this pair their privacy." Len glares at the photographer as he emerges from inside the shop.

"I can stay as long as I like," the photographer declares, like some vagrant refusing to leave a provincial park after dark.

Len just shakes his head. "You can't, actually. This is private property and I want you gone now. I've already called the RCMP."

The photographer mutters a few expletives but complies. Once he's gone, the security officers settle down and resume their former *incognito* places at the surrounding picnic tables.

"Len to the rescue," Granger growls under his breath.

I roll my eyes with a little guffaw. "You can't be serious."

"Damn straight I am."

"He just helped us out, and he didn't have to. Look, this is getting out of hand. More people have spotted you now, so can we go back to the hotel?"

He shakes his head but downs the rest of my mocha in one sip before grabbing my hand. "Fine."

We take our time strolling back through the picturesque village with our lumberjack posse following in our tracks. Granger insists on taking selfies at the bottom of the Blackcomb gondola with the grassy green and snow-tipped mountain behind us. I draw the line at him buying himself a Whistler Village t-shirt featuring a black bear with the phrase *GoT HoNeY*? But I can't deny that I enjoy seeing my community through his eyes, so I forget about the droves of fans altogether and decide to just relax and go with it.

➤

Evening finds us back in Granger's suite, watching the sun set over the mountains through his floor-to-ceiling windows. I lean my head into his shoulder and remember that I've never been up here without some kind of chaos at play, be it a party, a black-out rock star, or some other drama. I finally have time to relax into the overstuffed couch and appreciate the beauty of my surroundings.

"It's not just a nicer view, it's a nicer life, I guess," I tease.

"What? You mean the room? Honestly, love, it's four walls and a roof. It's a bed and a shitter and a place to unpack my suitcase at night. That's how I see it."

"If you feel that way, why bother with the suite? If all you care about is sleep, I'm sure there are less expensive options."

He laughs. "I don't give a shit about the suite, but my whole life is about image. This is what the world expects from a rock star. Can you imagine if I checked into a Motel 6? The vultures would be all over me. They'd say that I'd lost my fortune, which would only create bad press and tank my sales."

"That seems like a bit of a stretch."

"I wish it were, love."

"You can't deny that the view is beautiful though." I gesture to the mountains outside the window, their peaks rising around us like story arcs.

"I honestly barely see it anymore. One view is another is the next. I spent so many years in rooms without windows, maybe some part of me feels like my room with a view won't last very long."

"Rooms without windows?" I ask, lifting my head from his chest.

He sighs and shifts out from under me. "When I was growing up, the government didn't regulate the number of kids in a foster home—or if they did, they sure didn't give a shit. I bounced from place to place and was in about five of them until I was old enough for the system not to care if I disappeared."

"Anyway, he continues, "a lot of these homes were flats, sometimes filled with ten kids, so that the foster parents could cash in on the deal. They would load us up anywhere they could: bunk beds, walk-in closets, pull-out sofas, the laundry room—one time even a garden shed out back. Most of the time, the parents didn't give a crap about what we did, as long as they got paid. But they weren't all like that—I had one good family."

"Tell me about them." My voice comes out like fresh fallen snow, soft and full of crystals.

"I remember it well. I was ten, and I stayed with this couple for six months. They were so kind to me. They just had one other foster kid, a baby girl, so they gave me my own room with a view of the back garden, and my own matchbox cars to play with on the carpet. We ate dinner together every night. They took me swimming, to the park, and to church. In my own way, I loved them."

I'm almost afraid to ask, but I go for it. "What happened to them?"

"The wife, her name was Annie, she got pregnant. Told me it was never supposed to happen for her, but it did. Cried when she told me that they could only afford to have two kids.

They kept the baby girl, I don't remember her name, and I got shipped off. Those years are some of my last happy childhood memories."

My voice breaks right in two. "*Oh*...Granger."

"It's not about sympathy, Stevie, it never is. It's about survival. I took what was given to me and I adapted. I even used it to my advantage—I mean my freedom as a teenager. I was bigger by then, so if any foster father wanted to smack me down, I knew how to fight back. No one was really watching me, so I could do what I wanted, like take my guitar and fuck off for days. Seriously, I lost my virginity at thirteen to one of my foster sisters in the backyard loo."

"Are you telling me that you lost your virginity in an outhouse?"

"We were staying with a family in the country, and they didn't have indoor plumbing. She was sixteen, I think. The whole thing was both rank and incredible at the same time."

"Understatement, I'm sure," I scoff.

"I wrote a song about it: 'Hole in the Ground'."

"I listened to that one. I thought it was about death."

"In a way, it is," he explains. "The death of our innocence."

"Why haven't you told me any of this before today?"

"I can count the number of people who know about my childhood on one hand. Some of these stories, no one has ever heard. It's my suffering to deal with and writing songs helps."

"Do you think…" I stop and clear my throat. "Do you think it's impacted your life in other ways?"

"What ways?"

"Like partying and drinking perhaps?" I stare at my hands, unable to predict his reaction.

He removes his arm from around my shoulders and leans into me. "Not this shit again, for God's sakes. So I made some mistakes, but I've got it under control. I did the sweat ceremony thing and I've committed to meetings. Just because you led me home from the bar one time and took my shoes off doesn't make you an expert on this subject."

"I'm sorry," I whisper. "You're right—it isn't my place to draw parallels."

"Just forget about it. I think it's time for a subject change. It's getting too heavy in here."

"It's okay for things to be heavy every now and then," I argue. "You're not meant to carry this weight all alone—none of us are."

"Is that some kind of Indigenous wisdom?" His voice sounds tired, and offensive.

"No, Granger, it's human wisdom. You don't have to face everything alone. You're not in that windowless room anymore."

"Yeah? Are you sure about that?"

"I'm here for you."

"But for how long?"

"As long as you want me to be." I take his hand and mean what I say. With the photographers casting doubt, I can't control Granger Ellis anymore than the weather, but time is fleeting and I'm happy to be present with him now. Whatever forces, fates, or Lily St. Clair(s) the future holds, I am lucky to have this time with him today. From his tone and body language, I know that he doesn't trust my words, but all I can do is reassure him.

"I'm here for you, Granger," I repeat. "Not for this view, nor the fame nor the rest of the noise—I'm here for you and only you."

He looks at me like I imagine his only good foster mother once looked at him. It knocks the wind out of my chest, reminding me of the time I crashed into a tree on my toboggan as a little girl.

"But what if I'm not enough, Stevie?" Granger whispers.

I inch forward and swing my leg across his lap, until I'm straddling him face-to-face. I lean my forehead against his, closing my eyes and planting the softest kiss on his lips. It's not long before his mouth overtakes mine, sealing itself into my lips and teeth while his tongue probes deeper into my mouth. My hands drop to massage his shoulders before sliding around his neck. My nails graze his skull and he moans into my mouth, thrusting up against me. His hard length presses against the seam of my jeans while the moisture pooling between my legs makes me squirm.

"Sit still, Stevie, before you kill me," he croaks, tearing his mouth off mine. He runs his big, rough hands down my legs and curls his fingers around my calves. He twists me like a double helix until I'm sprawled across the couch, with Granger spreading my legs apart and positioning himself firmly between my legs.

He quickly unbuttons my shirt to expose the hot pink bra that I dug out of my closet just for him. His eyes drink me in and the extra effort proves worth it. The energy between us feels needy and raw. His look is sensual, but that same vulnerability still lingers in his eyes, along with a mirror of seriousness that I've perhaps never seen until now.

"You really are something, Stevie." He kneads my thighs with calloused fingers, almost like he's playing me. He strums one hand across my belly, which thankfully is smooth and flat, though it isn't tight. He bends his head to lick my navel as his talented hands tug my bra down to explore my breasts. After a thorough exploration, he sits back on his heels and starts to unbutton my jeans.

"Take this off," he says softly. "I want all of it gone and nothing between us."

At his request, I shrug off my jeans, throwing my shirt and bra on the floor as he sheds his clothing. His skin is hot to the touch when he settles back in between my legs. He's managed to put on a condom in the process and eases into me so slowly that the only way to describe the pleasure is "tortuous" somehow.

"Please!" I beg, and he shushes me, continuing to take his time, circling his hips in a lazy rhythm while he searches my mouth with his tongue. I close my eyes and feel him all around me, inside me and captaining my thoughts. Granger Ellis is everywhere—everything—my little glimpse of what everything means.

He whispers dirty things in my ear as our sweat-slicked skin glides together. For one sweet moment, the rest of the world disappears and it's just the two of us—not his past or mine, nor our futures. In the heat of the moment, *Actuator* doesn't exist, nor the paparazzi nor prying eyes. There's only Granger and I connecting in this way that I've never experienced with another person before now.

His breath hitches and he picks up the pace as I feel myself on the precipice of letting go. He shouts out something like a half-defeated war cry and we come together at the same time. Granger collapses on top of me and we both lie panting on the couch until he falls asleep in my arms. I watch him as he sleeps, tracing my fingers along the shaved sides of his head and into the mess of hair at its peak, while he exhales happily into my breast.

Lying so vulnerable like this, I can imagine that scared little boy bouncing from place to place and always looking to belong. His uncertainty about me and our future makes so much more sense now. His concern about Kit, his need for us to be seen together to validate the relationship and make it real—everything fits. But it is real. I know it deep down in my bones. I just need to find a way to help him open his eyes enough to recognize how beautiful the view outside his window really is.

Chapter Eighteen

"To Be With You"

Stevie

I'm tossing my sneakers into my locker when Richard comes up behind me.

"You missed two shifts last week."

Startled, I whirl around and grab my chest. "I wasn't on the schedule, Richard, so no I didn't."

His gaze is hard as he scans me from head to toe. "But you were supposed to be on the schedule."

I gather that he's referring to my last-minute vacation. "Granger told me that he spoke to someone about switching it." Richard laughs as if he just bit into a lemon.

"I guess you think you're pretty special now, don't you?"

"What does that even mean? I honestly don't have the time or energy for this, Richard. Did I miss a shift or didn't I?"

"I guess technically you didn't." His voice drops a few octaves at last. "But that's only because your big-shot boyfriend went right to the Regional Manager to get things moved around. As a result, Mandy had to work a double."

"I didn't realize." My voice is soft as my mind goes to Mandy. "I'll speak to her and offer to make it up."

"Don't bother," he snorts. "It's been handled."

"So, is there a point in this tirade then?" I already feel exhausted and my shift hasn't even begun.

"The point..." He punctuates each word by jabbing a finger into my breastbone. "Is that you better not start thinking that your shit doesn't stink. Do not go above my head like that again. I run things around here."

He steps back and crosses his arms, but that doesn't stop him from leering at me with a fairly laughable set of eagle eyes. "I'm still trying to figure out what he sees in you. Granted, you have big tits and a nice rear, but I'm sure a guy like that has T&A on tap without having to deal with your sorry ass."

I'm so shocked that I don't even know how to respond, but my whole body rolls like a tsunami. I'm not scared of Richard; he's rail thin and I could take him no problem, but it's like my body responds instinctively to the threat. I turn back around and slam my locker shut, before holding my head up high and pushing right past him. Before I'm in the clear though, he grabs my shoulders and knocks me against the wall, pinning my back against the bulletin board with the papers crinkling behind my head. He's so close that I can feel his hot breath on my cheek.

"Let's get one thing straight, bitch. If I go down for any reason, any reason at all, I'm taking you with me. This is my show." He releases my shoulders and his filthy hands trace my spine. I let out a whimper as they skim over my bum and linger there like smoke from a forest fire. After a few seconds, he pulls back his fingers, but not before delivering one hard slap to my ass.

I'm so surprised that no actual sound leaves my mouth. If it were anyone else—a hotel guest, or a customer at the bar—I'd be delivering a right hook to his head right about now, but instead I find myself paralyzed. This is my boss and I have a shift that started five minutes ago. By the time my brain catches up with my body, he's long gone. I wander out to the lounge in a daze where Mandy, who I'm serving with today, shoots me a worried glance from across the room. I gather my tray and notepad without sinking into my feelings, heading over to my first table by the fire, only to find Jayne sitting there in one of the high-backed leather chairs. Great. I take a deep breath and ready myself to suffer another passive aggressive beating from Jayne.

"What can I get for you today?"

"A clue, for starters," she snorts.

"Pardon me?" I grit my teeth and try to keep my temper under control.

"Look—Sally or Shauna or whatever your name is—I'm here to do you a favour. You can't seriously believe that Granger wants a relationship with you?"

My mouth drops open and I have to force myself to close it shut. "Will you be ordering food then?" It takes everything in me not to bite back.

"All this hand holding in public and romantic frou-frou dates? It's not him. Very few people know the real Granger Ellis."

"And you're one of them, I'm guessing?"

She crosses and uncrosses her long, skinny legs, which I notice are wrapped in tight, expensive-looking leather. "Of course I do. Did Granger ever tell you how the band came together?"

"Yes, he told me that the three of you moved to Los Angeles and met up with Ravi before making it big."

"That's part of it, but he left out the intense bond we all share from living together in a one room flat and staying up every night until dawn making music. Drinking together, laughing, fucking..." she says, raising an eyebrow. "You see, Granger and I were almost like one person. We'd get high, play music, and fuck until the sun came up. Sharing our deepest secrets and desires while we licked, sucked, and explored every inch of each other's bodies."

I try to steady my hands but already the empty tray shakes by my knees. "Why are you telling me all of this?" I can't help that my voice has already gone flat.

"Look, you might think from the way I've acted lately that I hate you, or that I'm jealous somehow. But that's not it. The truth is, I don't think about you at all. I am only trying to deliver a dose of reality. Granger Ellis is afraid to let anyone or anything into his life. If you haven't already noticed, he's addicted to things. If it's not one thing, it's the next, no matter how irrational the addiction becomes," she adds, giving me the once over. "I'm just trying to save you the embarrassment of being that forgotten lovesick fan that the trolls make a sport out of destroying. As much as you may think I'm the enemy, I promise you that I'm not—not this time."

Before I can even begin to formulate a response, she stands up and walks away. I don't turn around to watch her disappear because already I can feel the tears stinging my eyes. I'm not a crier—I never have been—but that seems to have changed since Granger Ellis entered my life. I set my tray down on the vacated table and search the room for Mandeep, who rushes right over when we lock eyes.

"What's going on, Stevie? I saw your face when you walked in here—you looked shell shocked." I swallow hard and shake my head. "It's Richard, isn't it?" she asks, sounding bitter. "I saw him come flying out of the back right before you. What did he say? He's been bitching about you taking time off to all of us."

"I am so sorry about making you work a double, Mandeep."

"He complained about that? What an idiot. I asked for the double since I have tuition due in a month."

"I hate to ask, but do you think you can cover me again? I just can't be here right now."

I know that Richard will flip when he finds out that I've left, but I'm in no frame of mind to serve people. "Say no more. It's not even busy tonight. Get out of here," Mandy says kindly. She takes my tray from the table and shoos me out the door.

I make it back to my locker in a daze and thankfully Richard is nowhere to be found. I don't even bother changing out of my uniform; rather, I simply grab my purse and leave the hotel, heading straight for my bike in the parking lot.

My bike roars to life and I drive without knowing where I'm going, but somehow I end up at Kit's. I buzz his apartment and he lets me right up. He's mid-laugh when he opens the door, though his smile falters when he sees my face. Still I push past him and flop down on the couch, which is littered with video game boxes and empty bags of chips.

"You live in a pigsty, Kit. What do your dates think?" I say without any real conviction.

"You know I don't bring women home, babe. This is my haven." He is uncharacteristically casual in low-slung basketball shorts and a tank top, with his blond hair sticking up in every direction.

"Haven of garbage."

"So push the Doritos out of the way, Stevie, and tell me what the hell is going on." He sits down beside me and loops an arm around my neck.

"I don't even know where to start," I sigh.

"It's him, isn't it? Granger?"

I start to protest but he cuts me off. "It's always him. I've wanted to say something for a while. I need to get it off my chest. I know I said that I was supportive of this whole fling, but I don't think he's right for you. I think this is dangerous."

He's way off track, but I'm curious about the overall theme of this speech. "Dangerous how, exactly?"

"He's not good for you. Stevie... you're sweet, incredibly smart, funny, sarcastic, spirited, and passionate. You love your family, your community, your friends, bartending, and your bike. He loves money, fame, and himself."

"And you're saying that he can't also love me?"

"I don't understand why you'd want him to love you!"

"You don't understand why I'm interested in being loved?"

"I don't understand why it needs to be him." He lets out a strangled breath. "Stevie... I...you must know that I..." He's trying to find the words that perhaps I've always half-wanted to hear from him, but after all this time and everything we've become to each other as friends, I don't want to ruin things between us.

"Kit, please stop. You're not even listening to me. I'm not upset because of Granger."

"Then what put that awful look on your face?"

It's clear that he doesn't believe me, but I decide not to tell him about Jayne. It will just add fuel to the Granger Fire, so instead I tell him about Richard. I tell him about the name calling, the idle threat, and his hand on my ass, as Kit listens without interrupting. When I finish he slams his fist down on the coffee table until the glass top rattles.

"Damn, I should drive over there right now and kick his ass. I knew that guy was a cunt the second that I laid eyes on him."

"You know that won't help." I dig the heels of my hands into my eyes. "I just need to figure out how to handle this going forward."

"Shit, if I can't beat him up, then you need to go straight to the hotel and get this sorted out. If he's harassing you, there could be others."

"Maybe not," I croak out. "But he does seem fixated on my relationship with Granger."

"Well, maybe he'll ease up once Granger and his crew leave." Kit eyes me like a hawk. The room goes dead quiet as I try to swallow the proverbial peach pit in my throat. I know Kit isn't trying to hurt me, and that a famous rock star like Granger isn't going to stay in Whistler forever, but hearing the words aloud is a different story.

"Hey, hey, hey..." Kit pulls my hands away from my face just as a single tear runs down my nose, dripping like a faucet onto my black workpants. When his eyes widen, I realize that it's only the second time he has seen me cry, and twice in a month no less.

"Ah, fuck," he mutters to himself, before leaning forward to pluck my purse off the floor.

"What are you doing?" I ask while he rummages through my things.

"Something I don't want to do, but that I have to do anyways." He pulls out my phone and opens up my recent contacts. "It's time to let the problem know what problems he has caused for you."

I shake my head, trying to decipher the meaning behind his words, but he disappears into the kitchen before I can speculate further, speaking in harsh guttural tones for a few minutes before returning and tossing my phone into my bag.

"What was that all about?" I ask, as Kit plops down beside me.

"Don't you mean *who* was that?" He squeezes my leg awkwardly. "I called Granger. He needs to know."

"Kit! That's the last thing I wanted."

"He needs to know." He repeats the words firmly. "He'll be here in an hour, but he had something to take care of first. You look exhausted. Why don't you lie down on the couch and I'll make you something to eat? Beer or tea?"

"Tea, please," I whisper, much too tired to argue. I toss a crinkled half bag of chips onto the floor and stretch myself out on the couch. Kit brings me tea and removes my shoes before covering me with a blanket.

I press my cheek into the buttery leather of the couch and sigh as he leans over to plant a kiss on my cheek. "I'm sorry, Stevie. You should never have to experience something like that."

I close my eyes and let my mind drift, aware only of the muted sounds coming from the television in Kit's bedroom. I wake up disoriented and sometime later to a big, calloused hand stroking my cheek. I launch upright with my blanket bunched in my lap, putting my ugly uniform on full display. I'd forgotten that I'd never changed out of my work clothes; in fact, I'm even wearing my nametag.

"Hi." Granger speaks up. His tone is soft but fire burns like the sun in his eyes. It looks like his beard grew several centimeters since yesterday and his hair is like a demolished birds' nest. He's wearing a black t-shirt and ripped jeans, with his inky black tattoos on display as usual. He's gorgeous—too gorgeous—as always.

"Hi?" I mean, in what parallel universe is Granger Ellis calmly sitting in Kit's house?

"Sorry it took me so long to get here." He strokes his hand down my cheek one more time before hauling me against his chest, hugging me so tightly that I have to tap his arm.

"Granger," I say, breathlessly. "You're squishing me."

He releases me and leans back to search my face. "Are you okay?"

I nod and he exhales as if trying to purge himself of bad air. "He's gone, okay?"

"Who's gone?"

"Richard."

"How?"

"As of right now, he has been transferred to another property up north, where I've been assured that his behaviour will be monitored closely. No doubt his attitude and the pending investigation will have him fired within the year. It's taken care of now."

"Granger," I moan. "It wasn't your battle to fight."

"Actually," he corrects me, "it was, and I'd appreciate your staying out of this. I created the situation by arranging time off for you. For the record, I actually bought the whole lounge out that night, to ensure that no one was impacted. It was your boss who chose to open it anyways and pocket the proceeds."

"But isn't that enough to get him fired on the spot?"

"It is, but they'll need to prove it by speaking to the staff and following the money. I didn't exactly ask for a receipt when I handed him a wad of cash. As we speak, they're pulling up every piece of security video to piece together the events of the night."

I'm silent as I try to process what he's saying. "Is there a security feed in the staff room?" I'm almost embarrassed to ask. When his eyes go dark, I wish that I'd kept my mouth shut.

"Because he touched you?" he growls. "He put his hands on you and I could kill him for it! I want to kill him. But if I kill him, I cannot be here for you, which is more important right now."

"Thank you," I whisper.

"That wasn't the only thing that happened today though, was it?"

"What do you mean?"

"I spoke to your friend from the lounge. She said my bandmate came to see you. So tell me, what did that conniving bitch say?"

"It's not important."

"It is to me."

I stand up from the couch and allow the blanket to drop to the floor, right before pacing the entire length of the room. "If you must know, she told me that you were lovers. She intimated that you were soul-mates."

He laughs and leaps off the couch. "Honestly, love, we were just two fucked-up kids—we thrived on righteous indignation and recreational drugs. We lived like paupers, partied hard, and yeah, we fucked. I owe much of my early career to her and Chad, in equal measure, but we were never soul-mates. I can promise you that." Granger shakes his head with a coy smile. "She's manipulative. You'll learn that quickly. If things don't go her way, she prefers that they go nowhere at all. But she needs to understand that the band is about all of us, not just her own needs. I'll talk to her, okay?"

"Can you not, actually? Talking to her just empowers what she said. I can let it go if you can." He stalks towards me and lifts me up, forcing me to wrap my legs around his waist for balance. "You're fucking amazing, you are. Even in those God awful polyester trousers of yours."

His lips meet mine with warm, urgent kisses, but I take a deep breath and pull away. "I may not agree with how you handled the Richard situation, but thank you for being there for me. You took my side—with him and with Jayne—no question. Granger Ellis, you're one of the most loyal people I have ever met."

His eyes soften at my words and his arms lock me in a vice grip. "I will always take your side and protect you. That's my first instinct, gorgeous girl. Now shut up and let me take you home with me."

The lights are off inside his suite, so I fumble around to find the switch. The light bathes the hallway in a dull yellow light but just as I'm turning away from the wall, Granger presses against me like a warm glove. His hips thrust against my backside and pin me like putty to the wall.

"Where do you think you're going?"

"Granger, what are you doing?" My voice comes out all breathy, but he doesn't answer. Instead I hear the sound of his zipper, followed by the crinkle of a condom wrapper.

"I wanted to do this the whole ride here." He grabs both my hands and braces them against the wall. I moan aloud as his hot, naked flesh rubs against the rough fabric of my pants.

"Keep your hands against the wall." He skims his palms down my sides and over my hips, pulling down my pants and underwear as if ripping off a bandage, before entering me in one swift movement. I cry out from the invasion, my voice laced with equal parts pleasure and pain. Despite the swift entry, I'm ready for him; of course, he can feel this inside me.

"Keep those hands up," he growls, while his fingers circle around to rub my swollen clit. Air hisses from his lungs as I thrust my backside against his front. "You drive me insane, woman." He picks up the pace and knots his fists through my hair, and I feel him tugging at my mess of locks as a low keen escapes from his chest. Apart from the sound of our breath, or whatever we have left of it, the hallway is silent. Granger's hands return to my wrists and he holds them a bit too hard, but I like the tension, I crave it.

"Fuck me harder, Granger," I whisper. He nudges my legs apart, bending me forward and slamming into me like a warrior. I know that he's close to coming, judging by the audio track playing from his lips, but he chooses to pull out instead.

"Turn around."

The moment that I do, he plunges his tongue between my lips with a low rasp. Digging my nails into his shoulders, I kick off my bottoms before wrapping my legs around his waist like a pair of human handcuffs. He hoists me upwards and plunges inside me again, releasing the most delicious sounding of groans. I'm totally covered in goose bumps beneath my shirt and bra.

I press myself against every thick inch of his body, braced securely against the wall. I sense the urgency in his eyes and know that the moment won't last long. His irises flare with possession and the orgasm overtakes me before I'm ready to feel it out. He answers by pulling me toward his mouth and swallowing my cries. The flex of his jaw reassures me because it's familiar. His muscles tighten before he pulls out, ripping off the condom and shooting his warm release onto my thigh. After he's spent, he disappears into the hallway bathroom and returns with a hand towel to wipe down the mess in my lap.

"*Thanks*… Stevie." His smile is uncharacteristically shy. "I promise that I usually have more self control around women."

I cock one eyebrow at him. "Do you now?"

"I mean, I used to—with other women." His face flushes beet red, which I find secretly adorable. He's totally unaware of the hole he's digging for himself.

"Relax, Granger. I know what you mean. I'm flattered, especially because my self control has taken a hit since meeting you." My voice grows softer as I finish my sentence, and Granger pulls me against his chest like a book he can't wait to keep reading. I'm pretty into our story so far, too.

While I imagine we look kind of ridiculous now, nestled together naked from the waist down, there are more important things in life than what you're wearing after sex, in those rare moments when the world is not looking, even at rock-god Granger Ellis. There's something about him that removes any hint of insecurity percolating inside me. I feel beautiful and cherished—not that Granger literally changes the way I feel about myself, but he helps me remember who I truly am.

"I guess we better get dressed, huh?"

"Or we could get undressed?" He wiggles his eyebrows, and I skirt off the gesture with a laugh and a shake of my head.

"Dinner first, then dessert."

I tug on my underwear without bothering with my starchy pants, while he nods and gives me a crooked smile.

"Deal."

Granger heads for the living room while I dash upstairs to look for whatever I was wearing yesterday. The moment I flick the lights on though, a horror-film-worthy scream unleashes from my lungs. There in the center of Granger's hotel bed lies a young woman—probably no more than twenty—wearing nothing but some oversized bracelet cuffs.

My brain catches up with my thumping heart as I absorb the nature of the scene. I know that those bracelet cuffs are Granger's, because I saw them near the bathroom sink when I left this morning. The girl's legs are spread wide, putting her perfect body on display, with those tiny pink nipples pointing skyward. I belatedly notice that she also has a huge tattoo of Granger's face emblazoned on her torso.

"What. The. Fuck?!"

Granger's feet thump up the stairs like terribly played trombone, reminiscent only of high school music rooms.

"What's going on?" He comes to a halt in the middle of the bedroom. "Jaysus Christ!" he shouts, though he doesn't sound too surprised.

"Seriously? What the fuck, Granger?"

He groans. "They do this sometimes."

"Who does what? What are you saying?" I'm more than aware of the hysteria drowning out my voice.

"The fans," he clarifies. "Sometimes they break into my apartment; others they bribe the hotel staff."

"Does this happen a lot?" My mind is going all kinds of places right now, boarding planes to countries I never wanted to visit and don't have any business getting to know.

Meanwhile, the girl hops to her knees and rubs her breasts to the tune of some impressively melodic moaning. "I'm here for you, Granger. I love you."

"Shut up!" I shout.

She shoots me a glare, whining at the object of her *crazy*. "I'll give you everything this ugly bitch doesn't think you deserve, Granger."

"Shut. The. Fuck. Up!" I scream so loud that even the birds take flight from the tree branches outside, but I've had enough of this—all of this—the taunts online, the paparazzo's comments, the looks I get whenever I'm with him, and that constant feeling of falling short somehow. Just moments ago, I felt so safe and secure in his arms, but the rational part of my brain knows that things will always be like this, at least on some level. I'll never be enough for rock n' roll—maybe to Granger, but not in the eyes of the big wide world.

"I can't believe this is happening," I whisper to myself, leaning against the wall and sliding my torso down the plaster until my bum hits the floor.

Granger is on the phone to the police when the girl suddenly rushes him. Her hands skim his chest and all I see is red. Immediately I lose it, launching myself at the bitch and tackling her to the ground. She shrieks beneath me and attempts to scratch my face, but this ditz is no match for me. Granger shouts overhead like a referee and it becomes obvious that I'm wrestling a naked woman in my underwear. Still, she asked for it and I can't seem to stop. Granger's strong arms lock around my body and break up our cat fight, whispering something in my ear that I can't make out very well. I don't know if I'm in a fog, or if the fog got into my head, but needless to say—things are foggy. At this point, I just want it all to stop.

Granger carries me into the bathroom and places me on the edge of the tub. "Stevie?" He squats down and checks me over with both of his rough hands. "Are you hurt?"

I shake my head no, but he just sighs. "The police are downstairs. Can you do me a favour and stay right here?" I don't look at him— instead I glance over his shoulder at my reflection in the bathroom mirror. My hair has that *just-fucked* look, my skin is flushed red all over, and my eyes look as if they've seen hell. Actually, they look like they've lived in hell and tried to change the place for good, but lost to the underworld every time. Still, I nod once to give permission and Granger stands up and kisses the top of my head.

"I'm sorry." He disappears from the bathroom like a dream that literally makes no sense.

I hear the commotion in the next room, beginning with the girl's cries upon being handcuffed and escorted away. The police radio buzzes with static, cameras click here and there, and there's the low murmur of voices as they piece together the events. A wave of fatigue hits me so hard that I almost fall forward off the tub. I don't know why I'm surprised, since I knew that a relationship with someone of Granger's notoriety would come with its own baggage, but somehow the incident has me rattled. Somehow this invasion is the worst day of loving Granger yet.

I manage to make it back downstairs with my pants on, where I find a uniformed RCMP officer taking Granger's statement. I sit beside him on the couch and try to answer their questions, perched stoically there as the seconds tick by like hours until they finally pack up and leave. As soon as I get up, Granger locks the door behind them and comes to me.

"Stevie?" he says, uncertainly.

I don't answer. I just stare out the window at the alpine landscape, sorting through the day's events in my mind.

"Sweetheart?" he tries again.

"It'll always be like this, won't it?"

Granger scrubs a hand up and down his face at my question.

"Don't let something like this drive us apart. Please don't."

"How can you do this? In a way, your life is no longer your own."

"Because I love playing music that much." He sighs. "But I love you too. More than you know. Tell me what you need, and I'll do that for you."

I shrug. "I don't know what you can do. Why is it up to me to figure it out?"

"Well, I'll find a more secure hotel next time. Double up on my security. Have my detail sweep the place beforehand. While not always ideal, I promise there are solutions, love."

"She was beautiful, wasn't she?" I whisper, as he rushes over and pulls me to my feet.

"Don't you do that. Don't you dare. Do I need to remind you of how we couldn't keep our hands off each other in the hall earlier? *You* are beautiful, Stevie, and you're all that I want." He shakes his head. "Don't you see? There are millions of her, Stevie. I've only met one *you* my whole life."

"Why does it have to be so hard though?" My voice cracks, but I let go at last and wrap my arms around him.

"Because the most important things in life are always hard. Easy didn't give me my career nor my success. Easy certainly didn't give me you. But it was worth the fight—you were worth the fight—and if you give us a chance, everything between us will be worth it too."

"It's worth it already," I whisper. "I'm grateful for what we have now." His arms tighten around me as I bury my face in his shoulder.

"Then relax. Let me take care of all of this, starting with you."

"I can take care of myself, actually."

He chuckles and presses a kiss to my forehead. "I know that. You're an independent, bartending, motorcycle-riding genius who doesn't need a man, of course I know that, but I wouldn't mind if you needed me. Being able to care for yourself doesn't mean refusing to share the load once in a while. We all get tired and need help. Quit your jobs and come to Los Angeles with me. We have another tour coming up in the winter—we could be together."

"That's a big bomb to drop on a girl who just witnessed a nude break & entry."

He laughs aloud this time. If I didn't know better, I'd think I could hear his voice echoing off the mountains. "Then take some time and think about it. But promise me to set aside your pride long enough to give my proposal the consideration it deserves."

"I will." I close my eyes and bask in the warmth of his arms while trying to ignore the cold reality sneaking up on us from behind. I've never been a big fan of forces that take you from behind (unless, of course, those forces are Granger) but I'm hoping that our bond will be enough to keep the fire lit between us for a long time.

Chapter Nineteen

"Home Sweet Home"

Granger

Stevie grips my palm like a goddamn sumo-wrestler. We're trudging up her mother's driveway, but I swear her hold will leave marks. I venture that'd be awkward before meeting her mom. "You must let up, beautiful—that's my guitar playing hand."

The door swings open, nearly knocking me in the nose. Next up, a mammoth bloke marches down the driveway, heading straight for my sorry self. I know what's happening ages before his fist collides with my nose, like Sunday Bloody Sunday, wrapping up the front door's business. Getting punched in the face is a theme in my life, at least wherever Stevie is concerned, but I'll take one hit for everyday I get to spend with her.

She shrieks on cue and comes between us, but no way is she getting in the middle of this one. I maneuver her behind me and bring my hand up to my nose. It comes away California-strawberry red but I make no attempt to stop the flow. Instead, I clench my fists and straighten my shoulders, imitating my security guys. As a former foster child, I've been throwing punches my whole life, but her brother is huge. I'm not sure how many more hits I can take on two feet. For Stevie's sake though, I'll take whatever he has to give.

His eyes are wild, and he breathes like someone ripped out his lungs. "Because of you, my baby sister was embarrassed. Because of you, her name and face are all over the Internet with ugly words about her."

"Dude, I know. I'm not happy about it either."

"Because of you, my sister feels *less than*."

"I know."

"You hurt her, you good-for-nothing Scotsman," he growls.

"Sounds about right. But I am sorry. Hit me with your best shot, man, but know that Stevie here is meant to be mine."

"If it happens again, we'll come after you—all of us."

I glance over his shoulder just in time to catch three imposing figures moving our way, all of them muscled and wide like samurai. They have dark hair, way different than Stevie's golden curls, but the whole family has the same soul-heavy, whiskey-brown eyes.

The shortest one cracks his knuckles and gives me a solid glare. Yeah, his message is loud and clear. "Your celebrity status won't save you here, asshole."

I take a breath and consider my words like I'm being tested— which I bloody well am. "Yes, I hurt Stevie, but I'll do everything in my power to make sure it damn never happens again. I care about your sister—just like you, I want to protect her." I address the brother looming before my very eyes, who I assume is Smith. I recognize him from the picture on Stevie's mantle. I gotta' say though, the look in his eyes is different now. Smith is looking at me like he's about to read me my last rights.

"Okay, then—as long as we're clear. Are we clear?"

"Crystal."

He gives me a sharp nod, which signals the others to relax. The flow of blood from my nose is more like lava than water. I wipe the remaining gunk on my shirt, congratulating myself for wearing something dark. Meanwhile, Stevie takes my hand and leans into my hips.

"I am *so* sorry."

"Don't be—really—I've had worse. I can handle a little brotherly initiation."

"That's not very reassuring," she whispers, stomping over to her brother. She shoves one of her long, delicate fingers into the centre of his chest like a spear, and not just any spear—this spear means business.

"How dare you! I warned you not to say anything!"

He doesn't look affected by her outburst at all. He just pulls her into a big bear hug, scooping her up until she levitates a whole foot off the ground.

"Mom is making your favourite."

"You think you can get out of all of this with a hug and a smile?"

"Don't I usually?"

"You assaulted my friend, Smith!"

His jaw flexes with a smirk at me over her shoulder. The look on his face is no kinder than a moment ago. "Baby sis, I had to make sure that he's actually your friend."

Her friend? My throat tightens. I should put an end to this shit right now, so I move in on Smith. "We are not friends; Stevie is my girlfriend."

The reaction is what I figured. My emphasis on the word "my" has her brothers bristling, but they leave it alone pretty fast. I don't give a shit about their response anyway; it's Stevie's I care about, and the smile across her face has my shoulders relaxing back into their sockets.

"Oh! You're all a bunch of testosterone-fueled meatheads! Forget it and let's just get inside before Mom kills us all."

I'm wearing a huge grin at this point, giddy that she didn't dispute my girlfriend comment. It brings us closer to putting this drama behind us and finally moving forward. The house is a rancher, with a wraparound covered porch. The inside of the house is small but well put together. I follow behind Stevie and her brothers as we head to the back of the house. When we reach the kitchen, flank steak simmers on the stove.

Stevie inhales and sighs out her next words. "Mmm…beef stew."

"She made you bannock, too," another brother says. I glance at the woman they're talking about, who's currently bent over the stove stirring a pot.

"Steven!" she shouts, dropping her wooden spoon and throwing both arms around my girl. Stevie laughs and hugs her back, while her mother kisses her cheeks repeatedly. "My baby…" she says with a sigh.

"I saw you last week, Mom." Stevie's face flames red.

"That was seven whole days ago." Her mother takes a step back, checking me out now. She stares right into me, and I use the opportunity to stare right back. She's short, just barely over five feet, with long black hair and caramel skin. In a way, she seems almost ageless, but her piercing eyes are the same colour as Stevie's, and they reveal the same old soul. Her lips are pulled tight, I figure because she doesn't know what to make of me yet. When she finally does speak, I almost wish she'd given me the silent treatment instead.

"So this is the man who broke my beautiful daughter's heart?"

Her words are simple, spoken without menace. It seems that she's stating a fact. I have to admit that her words cut right through me.

"This is the man who made a mistake," I counter. "The same man who cares very deeply for your daughter and will do anything to make it up to her."

I hear Stevie's quick intake of breath, but her mother doesn't flinch. "When a storm is coming, all the other birds seek shelter. The eagle alone avoids the storm by flying above it. My daughter is and has always been an eagle…the only question left is, what are you?"

I clear my throat, my gaze locked with Stevie's. "I am proud to be with Stevie and I will defend her honour at all costs."

"Then you are an eagle." She nods. "Come, let's eat."

We sit down at the table, and I learn that her mother's name is Alana. She is Lil'Wat First Nations, which gives Stevie her Indigenous roots. She has mentioned her heritage before, but *learning about it from her mother is very cool*, especially for someone like me, with no ties to my own history. I learn that the Lil'Wat are an Interior Salish people with a profound and harmonious relationship with the land. Like, they consider the land and people to be one.

Looking around the table, I realize that Stevie is different from her mother and brothers. Their family bond is undeniable, but my girl's freckled complexion and blond hair raises the question, for the first time, of her father.

"More stew?" Alana passes me the bowl, and I dig in shamelessly.

"Thank you. I haven't had a home-cooked meal in longer than I can remember."

"Well, you are always welcome here, Granger." My eyes sting— heck, even my spine stings. No way that she knows how much those words mean to me. Ever since I lost my parents, family is the one thing that I've always wanted, but I could never seem to get a firm grasp on the whole concepts. My bandmates have been the closest thing I have to family in a long time, and to be honest, they kind of suck.

"So tell us about you. Where are you from?" Alana asks.

I give my practiced media answer, you know, about growing up in Aberdeen, Scotland and the string-less guitar I found in a local pawn shop and nursed back to life. I don't offer any details about my parents because I hardly remember them, and she doesn't ask. Too bad Stevie is hearing these things for the first time, right here with her family, and I feel rotten for not sharing my whole story with her already. I know it's a taboo topic for me still, and sharing isn't something I do on the regular.

"Do you have any brothers or sisters?" Spencer asks of me, flicking his fork in the air.

"No." I shake my head.

"Lucky you," Stevie mumbles, giving me her signature roll of the eyes.

"Very funny, little one," Smith says. "But what would you have done without us growing up?"

"Have more peace and quiet, for one thing," she teases.

"But who would fix your car? Or change your light bulbs? Re-grout your bathtub?" Her other brother, Sean, sounds like my foster mother.

"I do all of those things myself," she protests, and he answers with a thunderous laugh, snaking a thick arm around her neck.

"I know, I know. But it's not like we don't offer. Face it, you love having us around," Sean says. She rolls her eyes again, but she doesn't dispute the statement.

"It must have been hard to bring home boyfriends with four older brothers?" I ask.

"What boyfriends?" Sean says, scoffing, and even Alana chuckles.

"I have to admit…I didn't have to worry about much with these ones hovering over my daughter. Let's just say that they kept a pretty close eye on her."

"Yeah, and on the rare occasion that someone actually showed interest in me, they became inexplicably disinterested very quickly," Stevie adds, glaring around the table. I don't miss how all her brothers avert their eyes. One even starts whistling like it's nobody's business.

"It wouldn't have mattered much anyway. Most people figured I was a bit of a freak, especially being two years younger with all the grades I'd skipped. I mean, who wants to take a fifteen-year-old to senior prom?"

"Only someone with a death wish," Spencer mutters, loud enough for anyone to hear.

"I was lucky to have the boys looking out for her with Stevie's father gone so often."

It's the first time that her father has been mentioned, and I'm dying of curiosity. "Is he…?" I trail off, but Alana shakes her head.

"He's alive and well. He retired down in Mexico with his girlfriend. We separated years ago, but he worked as a deep-water welder when Stevie was a child, which required a lot of travel and time away from home."

"That's dangerous work," I say.

"Even more dangerous for a marriage," she counters. "He's not part of the band. I fell in love with him on a girl's weekend in Vancouver, and he changed my life for the better by giving me these five gifts, but the distance was too much and I didn't want to move away for a man. Having roots in the community is very important to me."

"Stevie has said something similar before."

"It is Nt'akmen—our way. It's in the blood of the St'at'imc people. Our name, Lil'watul, literally translates to *people of the land*."

"There's so much history here." I glance around the room, in love with the atmosphere created by the old family photographs and relics of traditional art, which almost seem made by the mountains, oceans, and streams. "I'd love to learn more."

She grasps my hand in both of her much smaller hands. Her grip is firm and warm, like a living padlock. "Then come back and see me anytime. I would love to introduce you to our elders, for you to better understand our culture. You are always welcome."

My eyes start to sting and I whisper a quiet thank you. Afterwards, Alana serves us warm berry pie and ice cream for dessert. I wonder why three pies are placed on the table, that is, until I see how much Stevie's brothers love their mother's cooking.

"You probably had a big grocery bill when these guys were growing up."

She laughs and rolls her eyes. "Granger Ellis, if you only knew!"

Stevie links her fingers through mine, squeezing my hand beneath the table. I figure that means I've passed the test. Not that I was trying to be anyone other than myself, but her family's approval is important to me. Being here in my girl's childhood home guides me back to my old self again, at least what I figure is my old self, since I haven't spent time with that guy in a while.

At the front door, Alana kisses both of my cheeks and whispers something to me that I don't understand: *Kukwstumckacw*. I can't tell if she's saying one word, or two words, or three, but I let my grin communicate my curiosity.

"It means *thank you*." She speaks without blinking. "Thank you for watching over my beautiful girl's heart." I give her a nod, and the stinging feeling moves from my eyes to my nose. Bringing Stevie to my side, I pull Alana into a hug on the porch.

As we head out to the road, Stevie yawns. I have a package of homemade stew and leftover pie under my arm that her mother insisted on my taking home. All of her brothers shook my hand when we left, and even with the fullness of my belly, I feel like I'm walking on air. I open the driver's side door and Stevie tosses the keys in my lap as she slides in next to me.

"I shouldn't have downed that second glass of wine," she yawns. "My brothers pour like animals." She giggles, and the sound has me instantly hard. I need to get this sexy woman home, where I can smother her body before I lose my mind.

I back down the driveway and step on the gas, eager to get us home, but Stevie is asleep the moment I check on her. She breathes like feathers, with her face against the window and her cheeks tomato red. She is more vulnerable than anything I can dream up, just sleeping there against the window—it's like something inside me snaps apart and forms anew. The feeling is protectiveness combined with a sense of ownership.

This woman pressed up against the window, mumbling something about enzymes in her sleep, could be the family I've been searching for all this time. When I glance back at Stevie again, she sighs, and I wonder whether instead of *could be,* this girl has already become my family. If my first real family in this life comes with a band of brothers dead set on keeping me in line, well then, let's rock n' roll, love.

Chapter Twenty

"Here I Go Again"

Stevie

Given the tension in the aftermath of our recent media attention, Granger decides that I should get to know the band. Meanwhile, I'd love for him to develop a relationship with Kit, so he arranges a private dinner for everyone at the peak of Blackcomb Mountain. I was surprised that the band extended their stay in Whistler as well, but it's become apparent that where Granger goes, *Actuator* goes. He's the central nervous system and they are the limbs.

We ride the Sea-to-Sky Gondola just after dusk. Granger, Kit and I fill one car while Chad, Ravi and Jayne take the other. I stare out the window over the twinkling village lights below, which look extra bright when contrasted against the dark outline of the surrounding mountains. This view is like medicine to me, but it's not enough to ease my apprehension over the upcoming meal. It was tense enough trying to navigate the forced conversation at the mountain's base. Who knows what sitting through five courses will be like in the end.

The panoramic views from the modern restaurant at the peak are accentuated by an understated wood-slat ceiling and simple drop lights. The dining room is empty except for one long harvest-style table decorated with flickering candles in the very center. I take a seat next to Granger as Jayne sits across from him. Kit takes the seat to my immediate right while Ravi and Chad flank Jayne. I snort to myself as the thought *one big happy family* flashes through my mind.

No one really speaks for the first few minutes, other than Granger, who orders wine and a round of vintage scotch for everyone. The restaurant serves us a Hamachi appetizer, which is thinly sliced fish. It melts on my tongue like butter, and that helps to erase the bitter taste that sitting across from Jayne has left in my mouth. Although the bright spot of the evening is Ravi, who finally opens up and peppers Kit with questions about Australia. He even shares some of his own traveling adventures, and I find myself wishing that tonight's dinner was just with Ravi. Then I wouldn't have to deal with Jayne's perpetual smirk or Chad's evil glares.

Granger is no help either, having already started on his second scotch. He orders a tequila shot from the waitress as she passes by, as I note with irritation that his wine glass is filled to the brim. The next course of fried baby artichokes arrives and presents a reprise from the awkward tension. The table goes quiet and we scarf down the nubby green vegetable hearts, only to have a small plate with barbecued short rib and jalapeno-cheddar cornbread follow afterwards. It looks delicious, so I immediately dig in to embrace the feast—and that's when Jayne starts in on me.

"It's refreshing to see someone not obsess over her weight." She nods her head at my plate. "I mean, all those carbs and not a care in the world."

"Stevie is beautiful exactly as she is," Kit cuts in, obviously overhearing. "She gets plenty enough attention to prove it, believe me."

"Oh, I'm sure she does," Jayne says, all too sweetly. "Who doesn't love a sideshow?" She mutters the last words under her breath, but our table overhears no problem.

Kit pushes back his chair and the legs squeal as they scrape against the floor. "Are you for real?" For a moment, I think that he's about to throw the plate at her head, but I can't let him overreact. Besides, she's just trying to push my buttons. I change the subject in a last ditch effort to diffuse the situation.

"So how exactly did you all meet?" I specifically pose the question to Ravi. "Granger told me a little and Kit is a big fan, but I'd love to hear the band's history from the band itself."

With the change of subject, Kit sits down but nonetheless appears ready to leap into action any moment. Meanwhile, Ravi smiles and the wave of relief reaching his eyes is impossible to miss. "Well, I came in later, of course. These guys put an ad in the Los Angeles Times for a drummer. I showed up and got the gig."

Granger cuts in then, like a barn swallow diving across the porch. "Originally we wanted to become a four-piece band, but the three of us sounded so good that we decided to keep it that way." He slurs his words but still continues the story. Already he's moved from scotch to wine, but the first bottle is almost empty as the waitress sets a fresh one down on the table.

"With Granger's killer voice and *Actuator's* unique sound, we got a recording contract with an unknown label in Los Angeles pretty fast; from there we started playing out together at small venues," Ravi explains.

"When Ravi says small, he means wee little dumps where the dressing room is also the bathroom and you can't swing your guitar around on stage without knocking over someone's pint," Granger adds, with a hiccup that makes me cringe.

"Then we got an early hit with 'Hole in the Ground' and the rest is history," Ravi says, shrugging off the peak of their success and making me particularly aware of our location atop Blackcomb Mountain.

Ravi and Kit fall into an easy conversation about drum beats and DJ'ing, while I turn my attention to the main course of wild salmon appearing in front of me. I pick up my fork and try to squash any insecurities that Jayne has sent bubbling to the surface, because it seems a shame to waste a beautifully cooked piece of fish over one conniving bitch.

"But that's only half the story, really," Chad says, rolling his eyes.

"The easy half," Jayne slings her arm over the backside of Chad's chair. "You see, for a while, Chad and Granger lived in the same foster home as teenagers. Chad knew me from the neighbourhood. The second that Granger and I met, we got along like we'd been together forever, spending our nights sitting on the roof, smoking and watching the trains pass by." She leans forward in her chair as if telling a ghost story. "Granger always talked about learning the guitar. He was mad about one guitar in particular, which had its place in the window of a local pawn shop."

"One day, Chad stole money from the register of the grocery store, which happened to be his first workplace," Granger joins the conversation with glazed eyes, either from the memories or the booze. "Got canned for it, too."

"In a way, some might claim that I'm responsible for the great Granger Ellis' career." Chad raises his glass and toasts the air, a drop of red wine splashing across the table. The words are neutral but the intent behind them is deeply clear. Chad is marking his territory to ensure that I know Granger belonged to them first.

Jayne sighs and picks up her glass of wine for another sip. "From there we worked some crap jobs. I learned the bass guitar and we saved up enough money to come to America. We've been together now for more than fifteen years. We have the kind of bond that can't be broken by anything." She opens her mouth a little, as if preparing to put on lipstick. "Not even fame-hungry bartender whores."

"That's enough!" Kit shouts, shoving the table so violently that the glasses quiver in unison. I had no idea he was even still listening, but Granger's response surprises me far more than Kit's reaction. He doesn't even pretend to come to my defense. Instead he slumps over in his chair and watches the whole exchange with a blank look on his face.

At that point, Kit pulls back my chair so abruptly that I'm forced to my feet. He tugs me by the forearm and uses his own body to shield me before speaking. "You know what, Jayne? You're not just a cunt—you're a fucking cunt. We're going home, Stevie."

I give Granger one last look, staring at him with all the feeling in the world before turning my back and following Kit to the front door. My throat starts to close up as I wander along behind him, overcome with a mixture of shame and betrayal.

Ravi appears and walks in step with Kit until we reach the exit. "I am so sorry about this." He shakes his head with a sad shrug. "I wish there was more I could do, but they're like that, the three of them—like their own little castle, fortified with impassable walls. Take it from someone who knows."

"It's not your fault, Ravi," Kit murmurs. "But I won't let them treat her like that."

"Believe me, I understand." He nods before glancing in my direction. "You gonna be okay, Stevie?"

I'm not good, not at all, but I nod anyway. "Just make sure he gets back to the hotel safely, and maybe stay with him for a bit?" My voice comes out a little shaky. A look of understanding passes across his face, only to be swallowed up by something that looks like pity.

"You know I will."

Kit and I don't speak during our gondola ride down the mountain, but he lets loose once we're in the car.

"Is he really what you need in your life right now?" I notice that his knuckles are white from his grip on the steering wheel.

"He's just stressed." I find myself explaining. "He was nervous bringing us all together and he drank too much."

"It seems like more than that, Stevie."

"So he got a little drunk." I laugh and feel clearly the vibe of my own nervousness. "You drink, Kit, and so do I."

"Not like that, we don't. And when did this become about you and I? You're deflecting. It's not just the booze, Stevie. He didn't stand up for you. He took the band's side over yours."

"I don't think he really—" I start to speak, but he cuts me off with a snort.

"I'm worried that if he pulled this shit tonight, he'll always be that way. I mean that he'll always take their side."

"Well, don't worry about me. I know what I'm doing. My boyfriend had too much to drink at dinner and there's nothing else to it." I want this conversation to be over. I don't like the tight feeling in my chest.

Kit laughs ironically and fires up the engine. He doesn't look at me when he speaks, but I hear the disappointment in his voice loud and clear. "For an actual genius, you can be pretty fucking stupid sometimes, Stevie."

Chapter Twenty-One
"Big Talk"

Granger

The door to the library is barred shut when I get there. It may as well be locked, given the two fierce-looking broads stationed out front, both senior citizens. I approach them with care and hold out my hand. "I'm Granger Ellis. I believe we've met before?"

The shorter one with periwinkle glasses glares at my hand and crosses her arms. "We know who you are."

"Then you probably know why I need to see Stevie."

"And I need tits that don't double as a belt." The larger one with yellowish white hair snickers at me. "We don't always get what we want, now do we, boy?"

Yeah, fuck, there's no way I'm getting inside. These ladies are unrelenting—that is…unless…"I could make it worth your while?" The shorter one looks me up and down, probably wondering if I want to paint her like one of my French girls, or whatever. "You're not my type."

"Not mine either. Too skinny and too tattooed," the larger one adds. "Besides I'd probably break you in half."

"Oh, for the love of God. Come on ladies, that's not what I meant. I was thinking more like a limousine ride to one of your favourite restaurants in Whistler, followed by one night in a fancy hotel?"

"We can't be bought," the one with periwinkle glasses tries, only to be cut off by her friend. "Hold on now…hold on. A hotel, you say?"

"How does the Four Seasons work for you? I'll arrange for dinner at the restaurant there: *Sidecut*. I hear it's one of the best."

The larger one nods her head real slow and I can tell that I've already got her.

"Make it a suite," she commands.

"Say what?"

"You deaf, boy? Make it a suite at the Four Seasons and you have yourself a deal."

"Fine, a suite, you win. Just let me in there so I can get my girl, alright?"

They both soften at my last comment and shuffle out of the way to let me pass.

I rush toward the amenities room in the back, coming face to face with Joe. The expression on his face feels like a punch in the gut. His lips quiver, I figure with anger, as hurt goes a million miles per hour through his eyes.

"I ought to slap you silly for hurting our Stevie again."

"Yes, you should." My shoulders slump, but I straighten them out just as quickly. Being responsible for my actions is important, but so is not beating up on myself.

"I've fought alongside men with three times the balls of you, and that, sonny, is just a metaphor. I don't understand your generation, rock stars in particular. You have every possible privilege afforded to you, with all your money and fame. You have nothing but time and resources to spend making that beautiful woman happy, but all you do is sabotage yourself." He stares me down real good after finishing his speech, or *rant* is more like it.

"I know I do."

"If you're such a plague, you don't deserve her heart. You, sonny, should stay away. Go back to your demon-worshipping hole and never come back to Whistler again."

"You're probably right, Joe, but I can't do that. I just can't. I need her. I want her."

"So which is it? Do you need her or want her?" Joe scoffs. "Because to me, one sounds like dependency and the other sounds like entitlement."

"It's both, Joe. I need her, want her, and know that I don't deserve her. So do with me whatever you will, Joe, but afterwards please let me see Stevie."

"Why should I?"

I take a deep breath and answer him. "Because I'm better with her."

"But is she better with you?"

"I'll do anything and everything in my power to protect her heart, forever and always. I mean those words, and that's enough for me."

"You better mean it," he sighs out. "Or your balls will need protecting."

"Seems to be a bit of a testicles theme with you, Joe."

He cackles but gets interrupted by a hacking cough. "And I'm not kidding where yours are concerned, rock star. So yes, I'll let you pass, but you better watch your ass—and your balls—from now on."

"Yes, sir."

The old man places a wrinkled hand on my shoulder as I push past him. "Tell me, how did you get through the guards outside?"

I clear my throat. "I bribed them. Dinner and a hotel suite in Whistler."

"I should've known." Joe shakes his head. "Those traitors." He mumbles to himself and heads in their direction, thrusting open the front door, as if he's taking center stage. "Traitors, I tell you!"

At the end of the hallway, I find my girl sitting alone at a circular table in the amenities room. She's bent over a tangle of wool, but I don't miss the tears in her eyes. In a split-second, I decide to take this conversation elsewhere.

"Sweetheart," I whisper, as Stevie looks at me with flooded eyes. Watching tears spill down her face totally guts me. "I know we have lots to talk about, but we can't do this in front of the cavalry. I'm asking—actually begging—for you to please get up and come home with me." I close my eyes and prepare for a fight, but Stevie is already on her feet.

She doesn't say anything, but she still follows me outside. I assume that's a good sign. I catch a glimpse of her motorcycle in the lot and take that as my cue. "I'll have your bike picked up. Will you ride with me?"

She nods and climbs into the passenger seat of my rental car. Her face is like glass. We ride in complete silence to the hotel. There is so much I want to say, but to start now will spook Stevie and send her running for the hills. I'm waiting until she's captive between four walls with a door that locks behind us. For heaven's sake, I don't want her leaving until she realizes how sorry I am for what happened up on that godforsaken mountain. If nothing else, she must know how much she means to me. I park in front of the hotel, not giving two shits about the paparazzi as I toss my keys to the valet. She follows a few steps behind me, keeping her head down the entire time, as the vultures snap pictures and hit us with questions.

"Are you and Granger together?"

"What do you think of the rumours that he and his ex, Lily St Clair, are getting back together?"

"How did you snag one of rock's most eligible bachelors?"

"Is it true that you're just a waitress?"

"Do you know what Granger Ellis' estimated net worth is?"

With each word, Stevie shrinks into herself more. I literally want to kill them for it. Seeing the media shred on someone I love makes me want to rip their limbs from their sockets. But I place my hand on her lower back and lead her inside. She doesn't even look in my direction as we ride the elevator up to my room, where I lock the door behind us. The part that kills me is that she's still holding her knitting, with her needles clutched in one hand, kind of like drumsticks, the yarn against her chest, and the loose sky-blue end dangling past her bellybutton.

Chapter Twenty-Two

"Love Bites"

Stevie

"You said that you'd always have my back." I feel my throat tighten as I speak. His nostrils flare but otherwise his face is expressionless.

"I do."

"You didn't at the restaurant."

"I was wrong," he hedges. "I got messed up when I shouldn't have. My head wasn't clear."

I tilt my own head at him. "Why?"

"Why what?"

"Why did you get messed up? The dinner was your idea in the first place, and you left me stranded with Chad—and HER."

He moves his head from side to side, as if trying to shake away the memory. "It was just nerves. I was anxious and wanted it to go well."

"You hurt me, again."

"I fucked up, again."

"Why does this conversation feel like déjà vu?"

"I love you," he begs. "You have to forgive me." He tosses my knitting aside and takes both of my hands in his own. Tears form in his eyes and just like that I cave.

"I forgive you," I whisper. Granger answers by fisting his hands through my hair.

"I love you so much that it physically hurts sometimes." He kisses my jaw line as his hands travel down to my waist and he glides his rough fingers across my stomach until a sudden warmth floods between my legs. He grips my hips and thrusts against me—hard—

pushing his cock against my belly. I have to bite the inside of my cheek to keep from screaming aloud.

"I can smell how ready you are for me." He whispers sweet-nothings in my ear before his lips begin to nip at the sensitive flesh on my neck. My nipples pucker in response and I grind them against his hard chest with a low moan. He rears back as his eyes flash and scan my breasts. "I have to taste these. I'm going to die if I don't get one of those sweet buds in my mouth right now."

Without warning, he whips my tank-top over my head and shreds my bra with his hands, sending the shirt and two scraps of lace to the floor. I groan as the cool air hits my bare nipples and Granger releases a deep, vibrating moan before bending down to take one in his mouth. He sucks on it so hard that my vision starts to blur.

As much as I want him inside of me right now, there's something I want more. I hurriedly undo the button on his jeans and inch down the zipper, pushing them halfway down his legs and causing his dick to spring free. He's bare underneath as per usual. I slide my hands around to grip his firm ass and he pulses his dick against me with another pained groan. "I need to have you now, sweetheart."

"Shh..." I attempt to soothe him as I drop to my knees. He grabs his cock and pumps it with his fist before guiding it between my lips, which wrap around his cock as I take him deep into my mouth. I circle the head with my tongue, using my hands to pump the whole length of him, moaning and panting in the process.

"It feels so damn good." His breath is wildly erratic and I suck on him like a candy cane until he releases a muffled shout.

"You have to stop or I'll come."

I pop off him and glance up to meet his eyes. "So come, then."

He smirks and clicks his tongue. "Not tonight. Tonight I'm coming inside of you, Stevie."

He yanks me upright, hiking up my skirt to reveal my pink lace thong, which I hear tearing like a wrapper before it finds its lacy upper half on the floor. Meanwhile, Granger's fingers reach around to cup and squeeze my ass.

"Touch yourself." His tone leaves no room for argument, but I squirm when he first taps my clit before allowing him to grab my hand and replace his fingers with my own.

"Finger yourself." My legs rattle like stilts under the build up. "I want to watch you make yourself come."

I let my eyelids droop, thrusting two fingers inside my wet center as Granger removes his shirt and jeans with a hungry, wolf-tongued grin. His beauty is all muscles, nakedness, and tattoos like a totem. His aura burns with violet desire. He's lean but strong, with sculpted-cut abs and that delicious black insignia, spiralling its ink up both arms and halfway across his chest.

"That's right, love. Fuck yourself with those talented fingers." Granger strokes himself in time with my pace. My legs start to quiver beneath my waist and I scream out his name as the orgasm overtakes me. I slump against the wall as Granger steps forward to extricate my hand from between my legs. He slips my fingers into his mouth and hums against them. "Mmm, so sweet."

Granger takes another step backwards but surprises me by lying on the floor and beckoning me forward with his open palm. I drop to my knees and crawl up his body to straddle him, pausing to hold my breath before lowering myself onto his cock. I immediately gasp from the intense feeling of skin-to-skin contact while Granger shouts aloud and thrusts into me, just before his body goes still.

"Stevie?"

"I'm on the pill."

"I'm clean," he rushes out. "I get tested regularly."

"I trust you."

"*Thank you.*"

His fingers grip my ass as if nothing else holds him to this earth, and I start to float atop his hips. He feels so good and right between my thighs, especially in this position where he stretches me to my fullest. I feel the slow build of another orgasm arriving just as his breathing speeds up.

"Stevie, please," he groans, begging for release. I shout aloud as the second wave of pleasure pulls me out to sea—a smaller waved than before but ten times more intense—and he yells and swells as he rockets off inside of me.

We stare into each other's eyes while breathing like instruments, and I feel my sweaty breasts sticking against his chest. I lean forward to place both hands on his head, moving in closer to give him a sweet, chaste kiss. When I brush our lips together, he sighs like a little boy.

"I swear—every part of your body tastes like honey."

I smile and spring off him, only then noticing how my skirt is bunched up around my waist. I tug the fabric down and feel his warm release trickling along my leg. He must also notice the little stream, because he jumps to his feet and runs to the bathroom naked, flashing me a glimpse of his taut bare ass in the process. Granger returns with a towel to clean me up and I'm surprised by how gently he handles me, being so used to his gruffness, that rough everyday rock-star exterior of his. With his absolute possession of my body now, his hands gliding all over my body to clean my skin, I feel nothing short of cherished.

He retrieves my shirt from the floor and glances at my bra and panties sheepishly. "Fuck, I'm not even sorry about that." He grins and cocks one eyebrow, which earns him a liberated giggle.

"I'm not either." I watch Granger gather his clothing from around the room and make himself decent while peeking over his shoulder to check on me.

"I'll buy you new ones."

I roll my eyes. "I can afford my own underwear."

"I don't really give a shit if you can. Buying you underwear would be my pleasure." He chuckles before his eyes turn serious. "I meant what I said before. I love you, Stevie, and I do have your back. I promise that I'll get a handle on me."

"We have each other's backs," I answer. "I'm here for you, but you need to talk to me. Please don't shut me out."

He pulls me against his chest and buries his nose in my neck, inhaling as if he's trying to memorize my scent, before mumbling the following words against my flushed skin:

"You are the only one who's ever been in, Stevie."

Chapter Twenty-Three
"You Give Love a Bad Name"

Stevie

They say that pride comes before the fall, but I believe we see other things in its place sometimes: naiveté, willful ignorance, and self-loathing, for starters. I wish that he didn't have to fall. I wish there'd been some other way. But I'd be lying to myself if I didn't see it coming.

Chapter Twenty-Four

"High Enough"

Granger

"It's one more appearance, Granger. One more party before we blow this pop-stand and head right home," Chad tells me for the hundredth time.

My stomach hurts at the thought of leaving Stevie. Things are good between us right now, but who knows what happens next in our relationship—what defines the chorus of our song, what bars are destined for our coda? God knows that I'm running out of time to finish my next hit, but this one is not for sale. This one is Stevie.

"I already said no."

My scrub my forehead. There's pressure between my eyebrows and talking to Chad is like playing to an abusive crowd.

"This is about her, isn't it?"

"For the last time, it's not about her. It's about me. I'm tired of doing the same old shit over and over again. I need a change in my life. Getting healthy is the first step."

Chad paces the room. He throws his hands up in the air, just as he does always does—usually negatively, or else to get the crowd cheering. Right now I just want him to shut up.

"It's one last party. You owe it to the band. You owe it to me."

"How do you figure that, old pal?"

"I've been with you since day one. I've supported you, stuck by you, fronted you cash, carried your guitar case between shit-hole pubs in the suburbs of Glasgow. So yeah, you owe me."

I stare at the ceiling for a beat before answering. "You done?"

"I guess it depends on whether or not you're coming."

"Fine," I sigh out. "I'll come for an hour, but no Jayne, and I'm driving. You can find yourself another ride home."

"Whatever, suit yourself. You'll be missing out on some premium Canadian weed, top-shelf booze, and plenty of sweet young things, but it's your call."

Nothing to do but ignore the comment and point him out the front door. "Get out of my room. I'll meet you in the lobby in fifteen minutes."

I take my time getting ready, sitting on my couch for five minutes just to make them wait. True to form, Chad is waiting with Jayne in the lobby when I get there, but whatever. I don't have energy for an argument. I don't pay her any attention, fisting my keys and jerking my head instead, my signature gesture for them to follow. The valet has my rental car waiting and Chad climbs right into the backseat. Yup, that means Jayne takes shotgun. During the drive, they talk about some upcoming radio promotions for the new single, but I couldn't care less right now. I keep my eye on the road and crank up the car radio instead.

In fact, I ignore them during the whole ride to Vancouver, only acknowledging Chad when I need directions. He directs me to a high-end Westside neighbourhood—a mansion, specifically. It's by the water and has a gate. Chad shouts over my shoulder into the intercom, and the scene we enter would make Osiris and Tesla proud. I think about high school geometry class, which I failed, as I try to park the car, hoping to avoid getting boxed into the lot and following my lousy friends to the front door.

The house is full. Who the bloody hell is even here? Music plays in the background, and the lights are low and blue, making Chad look like a Smurf. It's fucking brilliant. Otherwise the party is half orgy and half Ibiza after-hours club. Someone passes a hookah around in the main room, with a full bar and serving staff. I would've loved this scene a month ago, but now it leaves me wanting for my girl.

"Can I get you a drink?" The way Jayne is acting is making me nervous. I know her tone well and dislike it plenty. Her voice used to make me feel alive. Now it just grates on my nerves.

"Just a can of Coke."

"Who are you and what have you done with Granger?"

I grunt, because who cares what she thinks. Jayne just heads for the bar and I chill out by the wall until she's back. I'm not in the mood for a show, so I just act like I'm someone else. A few guests still approach and pat me on the back, I guess to congratulate me on our new single, but no one asks for an autograph. At a party like this, there's too much ego and posturing for that.

Jayne returns soon enough, body-checking me with a can of Coke. "Come on, grandpa, let's go find Chad."

I shrug and follow her. She elbows her way through the thick crowd, probably hurting people. It's hot inside, and I'm thirsty as hell, so I throw back half my coke as we walk. Jayne leads us into a room and who knows why I follow her inside. Of course it's an empty bedroom. The door clicks behind me and the lock slides into place.

"The fuck this is happening," I mutter, turning around to face Jayne. Her smile is anything but innocent. "Jayne, you've got to be out of your head."

"We're good together, Granger," she protests.

"I'm not doing this with you—not now or ever again," I counter.

"What if I told you that I'll do all the work?" She doesn't wait for me to answer, pulling her shirt off in one fell swoop. Her bra is funky as hell, made of equal parts leather and lace. Her chest has always been small, and she still has those nipple rings I used to love so much. But the sight of her shirtless stirs up nothing else inside me. When I close my eyes, all I see is Stevie.

"We've been down this road before, Jayne. I've made it very clear that I'm not about to take that drive with you again."

Jayne looks at me like I just came out of the closet. "We have *history*, Granger."

"We do." I nod, but it's half-assed. "A history that I don't care to repeat."

"History has a way of repeating itself."

I laugh, taking another swig from my coke can and noticing the slogan *Enjoy Life!* scrawled along the side

"I learned my lesson, Jayne. You're an amazing bassist, a decent bandmate, and an okay friend, but you were a shitty girlfriend."

"You forgot the *best lover you ever had* part." She juts out her chest, which I deal with by closing my eyes. Unfortunately, the room starts spinning then and I have no choice but to look—not at her chest, but in her eyes.

"Let's not do this right now."

"Is this about her?" Jayne whisper, picking her shirt up from the floor.

"Believe it or not, no. You and I have been over for a long time. You didn't want me back until you saw me happy with someone else."

"Why should you get to be happy?" She yanks on the shirt, sideways, and gives me the stink eye.

"Oh Jayne," I chuckle out. "You really are a bitch, aren't you?"

I take a step backwards and place my empty can on the dresser, but the room tilts sideway and my vision doubles. "What the fuck's going on?" Fuck, why are my words slurred? It's almost like I'm having an out-of-body experience.

Jayne grins at me, but if I'm not mistaken she looks a little uncertain. "Your drink."

"My drink?" I blink at the red can, now too blurry to read.

Jayne shifts from foot to foot, and while I can't see her face, I hear her words clear as day.

"It was Chad's idea."

In fact, they're the last words I hear before blacking out completely.

➤

I wake up sometime later with a pounding headache. Who knows where I am—somewhere in Vancouver, alone, without Google Maps. No big surprise for me most days, but something is different this time. My stomach doesn't feel sick and guilty, nothing like when I wake up from a bender. No chance did I slip up and drink either—that much I know, at least.

I prop myself up on my elbows. Just my luck, I'm lying in bed with Jayne. Thank God she is fully-dressed. I almost want to take a picture for proof. We're in the same bedroom that she cornered me in before I lost consciousness. I know because my empty can of Coke is still on the dresser. Downstairs, the bass is thumping and the party is loud as fuck, but outside is different story. I just want to be outside with Stevie. I just want that black sky with all its damn stars. I nudge Jayne awake and she moans, satisfied, but her eyes are glassy and her pupils look enormous.

"Jayne?" I shake her again. "You ok?" She might be a bitch, but she's my bandmate and we go back a long way. I need to make sure she's safe before I jet off.

"Mmm…better than okay. I'm perfect." Her voice makes it obvious that she's out-of-her-mind high right now. Things could still be worse. She's in a good headspace, and I can't say the same for myself. My head pounds and the mounting pressure is so intense. Even keeping my eyes open hurts.

The bedroom door swings open and Chad wanders into the room. "Good, you're up. The party is insane downstairs. You need to make an appearance."

The crust of white powder around his nose tells me everything I need to know. His button-up shirt is open to the waist, and his fat chest is just a nightmare.

"What happened?" I groan, struggling big time to my feet.

"How the fuck should I know?" Chad immediately goes on the defensive. "You love birds came in here hours ago. The next thing I knew, you were in bed together."

"Hours ago?" I shout, my mind flashing to Stevie.

"Relax, man, you need to get your shit together. Here, take a hit." Chad hands me the end of a mostly smoked joint, which I consider for a moment before shoving it in his face.

"Nah, man, you need that more than I do." Chad holds up both hands in surrender, though his behaviour is riddled with its opposite.

"What I need is to get back to the hotel."

"If you want that to happen, you'd better get your shit together. You know weed always levels you out."

The cherry from the joint has almost burned down, scalding my fingers as I take a few quick puffs to relieve the pounding in my head, just before wandering across the room and dropping the end in my empty can of Coke. I run my fingers through my hair and straighten out my shirt before turning back to Chad.

"I don't know what the two of you had planned, but this shit ends right now. I'm done with Jayne's bullshit, but I'm done with yours, too. I'm leaving, Chad." Just like that, I head for the door.

"You're really going to choose some fat, boring whore over your best friend?"

I stop in my tracks, balling up my fists enough to cut off my own circulation. Every instinct in my body tells me to turn around and beat him to a pulp, but he's just goading me. I don't have the time or energy for Chad right now.

"I'm choosing the love of my life, actually. I choose her over you two sorry slags, and I'll do it again tomorrow, next week, next month, and then for years. I'll keep doing it until your selfish, shallow heads understand that Stevie is the rest of my life. You can be a part of that life, or you can remain a part of my past. The choice is up to you."

Now that I've said my piece, I couldn't care less about his answer. I bloody well crash into the walls on my way to the front door. The pounding in my head is not so bad—just a reminder of why joining my bandmates tonight was a terrible decision. Passing party guests, I get a few shouts and back-slaps, but the groupies give me a wide berth. My geometrical parking didn't work for shit, go figure, and the valet takes his sweet time freeing my ride. I'm anxious, pissed, and all around missing Stevie.

My forehead throbs like a drum. I fire up the engine and head for the highway. The wind has picked up since earlier, and the highway is dark like a tunnel. The only light comes from the moon over the ocean, plus the sting of oncoming headlights every few minutes. I pull out my phone to dial Stevie. Go figure, I've missed a few of her calls and texts. I try to type back with one hand, just to let her know that I'm coming, but it's useless. I toss the phone onto the passenger seat and press my foot on the gas. The sooner that I see Stevie, the sooner everything will be alright.

Thirty minutes later, I'm passing a mining museum on the cliffside as a long chill runs down my spine. The drive from Vancouver to Whistler means climbing one thousand meters in elevation, at least, and I'm speeding as I approach the next corner. The 'slippery section' sign catches my attention a second too late, and just like that, I lose control of the vehicle. On the same night that I managed to keep control of myself, I've allowed my car to swerve into oncoming traffic. Horns sound and lights flash. I might as well be onstage. I jerk the wheel and maneuver the car to the right, but at my current speed of one-hundred-and-twenty kilometers per hour, I won't be able to stop in time. Instead, I brace myself for impact as the car slams into the face of the cliffside.

By some miracle, I'm not dead. Somehow I barely have a scratch. The paramedic on scene treats me for a bloody nose before the cops cuff and escort me away to a holding cell in the town of Squamish. On our ride to the station, I overhear them muttering that the car is probably a write-off, but that is the least of my problems.

Only when I see that familiar set of whiskey-brown eyes staring at me through the cold metal bars of my jail cell do I realize that my problems have just begun. The disappointment reflected back at me is crushing. I imagine that Stevie's pupils have been replaced with shards of obsidian.

"You came," I croak, wondering when I last had a sip of water.

"You asked me to come."

As cliché as it sounds, Stevie was my one phone call. "But you still came."

"Yes, because I care about you."

"Is that enough?" I brace myself and wait for her answer, just like before I slammed into that hard-as-rock cliffside (I mean, it *was* rock). Sometimes, with Stevie, I do this thing where I act like a kid who pretends not to understand himself, but it's because she gets stuff so much better than me. Still, right now the silence is too much—and then she delivers the final blow.

"No, Granger. It's not enough."

"But I honestly have no idea what happened!"

Stevie just shakes her head.

"The police told me that you were twice the legal limit, and one of the officers mentioned that you smelled like marijuana."

"But I didn't drink anything, I swear!"

"Did you smoke marijuana?"

As bad as it looks, I know I can't lie. "Only a little bit, but you don't understand—I had to smoke in the moment. I needed to get myself right so that I could get back to you."

"Listen to yourself—do you even hear what you are saying?"

"I promise you that I didn't drink. Something must have happened—Jayne and Chad were there." At Jayne's name, her lips turn sour and I explain away her pain.

"Jayne cornered me in a bedroom and started to undress. She said something like *it was Chad's idea*, so maybe they drugged me..." I trail off, because one thing is clear: I'm only digging myself deeper into this mess.

"Does it matter?" Stevie's looking hard at the floor. "You had a choice to stay at the hotel or go to a party, and you went to the party. You did that knowing that you'd be with people that you don't trust yourself to stay sober around, including all the temptations and distractions you might encounter in that setting."

"But Chad and Jayne..." I start, but Stevie knows better and just cuts me off.

"Chad and Jayne are responsible for themselves. You are responsible for your actions and your choices. That's how life works, Granger."

"So that's it, then?" I belt out, pacing back and forth in my small cell. "I make one mistake and you abandon me?" I don't realize how immature these words are until they leave my mouth.

"Don't make this about me. The truth is, Granger, right now I don't trust that I'm the best thing for you. I think you have some healing to do. Perhaps it's the kind of healing that needs to be done on your own."

"But that's not what I want!"

She moves closer and wraps her fingers around the cold metal bars. I immediately cover her hands with mine, and touching her soft skin calms me in an instant.

"It's rarely about what anyone wants in situations like this—it's about what you need. That is what makes it so right."

"I should've said no to them." My voice snaps like a guitar string. "I should've come to you instead."

"But you didn't." She doesn't say this in an accusing way—more resigned, which hurts much more.

"But what happens to us?"

"You can't think about that right now, not until you figure out what happens to you." She pulls her hands away, and the loss of warmth hits me square in the chest. Seconds later, she's about to leave me here, giving me one last sorry look over her shoulder before she goes.

"I should probably tell you that your agent and PR team are all flying into town."

"Why?"

She hesitates for a second—the way I should've hesitated before I made every dumbass decision my entire life.

"It's all over the news. I don't know how it got out so quickly, but the crash, your blood-alcohol level...all of it. There are even pictures. It will be a media frenzy—hell, it already is. I'm so sorry, Granger."

"I don't care about any of that," I announce, stubborn as hell. "None of it matters without you."

She opens and closes her mouth, and when a single tear runs down her cheek my reputation is suddenly the last thing I care about. If I had superpower strength enough to bend these bars in two, I'd take her in my arms and lick away those salty drops. Her curly hair is out-of-control around her lovely head, haloed by the fluorescent police-station lights, and her skin is translucent and pale. She looks like an angel—one that I had for a brief time but lost, because fuck, I didn't deserve her in the first place.

I'll remember this moment for my whole life. Stevie is locked into the files of my mind, like a song you can't get out of your head, or your heart, or your goddamn DNA for that bloody matter. "Stay with me," I beg, noticing more tears on her cheeks.

"Goodbye, Granger," she whispers, just before disappearing into the light—as if the light was her real home all along, and for me just a symbol of where I aspired to find her again, someday.

Chapter Twenty-Five
"Edge of a Broken Heart"

Stevie

Unfortunately, claiming that I was surprised when Chad called would be the understatement of all understatements, but such is the nature of friendship. We prefer to think of it as something steadfast and unyielding—always black and white in its integrity—but in truth it is messy and complicated, just like life itself. As much as I want to hate Chad forever, to hang up the phone and hurl it across the room, he was calling about Granger, so I heard him out instead.

In consequence, I now find myself on the morning ferry to Bowen Island, the nearest of the Gulf Islands to Vancouver's coastline. I stand on the lower deck staring out at the Pacific Ocean, leaning against one of the sun-warmed parked cars. The car's trunk is stuffed to the roof with vacation contents, but the owners are absent. I sigh to myself and hear my breath getting carried away by the wind, wishing that I'd had the strength to say no to this little adventure.

I mean, if you can call it an adventure at all. It's been a month since I spoke to Granger and that was the last time I heard from him. His pleading on my doorstep at dawn following his release from jail seemed like life or death, but it was followed by radio silence. At first I was angry, palpably so, and then hurt, but now I feel nothing. Most days I'm just numb. I heard through the grapevine that after Granger's band bailed him out of jail the next day. They left town, back to whatever vapid, celebrity-drenched hellhole they crawled out of in the first place. Okay, so maybe that isn't fair, but I won't blame myself for smarting after everything that has happened.

I'd assumed that Granger went with them, but apparently I assumed wrong. Chad informed me of Granger's real whereabouts when he called. Apparently the band is taking a break and Granger checked himself into one of the best treatment centres in Western Canada. The ferry arrives at the dock before I'm ready and I have to rush back to my motorcycle. Whatever happens today, I can be grateful for the day off work and the wind in my hair, if nothing else. I don't know if Granger will want to see me. I called ahead and they didn't say *no*, but they didn't exactly say *yes* either.

The boat unloads and I follow the single windy road to the top of the hill. My bike climbs a little farther over the next hump before I see the sign for the centre. I pull into the driveway and park in the shade before taking a moment to look around. The simple and unobtrusive wood-panelled building blends right into the surrounding forest and is nothing like what I expected. I follow the path of rock stairs to the front door where I'm greeted by a fellow resident. I know because he immediately introduces himself by name, followed by his addiction and number of days in treatment.

"Monty. Day Twenty-Six. Cocaine and opiates."

Monty has wide blue eyes, a graying ponytail, and a friendly expressive face. Before I can even introduce myself, he leads me through the communal living space, which appears jammed with mismatched couches and scattered with what I can only assume are more residents. One plays guitar, another reads, and there's an older female visiting with two younger children. Monty waves hello to the guitar player and has me follow him through the double glass doors to the patio.

"He's out here. He's always out here," Monty says, shaking his head.

Outside, I find Granger sitting sideways on a lawn chair with a cigarette in one hand, facing a leaf-strewn pool. His eyes search my face but he doesn't speak at first; the way he looks at me is impossible to read. He takes a drag and exhales slowly, without his eyes leaving mine. Monty clears his throat. "Trading one addiction for another."

Granger responds by giving him the finger with his cigarette-bearing hand and I fight to suppress a laugh. I feel like giving Monty the finger too. Honestly, give the guy a break already! But no matter, because Monty sighs and backs toward the door. "Don't forget, man, we're on dinner clean-up duty tonight."

"I won't forget." Granger's rough-sounding voice is that beautiful, raw, Scottish drawl that I've been deprived of for so long now. I have to pinch my arm to keep my eyes from welling with tears. Then Granger stands up and snubs his cigarette out in the overflowing ashtray.

"Do you want to get out of here?" he asks.

"Is that allowed?"

He levels me with a look. "It's not a prison, Stevie, even if it sort of looks like prison." He stretches his arms above his head and in the process gives me a glimpse of his tight, rippled stomach. I can't control the rush of lust that floods my stomach then, but I really shouldn't be thinking thoughts like that right now.

"Let's go for a walk then," I chime, but in my voice I don't sound so sure.

➤

As it turns out, we have to drive to the trailhead, so Granger hops on the back of my bike. I scold him for not wearing a helmet but he just laughs and tells me that with the roads on Bowen, we won't be going fast anyway. Granger directs me to the mouth of a wooded trail and I park my bike on the side of the road. He leads the way and I walk beside him while taking the opportunity to study his face. It looks fuller now, and the circles under his eyes are gone at long last.

"Look, a deer!" He points into the distance and my eyes follow the line of his arm. "This place is filled with them, because they have no enemies here."

"Neither do you," I whisper, before I can stop myself.

"Stevie…"

I can hear the hurt in his voice, but he doesn't pursue the thought any further. Despite the sun sitting high in its throne in the sky, the ground is still damp from last night's rain and his heavy motorcycle boots leave deep footprints as they squelch in the mud. A bead of wetness drops from an overhead tree and runs down the side of his neck, only to disappear beneath the collar of his jacket. We walk in silence, but the air between us is charged with electricity.

Eventually, the forest opens up to a clearing with a giant tree at the centre.

"This Douglas fir is over a thousand years old. There's only two like it on the island. Stevie, meet Papa."

I study the tree and notice how the marks on its base resemble the face of an old man. "Pleased to meet you, Papa."

"Papa somehow managed to escape the clear cutting that occurred at the beginning of the century. His scars and marks are from the loggers' saws and axes but somehow he made it through all of that."

Granger steps forward and surprises me when he starts to climb the tree, because Granger Ellis doesn't seem like the tree-climbing type. He hoists himself up and balances his feet on a low branch as he reaches for something overhead. The shiny edge flashes in his hand as he makes his way back down to earth and hands the treasure to me. I turn the gold coin over in my hands as he explains the meaning of this little trinket.

"It's my seven-days sober chip. To be honest, I didn't think I'd make it through that first part. I don't think I'll ever be able to explain how agonizing those first few days were, but I came out here after my first week and hid this chip in Papa's branches as a reminder."

"A reminder of what?"

"As a reminder of what this tree and I have in common—at least what I'd like to have in common with Papa. After everything this tree has had to endure, it still managed to grow high and wide as it did."

"That's beautiful."

I feel my throat tighten around my own words.

"I want you to have it."

"I can't, Granger." I thrust the coin back into his fingers, and they immediately close around mine into a fist.

"You have to take it." I shiver at his nearness as he moves closer, his warm breath tickling my neck. "I miss you, Steven."

I change the subject, but his words mean more than I can admit right now. "You look good."

"I feel clearer."

"...and I want to ensure that you stay that way. My being here..."

"Is perfect," he cuts me off.

"Is confusing."

"Stevie, if the last thirty days have taught me anything, it's how much I need you in my life."

"Isn't this experience about taking away the need and making you whole?"

"That's bullshit, Stevie. I may be an alcoholic, but I'm still a man—and as much as I'm learning to be whole, that also means fully including others in my life. I can't be full without you. You are everything to me."

"But that sounds like need..."

"Fuck that, I don't need you, but I want you with every part of me and everything inside me. Need, want, have, possess, cherish—they are just words, Stevie. You are mine and I want things to stay that way forever."

"But—"

"I love you like I've never loved anything in my life, if I've ever truly loved anything in my life. Not my band nor booze nor even my music. *I. Love. You.* Do you even understand how much?"

He steps forward to slide his arms around my waist. The feeling of his bare forearms against mine sends a powerful jolt right through me. In his embrace, everything feels so right, but what about tonight, tomorrow, next week, or next year? My mind wanders and I wonder if his are just pretty words whispered within the safety of the trees, never to be tested by the real world.

"You say you love me, but what if tomorrow or the next day you decide that you love alcohol more?" I blurt out, and Granger hangs his head with a sigh that hurts.

"There's nothing I can say to convince you—I can only prove myself by taking action. I can prove myself by waking up each day and reminding myself of what I have and how I can cherish it. Give me a chance to prove this to you. Just one more chance."

"It's not about chances, Granger, this isn't a game." I take a step away from him, exactly as one would from a wild animal in the woods. Granger is enough like a wild animal in his life (and in the bedroom) that this actually makes sense. "It is *both* of our lives at stake. The truth is that I love you too. I love you so much that it makes my chest hurt." The fact is, I've loved Granger Ellis for a while now—perhaps even from the very beginning—but I've never said it out loud.

"You love me?" he interrupts, and I watch as his pupils dilate.

"I love you enough to understand that this, that us, isn't good for you right now. I love you enough to walk away." By the time I finish, I'm crying softer than the sky, but Granger gathers me back up in his arms.

"You love me…" He exhales the words like a prayer.

"Did you hear anything that I said?" I sob into his shoulder as he gently caresses my back and whispers soothing sounds into my ear.

"So walk away then, Stevie. Walk away and see how far you get." Even though his words sound like a threat, they somehow fill me with the comfort I've been seeking. "Look, I know that walking away is probably what you need right now, but I'm not done fighting for us. Just twelve more days and I will prove it to you, love."

I let the rest of it out, crying so hard that it leaves me hiccupping. I feel both selfish and relieved when I finally pull away, his eyes searching mine before he plants the softest, sweetest kiss on my lips.

It's one kiss but it tells me everything that I need to know—most importantly, that he's serious and won't give up on us.

"I should go." My voice is shaky and my eyes are wet, but Granger nods in consent anyways.

"I should get back also. Punctuality is a big thing here, as is routine. Break it and pay the price. Besides, it's my turn for dinner."

"You're cooking?" I can't help but sound a little incredulous.

"Just clean up tonight, but we take turns doing some prep."

"That's so..."

"Domestic?"

"I was going to say normal."

"Good," he says, sighing. "I think I need more of that, because the last few years, normal has been in short supply in my life."

"So that's why you like me? Because I'm normal?" I tease.

A smile spreads across his face before he throws his head back and howls. When he finally recovers enough to wipe the moisture from his eyes, he shakes his head. "You are a lot of things, Steven Tyler, but I can guarantee you that normal is not one of them."

Chapter Twenty-Six

"Show me the Way"

Granger

Here I am, standing on Stevie's mother's doorstep, bracing myself for the storm headed my way. I've only been out of rehab for three hours, but there was no question in my mind that Mama Tyler's needed to be my first stop. When Spencer, the eldest (and the meatiest) brother, opens the door, I automatically flinch, but he surprises me with a sigh that sounds like a vacuum. I get it, somehow, as if he put the thought in my head: this is Spencer's way of saying that I suck. He looks me up and down, letting his shoulders sag into his pecs.

"You're not even worth the energy." Spencer shakes his head. He acts like he's wiser than me and knows it—but actually that's probably all true. "You are nothing to me." He turns his back to me, but he leaves the door wide open. I don't know if that's meant as an invitation but I take it, wandering inside and heading for the back kitchen.

Alana sits at the table with a steaming mug of dark, sticky liquid. I swear, it's like she knew that I was coming. "Sit down, Granger." Her tone leaves no room for argument, not that I have one anyway, so I slide into the chair across from Alana, the same woman who I have to thank for Stevie's existence.

"I lied before..." I stop to clear the frog from my throat. "I lied about being an eagle. I wasn't an eagle then, but I am now," I explain. "At least I am trying to be."

She looks at me, unblinking. "An eagle flies against the wind and faces everything. If you are truly an eagle, then what are you doing sitting in my kitchen and not out looking for my daughter?"

Her words feel like a slap in the face. Stevie has been running through my mind on a nonstop loop, and there are many amends that I must make, but I don't even know where to start. Spencer joins us at the kitchen table next. He rests his thick wide arms on top and leans forward to freak me out. His knuckles change from purple to white, as he balls and un-balls his fists. There's fire in his eyes, and with his earlier words in mind, I have no doubt that he's itching to put me down.

"You obliterated my little sister's heart."

"I did." I nod and wish that there was more I could do.

"You were warned."

"I know, and I'm sorry." I ready myself for whatever happens next, but I'm a lucky bastard, because Alana takes control of the conversation instead.

"Why did you do it?"

With a long breath, I pull out the letters I wrote them both from my back pocket. "Because I didn't want to stop then. Because as important as Stevie is to me, the booze was more important. Because I convinced myself that I was in control, but my addiction always had the upper hand. Every single time." I pause and search both their faces, not getting much back. "I won't lie—I'm not fixed and will probably never be one hundred percent fixed, but I am healing and plan to work at it every day for the rest of my life, so that one day soon I can be the man that Stevie deserves."

Alana's eyes fill with what *looks* like compassion, but her mouth is set in a grim line. "I commend your commitment and dedication to your health, but that is yours alone to bear. I am not convinced that you bring enough into Steven's life to balance out the sacrifices she will need to make, and relationships require equal balance in the same way as the earth."

Alana swirls the liquid in her mug, looking hard at the surface. "I know my daughter is stubborn and sometimes struggles with letting others into her life, but she is a beautiful and caring soul who needs to be protected. She always takes care of others first and her primary concern in life is for the well-being of others. You need to be the man that brings her peace and comfort, not chaos and instability.”

“I know that recent history has shown you otherwise, but I swear to you both: *I am* that man.” My voice breaks, but I don’t even care. “I love Steven with every fibre of my being—with everything in me. When I close my eyes at night, all I see is her. When I’m playing my guitar or writing a new song, all I see is her. When I’m brushing my teeth…”

“We get it man,” Spencer cuts me off. “You see Stevie.”

“And she sees me…Stevie is the only one who ever has. I must have her in my life in whatever way she’s willing to have me. I know that I need to earn back her trust—that is, if I ever had it in the first place. I’ll do whatever it takes, but it would mean a lot to me if I had your blessing.”

“No,” Spencer snarls, but Alana makes him shut up, all by putting one of her tiny hands on his giant forearm.

“If Granger is who Steven wants then we will listen to her and support her.” She turns her attention back to me. “But, Mr. Ellis, it does not mean that we will force our Stevie to listen to you. I don’t know where my daughter sits with all of this, but I know that she is angry and hurt, so you very well may not get the audience that you are seeking.”

“Funny that you should mention an audience, as that’s partly why I am here. I have an idea as to how I might get her attention, but it’s going to take a little planning, and you and your sons are exactly the audience I need.”

Spencer snickers and raises his eyebrows. “So the big shot celebrity rocker needs two Lil’Wat Canadians to help him bring in an audience now?”

“Something like that.”

The two of them look at each other for a beat before bursting into laughter. Alana is first to pull herself back together. When she does, she faces me and asks a question to which the answer I already know that she understands. “What *took* you so long?”

Chapter Twenty-Seven
"Love of a Lifetime"

Stevie

It's been a full week since Granger's release and still no call. Not that I was expecting one right away—at least that's what I keep telling myself. I've been avoiding Kit like the plague, because I can't stand the *I told you so* looks he's been shooting my way every time we're together. I know he doesn't mean to be cruel; he just can't help himself. I take some comfort in knowing that he doesn't like seeing me unhappy, but there's always that small, insecure part of me wondering if he gets something out of it.

My brothers aren't nearly as easy to avoid. They've been calling me twice every day and treating me as if I'm made of glass. It's a strange feeling, because they've always been protective, but gentle has never been their thing. The date of Granger's release is circled on the calendar. Whether this was for moral support, posterity, or some indelible need to hear his voice again, I don't know, but now all I have is this big red reminder of what I didn't mean to him.

Fortunately, his treatment went largely unnoticed by the media, as it seems these days rehab is run of the mill. There was some brief coverage about his time off following a very stressful tour and then not a word. It didn't receive nearly the attention that my lack of celebrity nor the size of my ass ultimately garnered, but I suppose some topics sell better than others. There's obviously nothing I can do about that, so instead I try to remember my mom's truism about being like an eagle, observing everything at once from above while remaining just that—above the chaos, heartache, and toxic unanswered questions.

I've been puttering around my apartment for the last few days with some unexpected time off. My new manager at the hotel has been that *walking-on-eggshells* kind of nice, and for some reason gave me the whole weekend off with no demands for split shifts or overtime. I'm suspicious, but I would rather not look this particular gift horse in the mouth. So presently I'm standing in the middle of my living room in my pyjamas, holding Toto in my arms and feeling the same sense of listlessness that has plagued me for the last forty-eight hours. Then the doorbell rings. I release a strangled cry because I'm fully aware that one of my brothers has come to check on me, again. In fact, I don't even bother throwing on a robe as I greet my visitor with an irritated, "WHAT?"

It isn't one of my brothers though. My mouth drops open when I see Granger standing on my front porch. He scans me from head to toe and swallows hard. "Stevie."

The deep timbre of his voice instantly makes my knees go weak. I'm so surprised to see him that I momentarily forget my current attire—that is, until it dawns on me that I'm makeup free with my hair mussed up in a nest atop my head. I'm wearing an old pyjama tank top and a short set that is far past its prime, not to mention a little too small. Toto squirms in my arms and I stroke his back in response.

"Granger?" It comes out like a question, probably because it is one. *What the hell is he doing here?*

"Before you say anything, just give me a chance. I know that it's been a week since I got out, and believe me when I say that it's been a hell of a week, but it all needed to be right. It needed to be perfect," he explains.

"I don't understand. What needed to be perfect?"

I don't hide the fact that I'm gawking, but he's too gorgeous to bother controlling myself. He's wearing dark, torn jeans, a light gray Henley with the sleeves pushed up to display his beautiful ink, and those go-to motorcycle boots. His hair has grown out since I last saw him and he sports a few days' worth of beard scruff. He also looks like he has put on a bit of weight, but it suits him. He looks stronger and sturdier, like a tree I want to climb right here and now.

"I have something important that I want to show you. Do you trust me enough to come with me?" He holds out his hand and I observe the flutter in his long fingers for a moment before answering. His eyes plead with mine like there's some part of him that believes I might say no. But I can't say no—not to him, not ever—yes is the only true word in my heart.

"Not like this, Granger." His face falls before I can fully explain. "I mean not in my pyjamas," I spit out. "Here." I thrust Toto into his hands before pivoting on my heels like a deer. "Just let me take a quick shower."

I'm in and out of the bathroom in record time, rushing through my hair and makeup before throwing on some fitted jeans and a light cashmere sweater. Back in the living room, I find him sitting on the couch with Toto perched on his thigh. The sight of them together is so cute that I can't help but smile. I place Toto back in his tank and follow Granger to the waiting car. I don't question where we're going, because somehow I trust that it'll be in the right direction. I climb into the back of the black Escalade while he slides in next to me, signalling for the driver to leave. We don't talk much on the way, but he does ask about Joe and my family.

"Joe won a brand new car on a local radio show," I slant my eyes his way to gauge his reaction.

"Did he now? Well that's good luck."

"Yes, it's what I'd call unbelievably good luck. It also came with five years of maintenance and insurance costs covered. The strangest part is that he doesn't even remember entering a contest."

Granger shrugs but I don't miss the small smile tugging at his lips. "The man is eighty-five, love, I'm sure he's bound to forget a few things."

Even though my instinct is to keep pressing I let it go for now, but when the subject of Kit comes up, the air becomes thick with tension.

"Has he been around much?" Granger asks, in a way that seems forced and casual at the same time.

"Less than before, though I haven't been that social lately. Plus, it's been a little difficult to get our friendship back on track with his feelings for me out in the open."

"You likely never will."

"Will what?"

"Get back on track."

"We won't, or you don't want us to?"

"Both," he sighs out. "You are mine, Stevie, and even if he eventually accepts our connection, there will always be want for you. One thing I know from experience is how impossible it feels, trying to make the want go away."

I level him with my gaze. "While I appreciate your perspective, it's not yours to decide. He's my best friend, and you can't claim me as yours like some uncharted territory."

"I can and I have," he growls. I must bristle because he suddenly unbuckles his seatbelt and slides closer to me. "Stevie, I have no doubt in my mind that you are smarter, stronger, and braver than me. You don't need to be claimed or saved, but maybe I do. I just think the only way to save myself is to make you mine."

"But I thought the last forty-two days were about you figuring this out for yourself, Granger?"

"Yes and no, love. I mean, they were and I did. I understand now that only I am responsible for the choices I make. Only I am responsible for my own happiness. But I've also realized that a big part of my happiness is the light you bring into my life—so you better fucking believe that I'm going to grab ahold of that light with both hands and never let go."

"Oh…" I let out a whooshing breath, unable to think of another response.

"Yeah, oh."

As he leans in to rub his unshaven cheek against mine, the contact heats my skin and I curl into his body, wanting so much more, but the car suddenly stops and throws me back against the seat. I glance out the window to see that we've arrived in downtown Vancouver—also, we're stuck in traffic. I can't believe that we've already been driving for two hours, because it feels like just minutes have passed since we started talking honestly. Most of the ride was spent in silence, just being together in the car, feeling outside of time somehow, but it's always like that with Granger.

We edge forwards and the car eventually pulls over to the curb. I roll down the tinted window and see that we're parked in front of a theatre venue, with an actual red carpet stretching from the SUV to the double glass doors. Granger hops out and comes around to open my door, taking my hand gently and leading me into the theatre. It's dead inside except for one red-coated usher waiting by the auditorium doors.

"Good evening, Miss Tyler." The usher's smile reminds me of summertime. "Please follow me."

He takes us backstage, passing some stacked-up props, AV equipment, and tangles of cords. Granger leads me into one of the wings and the stage lights come on, followed by a ripple of applause. He tugs my hand and we walk together to center stage, only to be momentarily blinded by the bright lights. I blink and look across the crowd. Even though it's an intimate space, I can only make out silhouettes of bodies.

The stage around me is empty other than one microphone stand and two wooden stools in the centre, one with an acoustic guitar propped against it. Granger slings an arm around my waist and leads me to the first stool before taking the second one for himself and slinging the guitar strap over his shoulder. He clears his throat and leans into the microphone.

"I have no proper apology for you. You have no good reason to give me another chance, especially when you've given me so many already but I love you, Steven Tyler, and I'm hoping that is enough." He strums a few chords until someone in the crowd whistles. "I can't ask you to forget any of the hurt I've caused and I won't ask you to forget. I was what I was, and I am what I am now, which is hopefully a better version of what I've been previously. There's still work to be done, but I'm committed and cannot lose with you by my side. I want you to be mine forever, Stevie. Choose me, stay with me and be my girl. With you, I'm a better man."

The crowd starts to cheer and I don't know what to say. There are a few shouts and I recognize a few voices, namely the deep, hooting baritone of my brothers. Granger resumes strumming his guitar and surprises me by launching into one of my favourite songs.

We both lie silently still
In the dead of the night
Although we both lie close together
We feel miles apart inside
Was it something I said or something I did
Did the words not come out right
Though I tried not to hurt you
No, though I tried
But I guess that's why they say
Every rose has its thorn
Just like every night has its dawn
Just like every cowboy sings his sad, sad song
Every rose has its thorn

It's a beautiful rendition—too beautiful. My eyes well with tears and the audience lights up the room with their iPhone flashlights. I look out and immediately recognize the Wizards of Wool in the front row, snuggled up next to my mother. Only then do I realize that Granger has brought everyone I love together today, to witness the moment where he decided to bare his soul.

Though it's been a while now
I can still feel so much pain
Like a knife that cuts you, the wound heals
But the scar, that scar remains

Watching him sing, I realize that he's given me too much credit. I've been closed off for so long that *only* love could've opened me up, so the saving is mutual. Just when I think the song is about to end, an electric guitar wails and a full band appears from the wings. I do a double take because it's the actual band, *Poison*, and the lead singer winks at me as he comes across the stage. They sing together while I sit paralyzed, the last notes fading as I hop off my stool and rush over to Granger, throwing my arms around him until he practically falls off his stool. When he recovers, he pulls me into a hug that feels like proof of infinity.

"Thank you for saving me," I whisper in his ear.

"I'm yours," he whispers back, burying his nose in the crook of my neck.

"I love you, Granger Ellis, more than you can even imagine," I murmur. "But if you ask me to marry you on stage, I will officially kill you."

He tilts his head back and laughs heartily. It's a sound that warms me from my head right down into my toes.

"Aye, I won't ask you right now, but make no mistake sweetheart, the question is coming." I'm about to protest when he plants a firm kiss on my lips, making the crowd go wild once again.

The two of us stay like that—lip locked—while the band starts up another tune I recognize, but the music between Granger and me is all I can think about right now. As the band gets creative with their chords and choruses, a fire burns in my chest, and I revel in how beautiful this music between us truly is.

Epilogue

Six Months Later

Granger

She doesn't know. I have this ring burning a hole in my pocket, and Stevie has no idea. It's no ordinary ring, but then again she's no ordinary girl. I had the design approved by one of her tribal elders. It's made of white gold and onyx, carved into the shape of a raven, and surrounded by diamonds.

I've been told that the raven is mischievous and curious—that it symbolizes change and metamorphosis. In Greek mythology, the raven symbolized good luck and served as God's messenger to the mortal world. To me, this ring, like Stevie, is a symbol of my salvation, for she is nothing short of otherworldly.

My girl might say that she's not the marrying kind, but my girl says a lot of things. Today, she has to say *yes*. If not, it literally might kill me.

Stevie

He pulls up and lets the bike idle by the edge of the stone wall, which gives me an incredible view of the rolling green hills and craggy rocks of castle below. I inhale a crisp breath and lean my head between his shoulder blades, mesmerized by the indigo-blue water crashing into the gulley and sending whitewalls up over the shoreline.

I take Granger's hand in mine, warming his fingers in the wind. "It's beautiful here."

He shrugs and gives me a crooked grin. "I call it *home*."

We've been travelling for two months through Scotland and always skirting Granger's hometown of Aberdeen, in a way that I assumed was deliberate. There was an unspoken understanding between us that we'd visit his hometown only once he felt ready. We spent the first month in Edinburgh, followed by the Highlands. Granger seems so much clearer these days, and he's been writing a lot again. He told his agent that he needed time off to put together a solo album. The band is mostly understanding of his choice, well Ravi at least, and the others are going along with it because what choice do they have?

I know that they're all skeptical: the band, his agent, even his fans, but they haven't seen what I have from Granger. They haven't heard him singing by moonlight in that gravelly voice with only a guitar to accompany him. It is nothing short of transformative. It's our second month exploring the Scottish coastline and Granger was ready to fly home again the moment we rode into Aberdeen City yesterday morning.

Aberdeen is a port town in the northeast of Scotland. Granger explains that it wasn't much back in the day, but oil money made the city an expensive international destination. They call it the Granite City with its soaring gray stone buildings, quaint white shutters, and red doors dotting the cobblestone streets everywhere. My perspective on the city is incongruent with the dismal and gray landscape he describes, but it makes sense for him to project childhood memories onto this place.

I think it was important for him to see Aberdeen again, although it hasn't changed drastically from what he remembers. The process of coming home is never easy, as often our memories don't align with reality. Granger took me to his parents' gravesites: two unassuming marble squares resting side by side in the neatly trimmed grass. He didn't cry nor explain; we just stood shoulder to shoulder with our hands linked together, listening to the wind rustling through the trees, to the mowers, and the airplanes overhead. I think it was cathartic for him in some ways, at least I hope so. We spent that night in a quiet, simple hotel. We didn't make love but Granger let me hold him all night.

And now we are here, on the cliffside overlooking Dunnottar Castle. I don't know what the significance of this place is to Granger, but I do notice the way he stops and watches the land. He turns off the bike and tilts it to the side for me to hop off. I remove my beanie helmet and he grins and removes his own before tousling my already messy locks. The one thing about all this wind and salty air is that I've had a crazy mop since we arrived. There's been no taming it, as if it's very own weather system.

He takes me by the hand, leading me down the steep gravel path towards the castle. It looks medieval and haunting but there's something romantic about the ruined cliff-top fortress that captivates me all the same. The seabirds float on the gusting breeze as we near the stone structure, and I pull up my sweater to wipe the condensation from my face before speaking.

"It's incredible, Granger, it really is. But what are we doing here?"

"Seen enough churches and castles, have you now?" he teases.

"It's not that. This is the first castle you've brought me to without telling me why. There was the biggest castle, the oldest, the tallest...so why this one specifically?" He stares at me and those beautiful green eyes pierce right through mine, as some unnamed emotion causes butterflies to form in my stomach.

"We didn't have a lot of money growing up, I mean my parents didn't, but I do remember having one holiday before they died. We packed up the car and drove along the coast, stopping at little hamlets and tourist traps along the way. On the way back home, we passed this castle. I remember how all the windows were rolled down in the car, and how my ma's hair blew in the wind. I remember the smell of tobacco and perfume swirling through the air. And I remember feeling forlorn, knowing that our vacation was coming to an end. So I looked out the car window and committed this castle to memory. I told myself that I was going to get married here someday, so that I could be as happy as they were together."

"Granger…that's…I don't know if words are the right thing to answer you with right now." I'm struck to the spine by the depth of energy moving between him and me.

"Well, lucky for you, I don't need you to answer. Steven Tyler, I'm proud to say that I don't need to look out the car window anymore and imagine that future for myself. I can tell the little boy inside me to relax, because his someday has come."

"What are you saying exactly?" I think his real meaning is only now catching up with me. "No!" I blurt out without thinking, but that doesn't seem to faze him. It's not that I fundamentally oppose the institution of marriage, but the idea of chattel and antiquated traditions really gets my back up.

"Yes." He smiles and pulls me into the warmth of his arms. "I knew you'd give me trouble but goddammit, Stevie, I just don't care. I love you. Now make that little boy happy for fuck's sake and marry me already, won't you?"

"Married?" I manage to squeak out.

"I know you have your issues with the idea, but I've been plenty patient and you're killing me, woman. It's time to make it official and nothing you can say will change my mind on this."

"Okay." This time I speak without hesitation. "Yes."

"Yes?"

"Yes, Granger."

He laughs and hauls me against his chest, nuzzling his face into my neck for warmth, as if I'm a teddy bear that he'll never let go—though I am much more than a teddy bear to Granger these days. His proposal tells me that these days won't just be for now.

"Thank you." His whispering voice is carried away by the icy wind as he kisses the tip of my nose. "I won't be easy to deal with all the time, but I can promise to love you with everything I have for the rest of our lives."

He turns me in his arms so that my back faces his chest, and together we stare out at the waves crashing like poetry against the rocky shore. I know that he's right about one thing: if the start of our relationship is any indication, this won't be easy. Easy doesn't always equate to better though. Easy is light and fluffy—it's bright days and cloudless skies—but life also holds heaviness, dark clouds, and turmoil in equal measure, and sometimes you have to really fight for the things you love. You fight for them because you know it will be worth it in the end.

I have learned from Granger about the complexity of what it means to need someone as a force in your life. I think we need the energy and people around us to move and be moved and allow to move us, for this is what brings us together as who we are and always wanted to be. Granger might have his addictions, and I might have my thoughts on those needs, but we also have each other darting through the emerald green Scottish countryside on the back of a motorbike—wind in our hair and hope in the sky.

Perhaps the needs that find unity in a place like this belong to the same higher order that we are intended to surrender to in love, just as the ocean surrenders to the tide. Not only will life with Granger be everything I didn't know that I needed, it now forms a world that I can no longer live without.

The End

<u>Stevie's Playlist (songs from InterPlay)</u>

To Be With You – Mr Big

Africa – Toto

Pour Some Sugar On Me – Def Leppard

Cherry Pie – Warrant

It's My Life – Bon Jovi

Working For The Weekend - Loverboy

You're All I Need – Motley Crue

Here I Go Again – Whitesnake

Love Hurts - Nazareth

Every Rose Has its Thorn - Poison

Acknowledgements

Where to begin? The editing process on this second edition has been exhilarating, cathartic, and at times frustrating—but so damn worth it. A huge thank you to Kelsey Straight for her great work, not only with editing but also in helping me to craft and uncover Granger's voice. Kelsey is an actual real-deal literary rockstar.

Thank you to Whistler—a place that I hold dear to my heart and a truly magical piece of this beautiful province of ours. A visit to Whistler always results in some of the most unforgettable experiences. www.whistler.com. As well, thank you to the Lil'Wat First Nations for the inspiration I garnered from your environmental stewardship, your incredible connectivity of spirit, and your resilience in the face of injustice.

Thank you to Tamsin Lehn, my book club readers, and to Megan Watt and the TSPA for their guidance and invaluable connections. Also, a special thank you to Diana Chan—Whistler businesswoman extraordinaire, mentor, and cheerleader—your ongoing support has meant so much.

To the reader, for being gracious with storylines and characters that don't always fit into the mold, thank you. Your patience, especially as I delve into topics that can be thought of as *taboo* for romance reads, means the world to me.

And most importantly, thank you to all the Granger's out there, and to anyone who has ever struggled with balance and moderation—you are the true idols. Keep fighting the good fight. www.aa.org

It does not matter how slowly you go, as long as you don't stop. – Confucius

For more titles by Jennifer Watts: www.jenniferwattsauthor.com